GUNS FOR SONORA
J.A. GREENE

Publisher, Copyright, and Additional Information

Guns for Sonora by Jeff Greene

Copyright © 2023 by Jeff Greene

ISBN- 979-8-9880352-0-6 (Paperback)
979-8-9880352-1-3 (eBook)

Editing by Editor Name
Cover design and interior design by Rafael Andres

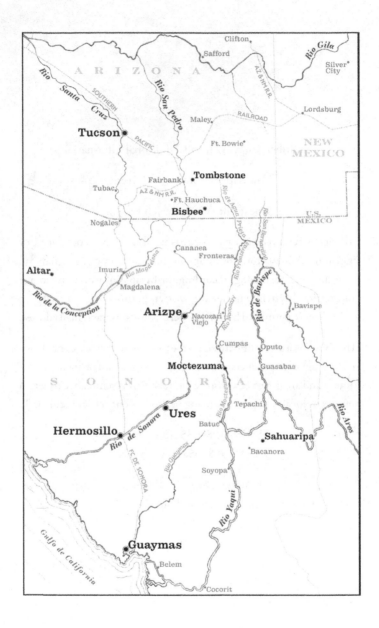

CHAPTER 1

SONORA, 1888

Connor guided his horse and mule around the switchback, turning west and slanting downward. The sun's position promised another two hours or so until camp and a spartan meal. Seen from a distance, he was not physically imposing with only average height and a lean one hundred and seventy pounds. Hard work showed to good effect in his wide shoulders and thick chest. He had brown, shaggy hair and eyes that presently narrowed against the glare above the worn, dusty clothes, thick canvas vest, and jacket. A Winchester '73 model rested across his legs, secured by a makeshift leather sling over his left shoulder. Over his right shoulder a canteen was suspended for easy access.

Connor scanned the trail ahead, thoughts drifting back to his first time in Mexico. He'd enlisted with Col. Mackenzie's Fourth Cavalry in early 1870 after working in his older brother's Irish crew, laying track for the Union Pacific. His mother had seen him apprenticed as an accountant and been disappointed after six months when he joined his brother out West. He'd witnessed the Golden Spike being driven in at Ogden, Utah, in May of 1869 and the completion of the first transcontinental railroad. His older brother, Colin, a Civil War veteran, had saved to buy a farm and headed out to Oregon. Connor had hugged his brother and drifted South, enlisting at Jacksboro, Texas.

As a young corporal, he'd ridden for fifty straight hours with the three-hundred-and-seventy-plus men of the Fourth Cavalry. They'd crossed the Rio Grande to attack and punish the Kickapoo, Mescalero, and Lipan for their raids from villages near the Rio San Rodrigo at Remolino, Mexico. Guided by the Seminole Negro Indian Scouts, they had traveled a night, a day, and another night through dry, dusty, rugged terrain to reach the village at dawn. Cartridges stuffed in pockets, he had joined the charge through the villages, firing at surprised warriors erupting out of lodges, scattered by the frontal assault. They returned with prisoners and captured horses, covering about one hundred sixty miles, snatching sleep in the saddle. Some would fall off their horses, remount, and press on. Others leaned forward, arms around the necks of their horses, and drifted in and out of sleep. He'd learned a lot about stamina, determination, and himself by the time they re-crossed the Rio Grande and in campaigns before and after, on the southern plains. Connor had received many more hard lessons in the intervening fifteen years.

Connor had been back in Mexico many times since Remolino, both as a civilian packer and sometime scout against the Apache. He had been the pack-master on this most recent run. Facing west, he felt a slight breeze and the pack mule pull back on the lead rope. He pushed up in the stirrups and twisted left to look back. The first shot slammed into the canvas vest pocket over his heart. Horse rearing, brogans coming out of the stirrups, his butt slipped over the cantle from the impact. More shots, a burning in his upper right arm as he hit the ground, with butt, back, and head in quick order. Intense pain exploded as he rolled right to avoid being stomped by the panicked animals, over the edge of the trail and down the steep slope. He rolled and bounced downward, toward the east turn of the next switchback. The forward buckhorn sights of his .44-40 Winchester gouged his left temple as he picked up speed. Rolling down, tangled sling and canteen, the rifle barrel jammed into the ground as he spun, propelling him up a foot into the air before he slammed back to earth.

The scrub juniper stopped his rolling descent with a brutal, rib-cracking jolt. Twenty-five feet above, the horse and mule ran back up the trail they had just traversed, fleeing the gunfire. Shouting from the ambush; two or three voices registered with the pause in the firing. He couldn't see the bushwhackers—the rolling descent had taken him out of their line of sight. Right side wet and raw, ripping pain sawing at his heart, Connor lay stunned.

Digging his heels in to push away from the juniper, he started rolling again, stopped this time after another twenty feet by a modest line of rocks and boulders, the largest maybe four foot high. Blood from his temple blurred his left eye's vision. Connor tried to slow his breathing and think. He weakly tried to assess how bad he was wounded and how long he had before he bled out. Random thoughts without conclusions. Blood on his chest, oozing through the elliptical gash in his vest pocket, exposed mangled brass casings of the .44-40 rounds in the cartridge loops inside.

Feeble at first, he struggled to untangle the sling, the canteen abandoned, its tin seam split and water draining. Up, onto his knees, then easing over the line of rocks. Shirtsleeve swiping at the blood blurring his vision. Two, maybe three minutes gone. They would be closing in soon, more voices, Spanish. Hat gone, covered in dirt, blood, not able to walk, each breath a searing pain, he started to crawl. His actions were driven by some primal, unconscious response. The low line of rocks slanted away from his attackers as it went up toward the trail he had just ridden. Crawling, dragging his rifle, likely useless from dirt and debris, Connor made slow progress up the slope to the trail. Rocks provided low cover and concealment.

He could hear them coming, rocks clattering as they worked their way along the steep slope. With a cautious glance between rocks, Connor could see two men coming, gravity causing them to drift downslope and to their left. Maybe seventy-five yards away, they were moving slowly and cautiously, rifles up, separated by fifteen feet. Connor, wounds leaking and body damaged, needed to escape and gain time. Time to clear his brain and work out the survival choices, if any. Time to stanch the bleeding and increasing weakness. He was closer to the trail now, still not able to stand. Breath coming hard, deep breathing not possible without spikes of agony. Connor tried to suppress the shock and focus on staying alive.

At the trail, he glanced right and saw another man coming out of the boulders and scrub, leading a horse. The other two were still moving slowly downslope and short of his concealed path behind the rocks. Decision time. Cross the trail and risk exposure to reach high ground above the trail, or stay below it. Below, he would be visible to the rider as he came back up the trail. The rider was looking left in the direction of his partners. Connor observed he was above the rider's line of sight and as yet undetected.

Connor rolled across the narrow trail and lay on his back, using his heels to push himself up the steep slope, finding modest concealment behind low brittle brush and broken granite. He lay still, six feet up and back from the trail. The third man was mounted and moving toward him on the trail, eyes focused downslope. He would pass below him soon, rifle across his saddle, hand around the rifle bridge, finger near the trigger. Left hand guiding the horse with the reins.

The wounded man had little time to consider his choices. His rifle was clogged with dirt and, maybe worse, the barrel could be bent, making it dangerous to fire. The short barrel, double action .44 caliber in shoulder harness, under his right armpit was also covered in dirt but still with him. Connor was a left-handed pistoleer and the pain on that side made arm movement, even to unholster, hard, maybe impossible.

As the rider came past his position on the slope below him, several things happened nearly at once. The men on the lower slope passed the line of rocks that had concealed his upward crawl. Glancing right, one saw the blood spoor and then looked farther up toward his partner on the horse following the trail. Connor, left arm held tight against his rib cage, leaned forward, away from the steep slope. Gravity accelerated his body out and down, right hand gripping the barrel of his rifle. He used the fall forward and height advantage to swing his rifle overhead, then down from above at an angle toward the rider's head.

Whether alerted by his companero or the noise above, the rider turned in the saddle to his right, eyes widening as the descending rifle butt hit his forehead and skidded across his eyes. His feet still in the stirrups, he slumped back, stunned in the saddle, horse rearing. Connor released a mixed grunt and cry of agony, falling forward into the rider, losing the Winchester. He grabbed the leg of the rider, pulling it into his right shoulder just as the panicked horse set off down the trail.

The rider's right leg came out of the stirrup but Connor was not letting go, even as his lower legs were dragged alongside the horse. Ripping pain had him seeing grainy black dots in his vision. The rider slumped to the left side of the horse, his head bouncing against its hindquarters. The combined weight of the two men slowed the horse down to a canter, then to a walk after about eighty yards and around a switchback turn. The horse came to a pawing stop and turned while Connor got to his knees, then to his feet. Gasping, making incoherent sounds as the pain in his chest surged with each breath, he tried to mount from the wrong side of the horse. He barely managed to get across the lap of the unconscious rider before a rifle shot sent the horse off again, down the trail.

Lying across the rider's lap, right arm hooked under and around the horse's neck, a leg in the stirrup, he held on desperately. The movement of the horse slamming the saddle up into his mangled chest forced out low-pitched cries and blocked any ability to think. With no further shots, the horse finally slowed, then stopped again. Sliding off the horse, Connor felt his feet touch the primitive trail. Mumbling gibberish, hoping to steady the horse, he spotted the reins and got his right hand on them. Feet planted in the trail, thighs trembling and knees barely keeping him upright, he moved slowly around the front of the nervous horse, trying to calm the beast.

On the slumped rider's side, Connor could see the man breathing but unconscious. His head battered and cut. The rider's rifle was caught between saddle horn and his right leg. Connor nudged the rider's left leg out of the stirrup and used his right shoulder to push him off the horse. The gunman fell off, hitting his head, and lay still. Looking down, Connor realized he knew this particular bastard. Emilio, with an unknown last name. Just a few days before, they had been riding together, running a load of guns and ammunition to the Yaquis, a day south and west. This was to be his second and last trip, the one that paid his debt to the bank for his land along the lower reaches of the Blue River in eastern Arizona Territory.

The trip also squared his commitment to the Yaqui woman who had attracted and recruited him in Tucson. Right now, he needed to escape the immediate danger.

He needed to get somewhere where he could sort out his condition and determine how to get back out of Sonora. Connor guessed he was still two hundred and fifty miles south of the international border. Maintaining a death grip on the horse's reins, he picked up Emilio's rifle. He paused as a wave of darkness threatened to topple him, then slipped it into the rifle scabbard. Holding the horn, left foot in the stirrup, he took a deep breath and pushed up. He didn't make it. As the skittish horse turned in circles, he used its momentum to try again. This time he got his heel over the cantle and finally his knee over. The chest pain was blinding, pulsing.

Up in the saddle, taking short, shallow breaths, his eyes cleared enough to see. Farther ahead he saw his horse and mule, one down and the rope between them tangled in what looked like greasewood and cholla. He moved in that direction while still slumped half forward on the horse's neck. Looking back, he couldn't see his pursuers yet, but they were coming. Likely they were retrieving their horses hidden behind the ambush site.

Coming up on his two animals, he didn't want to dismount. He was seeping blood and not clear how bad his chest wound was. Connor grimly noted there were no bubbles so his lung was intact. The mule looked okay but the horse was down and had been hit at least once in the melee. He wished he could change saddles but that was going to be too much in his current state.

Dismounting was an agonizing process, as he went on one knee to untie the saddlebags and bedroll. Tying off the bridle to the greasewood, he used his right arm to swing the bags and bedroll over the mule's packs, tying the leather straps to one of the other packs on the mule. Connor doubted he could move effectively enough to manage both horse and mule, but he needed time to sort through the packs and saddlebags. The mule also had water canteens, which were still filled and essential. He wasn't up to finishing off the wounded horse so he cut the lead with his belt knife and reattached it to his newly acquired horse's saddle horn. The mule seemed less skittish, maybe from their longer association.

A day's ride up the trail was where he had left the band of gunrunners, three of whom had just tried, and might yet, kill him. Down trail, the two still functional would be coming. It was critical to find another way home. Another half mile and he came to a spur on the mountain that headed generally north and east. A quarter mile down the spur was a clump of boulders that would provide cover and might be defensible for a short while. He turned off, knowing that his pursuers would not miss the sign. Pain and defense trumping stealth.

Reaching the boulders, he worked his way among them and tried to see where the spur went or how it ended. Connor could see that another couple of hundred yards farther, it petered out into a steep but navigable slope, then into a downward-slanting draw. Following the draw might lead to the trail he had been taking but beyond the ambush site. He was exhausted from the pain and blood loss. He would make what stand he could or even try to buy them off with his share of the money. For now, he was done. He found a spot where he could observe the trail while remaining unseen among the rocks. Connor looked west, aware that the sun was low on the horizon. There was a stunted mesquite near his position, casting a long shadow toward the draw he hoped he could use later. The light breeze was picking up.

Securing both animals to some brush, he took a gallon canteen off the mule stumbling back for his saddlebags and the rifle. Opening his saddlebag, he took out a pint flask of rye whiskey and a clean blue cotton shirt. Connor took several minutes to gather himself, then set his belt knife to the shirt, cutting strips. Then he heard the hoofbeats of his ambushers. Emilio was propped up and his hands tied around and in front of the first rider, who looked at this distance like another one of his former associates, Felipe. The way Emilio's head was rolling loose, Connor could see that he was out of the fight for now. The third rider was Alfredo Cruz, the only one of the three who had given his last name. As they passed the turnoff to the spur, they slowed and looked to the boulders where he was concealed. Alfredo dismounted and, with rifle, led his horse upslope to a position where he could observe. Felipe and Alfredo shouted back and forth, and then Felipe, with Emilio, took off up the trail toward where the gunrunners had last camped.

Connor had a lot to do and not much energy left. Sliding off his vest first, then his bloody shirt, he finally could see the damage. The bullet had smashed into his chest at an angle as he turned in the saddle. The slug had passed through the doubled canvas and across the top of two cartridges, through the underside of another, mangling both before penetrating his pectoral muscle at an angle, coming to rest against the outside of a rib. He could feel the slug resting there. His right shoulder had a bullet graze that was leaking a bit but he ignored that for now. He had to hope that Cruz would stay put until he got some reinforcements.

Tearing off the left and right sleeves, he cut the clean shirt into strips below the fourth button, intending to put the upper part of the shirt back on over the wound after the repairs. Then he would tie the other strips around his chest, over the covered wound, and tie off on the right side of his ribs. Ribs could use a tight wrap, but that required someone to help. A quick glance told him that Cruz was staying put on the slope, partially behind the cover of some rocks.

He found a relatively clean area on the shirt he had removed, tore off that portion. Next, he removed his sewing kit from his other saddlebag. Opening the canteen, he took a long drink and then used some to rinse his hands, soaking a strip from his clean shirt and gently cleaning around the wound and the area above the lump from the slug. The rye whiskey was used to clean hands, needle, belt knife, and around the wound. He also soaked a strip of clean cotton shirt with the whiskey.

Making a cut with the knife below the spent bullet, he wrapped the soaked shirt strip over his index finger and pushed through the cut and into the bullet path in his pectoral. Awwwwwrrrrrr! Taking fast, shallow breaths, Connor felt his fingernail touch the slug and start to work it out. Swearing and groaning, he had to stop as his vision blackened and he started to hyperventilate. Feeling it reach the surface of his skin, he took his finger out of the channel and used the knife tip to work it the rest of the way out. He just sat for a minute, breathing fast but struggling for oxygen, as the blood ran out of entry and exit wounds. Applying the good rye to the wounds, he applied pressure with a pad made from the cotton strips.

Connor thought of himself as a reasonably hard man, capable of doing what was required. This was going to be a severe test. He had no intention of dying here. As he sat panting, feeling the waves of pain roll through, he told himself, just a few more minutes and he would try to suture the wounds. The blood was soaking through the compress. Starting with the exit wound, he used a bent needle to penetrate the skin on the bottom of the cut, through the top, and then through the bottom again. He didn't have the will, strength, or dexterity to tie off each suture, just at the last of the six loops. Making another compress, he held it on the exit wound and gathered his wits for the entry wound. This wound didn't have clean edges so he would need to tie off each suture. He poured more whiskey into the wound and took another snort. Holding one end of the thread in his teeth, he started again with the needle. Eight stitches, poorly tied off, a fresh compress, and a quick prayer completed the repairs.

Dribbling more rye on both wounds and the shoulder graze, he held the compresses against the wounds and waited to see how much bleeding would continue. Maybe he passed out or just fell sleep, but when he came to, it was almost dark. The compresses were soaked, but lifting them off, the leakage was much slower. He applied more whiskey then tied the new compresses in place and slipped on his half shirt and buttoned it up. He made a sling to keep from moving his left arm and tearing out the stitches. He was weak but certain that he needed to move or die here. At this elevation, it was cooling off fast.

Connor felt light-headed but the throbbing pain was more manageable, especially after a sip of water and a mouthful of rye. Reaching in the saddlebag, he retrieved a bag of jerky and ate some, with generous sips of water. It was salty, and that was about all that registered as he chewed and swallowed. Dumping Emilio's saddlebags, he found two cans of pears, which he set aside, some rough ground corn, a bag of pinto beans, and unground coffee. The other side had two shirts, one of which he slipped on. He threw out most of the rest, keeping a box of .44-40 cartridges, a rifle cleaning kit, and an awl. It felt like Christmas when he discovered a flask of what smelled like mescal. Bacanora, high-proof stuff, made from the agave pacifica—the fiery alternative to the tequila distilled from the blue agave. It was famous for giving courage and making heroes of mortals, at least for a time. He took a deep sniff, grunting as the strong smell reached his lungs, causing a spasm and sharp pain in his injured ribs.

There was also a small canvas bucket, which Connor filled with water for the horse, and then for the mule. He had owned the mule for several months, brown, medium sized, and not prone to panic. Even so, the mule would soon be on his own if it proved impossible to handle in his wounded condition. It was loaded with mostly food and water, a small shovel and oats. He tossed handfuls of oats in the direction of both animals, not wanting to get up. He ate one can of pears. He repacked Emilio's saddlebags with mostly food, along with the Bacanora and the small amount of whiskey remaining. Using some deadfall within reach, he made a small fire to brew coffee but mostly to reassure his watcher that he was still functional. He lay spent for a couple of hours, drifting in and out of consciousness. Waking, he realized it was dark, halfway through the night, judging by the moon. Struggling to shake off his torpor, Connor drank off the now cold coffee and slipped from the boulders with the horse. He walked slowly alongside the animal, good arm crooked over the saddle horn for support, the same hand holding the reins. The mule, on a lead, followed. Reaching the end of the spur, he took a deep breath to fight the dizziness and started to slide off and down the spur.

CHAPTER 2

He moved slow, pausing often to manage the throbbing pain and staggering gait. In places, he sat on his butt and slid while the animals sat back on their haunches as they, too, slid down the spur. The quarter moon made it hard to see, and although only about a hundred and fifty vertical feet to the draw, the slope off the spur was longer and convoluted as it zigzagged. He lost track of time and concentrated on not passing out or losing the animals as they made their slow descent. Connor heard coyotes yipping in the distance and occasionally small game moving during his frequent pauses. Fortunately, there were no telltale rattles from snakes. Reaching the draw, the slope was less precipitous and he mounted the horse and allowed the mare to pick its own way down. The draw widened and narrowed as it twisted downward. The sky was starting to lighten, and although he had only traveled about two and a half miles, he knew that he had to rest. He had to find a place where he was out of sight and he could defend if needed.

To his right he saw a large area of broken boulders that extended from halfway up to nearly the top of another ridge. There was vegetation visible in the growing light. Mostly mesquite and some small juniper mixed with catclaw, prickly pear, and other low, thorny vegetation. He dismounted and slowly worked upslope toward the sheltering rocks. A little way up, he tied off the animals and, returning to the trail, attempted to brush out the signs of his departure from the draw down from the mountains. Connor's fieldcraft was not exactly the best, given his condition, but the men behind him were not skilled trackers. Hopefully they would hurry on to the main trail leading out of this part of the Sierra Madre. When they didn't find him, they might return but also might just continue on toward the border. They might expect he would die or try to intercept him closer to the border.

Returning to the animals, he led them farther up and entered the jumble of boulders. Working deeper in, there was a four-foot split between two boulders that went up and then left, going on for about twenty feet before opening up to about ten feet wide. It continued at that width before making a hard right upslope after about eighteen feet. Leaving the animals at the turn, Connor walked up far enough to see that there was room for the animals to file onward to a point near the crest. Part of the passage was mostly covered by a slab of rock and offered some protection from the elements. There was some thin grazing in the wider sections and Connor grabbed the rifle and hobbled the animals before returning to where he had entered the maze of rock. The sun was fully up now although he was shaded, resting against a rock where he could see any pursuers coming down the draw.

At this altitude, it was cold in the morning but Connor was feverish. He walked back up to get his canteen, blanket, the can of pears, and cleaning gear. Emilio's rifle was the same model and caliber as his had been, significantly older but well maintained. He emptied the rifle, cleaned it, and reloaded. It was slow going, relying on one arm and hand. Taking off his half shirt and bandages, he could see the wound was still seeping and felt hot and painful. He cleaned it as best he could and, without removing the sutures, doused it with more whiskey. Reapplying cleaner bandages, he closed his eyes.

His current situation was the result of two things—money and a woman. The proximate cause of his current predicament was, without doubt, Issac Weaver. Weaver had been the leader of this gunrunning venture, and in hindsight, it had been stupid to cross him. Connor was a steady, thoughtful man, not usually given to reckless action. But trying to cheat or intimidate him were things that would put his back up. Weaver had gone way beyond that, trying twice now to kill him.

The expedition had consisted of five packers, each managing three mules apiece. A sixth packer managed the mules, carrying food and water in addition to what the packers carried with their personal gear. Each mule carried twenty rifles, with three hundred rounds of ammunition for each. The sale of the guns, ammo, and mules would net Weaver between eight and ten thousand dollars, assuming no losses along the way. Considering most men made between thirty and seventy-five dollars at very best a month, that was a good haul for two to three months' work. Of course, if caught by "La Gendarmeria Fiscal," also known as the Rurales, the return on investment would be very unattractive. His accounting experience was not necessary to figure that out.

If caught, the Rurales would split the contraband between them. The surviving prisoners among the contrabandistas would be faced with a stark opportunity. They would be allowed a chance to run for their freedom. As the Rurales were fond of saying, the prisoners "got away, but just a little way." The Sonoran Rurales were under the command of Emilio Kosterlitzky, the Russian-born, German-raised veteran of the Yaqui and Mayo Indian wars. He enjoyed the rank of major in the Guardia Nacional and lieutenant in the Rurales, appointed by President Diaz directly. Kosterlitzky had been, since 1886, Chief of Military Intelligence for Sonora and Sinaloa. He was likely to have a decidedly dim view of gunrunners.

Besides the six mule handlers, of which Connor was one, there were four gunmen hired as escorts and Weaver. As this was his second trip, Connor had asked if he could take some rifles along on his own account, for sale. Most of the group carried extras to pad their wages, three hundred dollars for the packers and six hundred for the escorts. In Connor's case, he brought an extra mule and twenty rifles, which would bring his net earnings to around eight hundred dollars. He knew this was pushing it, but he also knew that Weaver needed him. Not only was he tough and experienced, he also was good at weapons repair and carried spare parts and the tools to use them. This was appreciated by the Yaqui customers. He was also trusted to escort their guide's sister, returning to Yaqui territory with her brother. She would manage Connor's extra mule and rifles.

Weaver wasn't happy knowing he was potentially fostering a future rival in the business. Weaver was about ten years older than Connor. Taciturn, he was an experienced leader, having been an officer in the Confederacy. Weaver was not troubled by laws or rules other than his own. He projected confidence and a willingness to use violence if required. That said, his gunmen seemed loyal and disciplined. Maybe because he tended to be successful when it came to illicit enterprises and made sure his men shared in it. He was a survivor of many dangerous situations and that inspired confidence too.

Each night on the trek in, the guide, Anastasio Maldonado, would join his sister, Mariela, and Connor. Anastasio was near Connor's age, lean with dark, thoughtful eyes. Civilized in some ways, but capable of reverting to something more primitive. Mariela shared that trait too. Shorter, maybe five foot four inches, she had cut her hair to about four inches and wore it under a hat. She wore men's clothes and her breasts were compressed in some fashion, but even so, she looked very lumpy chested for all her attempts to blend in with the other hardcases. Conversations were short and stilted due to the exhaustion of that day's trip and the language limitations. Spanish was the lingua franca, but Connor gradually picked up some Yaqui words and phrases. Connor tried hard to stay respectful of both siblings, sharing his knowledge of weapons and the limited camp chores during the journey.

One night, Connor asked Anastasio, "Do you think there are enough Yaqui to stop the Mexicans from taking your lands? Better weapons will help, but are they enough?"

Anastasio frowned and rocked side to side as he sat cross-legged by the low fire. He replied with eyes on the fire, "It depends on how many Torocoyori there are; even the Apache found the Apache Scouts hard to overcome."

Connor knew that Torocoyori was the word describing Yaqui who went over to the Mexican side in the struggle. Connor nodded, impressed with the insight and realism.

He was surprised when Mariela said, "What other choice do we have, Senor? We are losing everything to these thieves!"

Normally, she listened quietly to the conversation, but her eyes seemed to spark as they locked with his. He knew the Yori, as they called the Mexicans, also was synonymous with "stealer of lives."

Connor nodded and tried to keep his doubts about the ultimate success of their resistance out of his voice.

"I hope that you will be able to negotiate a reasonable peace and that it will come soon. I hope that you will all survive to experience it."

That somber thought seemed to deaden further conversation for the night as they repaired to their blankets. Tomorrow promised another challenging day.

Anastasio would typically fill him in on what to expect the next day in terms of terrain, occasional water sources, and potential danger zones. He would also respond to questions about the Yaqui struggle to preserve their independence and the history of the eight pueblos at the heart of their culture. Both had been incensed when Governor Torres began to redistribute Yaqui lands along the river.

Anastasio told a story about this injustice. "Two of my cousins were told that they owed taxes. They were told to either pay or give up their land. Of course, they argued and refused to pay. They couldn't pay! When the soldiers returned, they hung both from a low tree, their feet about two feet off the ground. That is where we found them. We never found the rest of the family. Except for one young daughter. She was found floating in the river."

There was a matter-of-fact way to how Anastasio told the story that made it even more grim. His intense stare said he would never forgive. He and his sister had joined with Cajeme, leader of the uprising. He had some early success, but after his defeat in battle at Buatachive they had traveled north to relatives near Tucson. Now they were returning, along with guns for the Yaqui holdouts in the Bacatete Mountains.

While Cajeme had been fighting and ultimately losing, Connor had been packing and scouting for the U.S. Army in pursuit of Geronimo. Now, Cajeme was dead but not his cause and the fight. Geronimo, along with most of the Chiricahuas and Warm Springs Apaches, had been shipped off to exile in Florida. Small numbers of renegades were still a danger, particularly south of the border. Connor made the distinction that at least the Yaquis were semi-civilized farmers. Their fight was not north of the border. Although more numerous than the Apache, he doubted that their fight would end better for them. They had a long history of resistance, but submission, exile, and death seemed the more likely outcome.

Connor recognized that Tucson was the northern gateway to Sonora. Tucson had a considerable Mexican population and the cultural connections with Sonora. It also had a growing Yaqui population, so it wasn't surprising that he had met and been recruited by Rosangela Lazaro there. Connor was beginning to realize there were opportunities besides ranching worth considering as he thought about the future. The economies on either side of the border were heavily linked by mining and the processing of ore. Silver, gold, and more recently, copper were mined throughout the region. Copper in particular required scale in both mining and subsequent processing. Large companies and their subsidiaries, like Phelps-Dodge, were investing on both sides of the border. The economic and job opportunities were attracting Americans, Mexicans, and native peoples, especially Yaquis. Contributions from Yaqui wages were funding the resistance and the weapons they needed.

After reaching the rendezvous point with the Yaquis, two days were spent working out payment. It was a combination of barter and cash. Some payment in Mexican and U.S. gold and silver coin, some in gold and silver valuables, and the remainder in heavily discounted paper currency. Anastasio and Mariela spent time with the twenty or so Yaquis that had come up from the south. Connor joined them to eat and to say farewell on the final night. Before turning in, Anastasio gave him a surprised smile and abrazo when he tossed him a bag of spare parts and some extra repair tools. These were in short supply, short of cannibalizing other weapons.

"I hope you will be able to use these," he told him seriously.

He also got a bigger smile and a more enjoyable hug from Mariela when he presented her with the Winchester carbine and two boxes of ammo. He had loaned it to her on the beginning of the trip, and the carbine with the shorter twenty-inch barrel had become an extension of her existence.

"Thank you for managing me and the mules. I appreciate your strong support on the trail," he told her. "I wish you a safe journey and will think of you."

She had impressed him in critical moments and he appreciated her loyalty. Connor found he liked her—they had a bond, forged during the treacherous journey, and he wanted to acknowledge that in a concrete way.

She gave him another quick hug and sighed into his ear, "I hope we meet again, Senor Connor. You are easier to be with than the mules."

They both laughed at that and moved apart. Connor speculated that, at this point, his smell was indistinguishable from the mules he had shepherded south.

Connor had sold all his rifles and ammo and needed to collect the final two hundred dollars owed for packing in Weaver's rifles and ammunition. The events of the trip had created something deadly between them, and Connor expected trouble in getting paid. He waved to Anastasio, packing for departure with the rest of the Yaquis. He walked toward Weaver and two of his escort gunmen sitting by a small fire when Anastasio intercepted him.

"Safe journey, Connor. My sister says to tell you that you are always welcome. Ask for us in Belem."

After shaking hands, Connor replied, "Thank you, my friend. I hope that there will be peace for you, and we will be able to enjoy that together. If you or your sister ever return to Tucson, ask at the Torim Pulcheria or leave a message with Ray Witherspoon in Clifton. I will find a way to meet you. Tell Mariela that I will work on improving my prospects."

They both smiled at that. Connor steeled himself for the next conversation.

As he walked up, Weaver said, "So you are pulling out now?"

Connor nodded. "Just as soon as I collect the rest of my pay."

Out of the corner of his eye, he could see Cruz and the gringo gunman, Haggerty, speaking in low voices, glancing his way as they talked. Haggerty, gray-brown hair, heavy shoulders, and a small paunch, was the first to answer.

"Didn't you make enough on those rifles we protected for you on the trip down?" Haggerty was Weaver's Segundo and shared Weaver's antipathy toward Connor. Connor considered the odds and calculated that this was not the time or place to settle any issues other than what was owed him. Besides, there was a size advantage to Haggerty that almost certainly required gunplay to even the odds.

Connor didn't react, looking over to Weaver. He was probably north of fifty years old, with a tanned, weathered face, tobacco-stained teeth, and a mustache above a reasonably fit six-foot frame.

"I think you cut into my sales, Connor, costing me about two hundred dollars of profit on those four rifles I have left," Weaver said. "I'd say we were about even."

Connor was disappointed but not surprised that Weaver would try and screw him. Weaver was wearing a slight smile, confident he had picked his time and spot well.

Connor gave Weaver his most sincere and earnest look.

"I wish you had told me that you needed some help with selling. Why don't you get those rifles and some boxes of ammo if you have any left and I will sell them right now for you. Will that settle it? You better hurry. Your customers are about to leave too."

Weaver glared at him, trying to see any holes in the proposal. The prospect of more profit won out. He turned to Cruz.

"Get the rifles and a few boxes of cartridges."

The Yaquis were just about packed up when Cruz returned, four rifles and the same number of cartridge boxes. Connor took them and walked up to Anastasio.

"I have some rifles left to sell—I will throw the ammo in with them. Can you see if there is any interest? It may be a while before we are back."

Connor waited as Anastasio conferred with the leader of Yaqui warriors. They chattered and sorted through pockets and bags. When he returned, he apologized and handed him a rawhide bag.

"Amigo, this is all we have—is it enough?"

Connor opened the bag and started to sort through the miscellaneous coins and paper money. He took roughly half or around ninety dollars in coin and another fifteen in U.S. paper money out of the bag, stuffing it in his pocket. That left about eighty in the bag, still better than the cost of the rifles.

Looking at Anastasio, he said, "It is enough. Will you stay long enough for me to ride out? I don't trust these bastards we rode with."

Anastasio nodded his understanding and walked back to the leader of the band, talking in a low voice. They stopped their packing and turned to watch what happened next.

Walking back to about ten feet from Weaver, Connor stopped, held up the bag, and asked, "Will you pay me what you owe me now?"

Haggerty squared up his shoulders and flexed his hand near his holster.

Weaver responded, "Hand over the money and we will see."

Connor looked at Weaver. "I hope we are not going to start shooting. These Yaquis might just decide to join in. After all, you have a lot of their money and I think they know your prices were pretty stiff."

Weaver didn't enjoy that thought and glanced at the Indians who were watching intently, impassive but dangerously opportunistic.

Uncertainty about how his customers might react added to the scales as Weaver replied with a growl, "Hand it over."

Connor tossed the rawhide bag to Weaver and then turned to Haggerty, flipping a silver coin to him, glittering as it rotated in the air.

"Thanks for your protection, Haggerty; that should about cover it."

As the surprised Segundo reached to catch the silver piece, Connor pivoted, walked to his horse, and mounted. Leading his mule, he put spurs in, riding out.

He heard Weaver shout, "Come back, you son of a bitch!"

Without looking back, he kicked his horse into a canter down the trail.

CHAPTER 3

He woke, hot and fevered, chest hurting with each breath. No sign of anyone going down the draw below him. After a slug of rye and a deep drink of his water, he forced himself to his feet and retrieved the Bacanora. He mixed some cornmeal, jerky, and water in his coffee cup. After soaking it for a few minutes, he gobbled down the slightly salty, grainy slurry. Connor used some of the 100-proof mescal to clean his knife and then peeled off his dressing after adding a little water to loosen it where it had dried to the wound. Red, angry, and some pus draining from the exit end of the wound, the infection was not a good sign.

Taking a rod from his pistol cleaning kit, he cleaned it with the liquor and threaded clean cloth through the eyelet used for swabs. He removed the sutures, entry and exit, pausing for a few minutes to recover from the blurred vision and explosion of pain. Swabbing the entry and exit wounds with the alcohol-soaked cloth, he steeled himself to run the cleaning rod with the Bacanora-soaked cloth through the bullet passage. Up, down, and then several more times, his head rolled back; panting fast, he felt tears on his cheeks as he cursed and saw stars.

Changing cloth, he added more alcohol and cleaned the passage again. This time he did pass out for a few minutes before cleaning the entry and exit points yet again. He let the blood drip from the lower end, then leaned so the other side was higher and allowed the blood to drain from that side too. Applying pressure left then right there was no pus and only blood released. After thirty minutes, he started to re-suture both ends, taking his time and tying off each stitch. Finished, he lay back against the rock and stared out, unthinking, waiting for the pain to subside and allow coherent thought.

Opening his eyes, it was almost dark again. Walking back up to the wider passage near the animals, he sat under a stunted mesquite, gathering fistfuls of fallen sticks and bark. He used a stout stick to gouge out two six-inch-diameter holes, twelve inches deep, with a passage between the two at the bottom. He started a fire with the twigs in one of the holes. With air and more fuel fed in from the other hole, opposite the fire, he hung a small pot of water using a makeshift tripod and the pot's bail. There was almost no light or smoke from the fire's chimney. He retrieved some shredded willow bark from his pack, dropped it in the pot, and let it boil. He felt weak and listless.

Hopefully the willow bark tea would help with the fever. Pouring the tea into his coffee cup, he poured more water, added dried beans, and took stock of his situation while he waited for it to boil and then simmer. He hoped that his infection and fever would subside. Connor wasn't sure he could go through another attempt to disinfect the wound. He took stock of his current situation. He had three blanket-covered canteens, two still filled and one half filled. His fourth canteen had been ruined at the ambush site. Enough food for about a week on the mule, along with oats for maybe half that time for the animals. They would have to forage for themselves as they stopped, when possible. Rifle, revolver, and ammunition for protection, it would come down to his ability to recover and his physical stamina. He had to acknowledge that his gun skill and reactions had been significantly compromised by the ambush.

Eating the beans, mixed with one of his remaining cans of tomatoes, Connor decided to rest for at least one, maybe two days. Then he would have to move south, then go east, across the Rio Yaqui to find a place where he could recover with some degree of safety. He estimated he was at least two hundred and fifty miles south of the Arizona border. With luck, Weaver and his gunmen would have left the area. Connor moved up the passage above the animals, knowing they would alert him if anyone came up from that direction. He boiled another large cup of willow tea, rolled up in his blanket, and slept.

In the morning, he took off the dressings and assessed his wound again. Still some discharge coming out the lower exit wound and still some heat there, but not like yesterday. Now he really felt the effects of his roll down the mountain. He could see the bruises and he felt like he had received a thorough beating. His ribs were injured, making deep breaths very painful. Feeding and watering the mule and horse, he gave them a feeble, one-arm rubdown and carefully moved through the sheltering rocks looking for an area where they could graze a little. He found a small area about fifty yards from where he had slept, hobbled them, and returned to his packs, then found an observation point to watch his backtrail.

Drinking more tea, he pulled his revolver from his shoulder harness where it rested near his saddlebag. Although it was May, he was still at about a thirty-five-hundred-foot elevation and the mornings and nights were chilly. His left hand was his dominant and his pistol hand, even though he fired a rifle from his right shoulder. Reloading would be slow. With his wound, he could fire the rifle, albeit with his left hand just above the receiver due to his chest wound and limited reach. The pistol was another story. Since his shoulder harness was set up for a left-handed draw, he would have to put it in his belt so he could draw and use with his right hand. Connor had often practiced drawing, extending and firing in one fast, smooth motion before this latest catastrophe. It was not uncommon for him to go through a couple of boxes of cartridges a month, practicing. Inside twenty feet, he was confident of hitting a man-sized target, even moving. He had also practiced shooting with his right hand. He was not near as fast that way, but still functional.

Connor didn't think of himself as a shootist, but he was more than competent. He wasn't fearless; rather, he was a fatalist when committed to action. He had the self-confidence, trusting his survival chances to emerge maybe not unscathed, but alive. Connor knew from many skirmishes during his time in the Army and as a civilian contractor that he could hold his end and act with intelligence. People seemed to pick that up from his demeanor, finding it reassuring or a bit intimidating. Depending.

He remembered entering that bar in Tucson two years earlier and meeting Rosangela. He had come down from the Blue River in eastern Arizona, near the New Mexico line. He had just put a down payment on a section of land on the east side of the Blue, about twenty-five miles north of Clifton, near where the Little Blue joined the Blue. He had cut timber for a cabin and left it to season. Looking east and west were the San Francisco Mountains, with peaks above eight thousand feet. He had come down to Ft. Lowell to sign up as a packer or scout, whatever was needed. Connor needed someplace acceptably clean and reasonably inexpensive, with food and lodging for a few days.

When he saw her, she was behind the bar, serving drinks and bringing out food. Not beautiful but hard to take your eyes off her. Dark hair pulled back, tall, broad shoulders with a deep, downward-slanting bosom. Waist not girlish but with clear demarcation between it and her wide hips. He moved to the bar to order a warm beer and get a closer look.

"What will you have, Senor?"

"Beer, Senora."

She gave him a quick appraisal, dusty, fit and athletic with heavy shoulders. He tried to discreetly do the same without seeming too obvious, now that he was closer. She was at least thirty, but the wrinkles were not severe—character lines as they say. Her nose was prominent, extending out a third of its length then down at an angle. Up close, he liked the way her cheekbones broke the planes. Not beautiful but interesting—*arresting* maybe a better word. It was late afternoon and he was hungry.

"Am I able to get something to eat, still?" he asked.

"Chili and tortillas," she replied, nodding to a small table with two chairs by the wall as she moved toward the kitchen.

He thanked her politely then moved to sit down. The chili and fresh tortillas were great after the bland trail food he had been consuming. The meat tasted like goat, stringy and pungent. He resolved to buy some ground chile to spice his food before he went out again. The beer was lukewarm but welcome. Later, he paid at the bar and asked about a room and where to get a bath or a least a couple of buckets of water.

"Wait a little and I will have a boy come by and take you to a place and bring water. When you are clean and rested, come back. I have a question for you."

He returned, a triumph of hope over experience, but she was interesting and why not? It was not like there was something better to do. He stood at the corner of the bar, clean, shaved.

Rosangela rightly assumed the improved appearance was for her. "You look much better, Senor—less wolf, more man. Is this the life that you prefer, always moving about?"

Connor found himself replying, "I have been doing this for a long time; it has always seemed a logical step after I left the cavalry. Now I think it is time for a change. Do many men say that after talking to you?"

Now that he was clean, he could appreciate that she smelled good—soap, lilac, and tobacco. He struggled to maintain eye contact against the desire to visually enjoy the rest of her.

She smiled at that, responding, "Some do, but they seldom make the change they say they want. It takes perseverance and dedication, Senor."

He suspected that she was alluding to what it would take to sustain her interest. As the night wore on, he felt sure of it. Connor also thought it might be a challenge.

They carried on a desultory conversation, gradually becoming acquainted, interrupted by breaks to serve the other customers. There was another, older man also tending bar and waiting tables. There were about thirty or so patrons, mostly men, many Yaquis judging by the language dominating. Workingmen, eating and drinking.

"My name is Connor," he told her. "I am working for the Army as a scout but mostly a packer. I bought land farther north for a small ranch when the Apache are finally settled."

Her name was Rosangela, a Yaqui, born near the river of the same name that emptied into the Sea of Cortez. They conversed in Spanish and she was perfectly fluent.

"I arrived two years ago after the second battle of Anil. The Mexicans won the rematch and there was a serious outbreak of smallpox. Like a number of the Yaqui, I found Tucson a good place to regroup or perhaps restart," she told him between sips of their drinks.

He shared a few stories of his experiences, usually ending with an amusing anecdote at his own expense. Connor had been with General Crook on his expedition into the Sierra Madre to bring back the renegade Apaches. It had been well covered by the local press both during and after they had returned. As they talked, she slid her hand on the countertop so that their fingers occasionally touched. He covered her hand with his and she let it remain until she moved to serve more drinks for other customers. When she returned, they shared a long look, wondering what was next and how to move the story forward. She liked his polite confidence and could see that he was physically quite capable as well as intelligent.

Rosangela broke the silence first. "Will you come back to see me again? I can see that you are a man of perseverance." The last was added with a smile.

"I am," he replied, "and I will. I am hoping for much more from you. I could look at you all day and I find the conversation engaging. I hope we can talk outside of your establishment. Will you permit it, Senora?"

The direct change in tone was to her liking and confirmed her desire to explore a deeper relationship. She had learned that he needed more money to pay off the bank for his small ranchero and purchase calves to launch his business. She somehow doubted that he would be content working a small cattle ranch in the middle of nowhere.

"Come back tomorrow and we can talk some more. I sometimes hear of opportunities to make more money, in a shorter time. We can talk of other things as well."

He was reluctant to end the dialogue but also knew when it was time to make his exit. He paid, thanked her, and brushed his lips against her fingers, rising, then moved to the door. Connor had spent much of his life in the company of men, but it occurred to him that he had a strong desire for something different.

She thoughtfully watched him lithely weaving to the door and turned to the older man helping her tend to the tables and bar. Her uncle, Javier, cocked his eyebrow quizzically.

"I think he could be useful, maybe reliable for what we need," she responded to his unspoken question.

"Right now, our need is first for money, then arms and then for men to deliver them in Mexico. Much work to do," Javier grumbled. At that point, he spotted Anastasio Cuca, Cajeme's second in command, enter and move to the bar. Javier motioned with his eyes for Cuca to follow him outside and then he followed him around the corner, away from prying eyes.

The Sonoran government had agents, and they were very active in towns like Tucson. The Yaqui and, until recently, the Mayo had long been a problem. They had always asserted their independence and resisted the dominant culture. They had their own version of Christianity, but influenced and mixed with older beliefs that preceded the Spaniards and later the Mexicans. Cajeme, also known as Jose Maria Leyva, had served with the Mexican revolutionaries against the French. His experience in the military had helped him to fend off the Mexican forces in the first battle of Anil, as he had years earlier at Capetemayo.

Times and fortune had changed, and the Yaqui were being hard pressed by the forces led by Col. Torres and his kin, Governor Luis Torres. Thousands had submitted; some had been removed to work at haciendas against their will. Thousands moved to areas outside government control. Others were prepared to fight on. They needed guns and ammunition to continue effectively. Javier consulted with Cuca to learn what was most needed and how to get it to the rebels along the Yaqui River and adjacent mountains.

Javier was thin, of medium build and height, aged beyond his forty-five years. Cuca was stocky, broad chested, and his face less angular. Both had trust in the other, based on their shared hardships against the Mexican soldiers over the last ten years. They quickly identified a place to meet for final coordination of the delivery site. The agent would meet outside the church of San Francisco Javier, in Batuc, Sonora.

Batuc was along the Moctezuma River, not far from its confluence with the Yaqui. There were a number of Yaqui living there and in the neighboring village of Shaqui. It was roughly halfway between the Yaqui fighting from their refuges in the Bacatete Mountains on the north of the Yaqui River and the U.S. border crossing. The first week of April 1887 was the time set. It would take that long to raise the money for the gunrunners and find a competent leader willing to take the risk. The long trek to Batuc, especially while avoiding the Rurales, would be about forty days. Javier would send a guide and contact for the smugglers. Cuca would send an agent to meet the guide and coordinate the final rendezvous and exchange of payment for the weapons and ammunition.

Anastasio Cuca left Tucson directly, not wanting to chance being seen by the spies of Governor Torres. Javier returned to the bar and talked with Rosangela.

"We will need to get at least a few men with the gunrunners to keep eyes on them," he told her. "We will need to pay them something up front and the rest at the rendezvous."

"I will work on that and on finding someone to take the guns. I will talk to people in Nogales and El Paso and see if they have some possible names or contacts," she responded.

She thought that maybe this Connor, if properly motivated, could be her eyes and ears on this first run. She had no doubt that there would be more deliveries, and maybe at some point he could take over the deliveries, with her guidance of course. She looked forward to working on him some more in the time ahead. She could see he was attracted to her, and she liked what she saw too.

CHAPTER 4

SONORA & ARIZONA, 1887

Sonora was oriented with its long axis northwest, beginning at the U.S. border going southeast and terminating at the Sinaloa border. The eastern side of the state shared a border with Chihuahua. The southwestern side of Sonora was bounded by the Sea of Cortez. The eastern side of Sonora was dominated by the western slopes of the Sierra Madre Occidental with a number of peaks above eighty-two hundred feet. The continental divide followed the Sonora-Chihuahua border for a while south of the U.S. border and then veered into Chihuahua State but roughly paralleling the border. The area along the border with Chihuahua was rugged in the extreme. A number of rivers flowed from the Sierra Madre, the Sonora, Yaqui, Moctezuma, Aros, and Mayo to name some of the bigger ones.

The first trip had been successful as a trial run. They had taken a variety of weapons, primarily rifles of various calibers and revolvers along with ammunition. They had moved fast and managed to avoid the Rurales. They had avoided all the towns, traveling along the San Pedro River, south across the border and then to its headwaters above Cananea and its mines. Circling to the east of the town, they had hit the southeast-flowing Sonora River, leaving it when it turned southwest. Striking out cross country, they reached the Moctezuma River and followed it south to Batuc. They stayed in the rougher country away from the river to avoid travelers, towns, and more importantly, the hard-riding Rurales.

Traveling at a slow pace in the early evening and mornings, they camped during the day in remote and concealed places. If there was no water, a small party would slip to the river and replenish. It took thirty-five days to reach the rendezvous and make the exchange. Issac Weaver was an old hand at moving back and forth across the border. He brought three men with him to provide security and they seemed to know each other well. He had moved guns before, although his prime source of income was stolen horses and cattle, moved from either direction across the border. Weaver used Connor to communicate with the other mule skinners, who recognized his experience and accepted him as their acting leader for all things pack related. All of them were using hide aparejos because of the rough terrain they expected to cross, rather than the cross-tree saddles.

Outside of responding to Weaver's instructions, he and the packers didn't interact too much with Weaver and the guards. Weaver was what Connor would describe as a prime asshole, with a tendency to rely on intimidation and a bullying manner when talking to the mule skinners and the guide. He was a little more circumspect talking to Connor, seeming to know some of his background, which earned a little respect. There was a clear hierarchy and Connor was happy to watch and learn, maintaining a low profile. Besides, any disagreement would likely not end well and Connor was not about making friends, just getting out and back and collecting his payment.

After the exchange with the Yaquis, the group split up and the return was a lot faster, not having to worry about managing the mules or getting caught with contraband weapons. Still, Connor wanted to avoid contact and questions as much as possible, so he tried to avoid towns and the better used roads on the return. He also thought through his story about why he was in Mexico at all. He took the precaution to agree on a story with a friend of his in Ures and another in Nacozari. In the event of questions, they were to say he had been providing backup security, if it was needed, for payrolls during the preceding few months. His story was that his contract had ended and he was heading home. The alibi cost him a couple bottles of whiskey and would get a little flimsy if questions moved beyond, "Do you know him?" and "When did he leave?" It was still better than nothing, but not being stopped was even better.

Arriving back in Tucson, he was in for a surprise when Rosangela intercepted him about two blocks from the bar. He had been thinking about her a lot, the closer he got to Tucson. He admitted to himself that he liked and wanted her and the last nights before he had headed south had cemented that. He had agreed to help with the guns after his contract with the Army had ended. Connor had needed the money and he felt a strong attraction to the woman. They had grown closer with each trip back to Tucson, between returns from the field with the Army or the Indian Scouts in pursuit of renegades.

One night, she had come to his room. She hugged him without a word and he kissed her back, and then again as his hands slipped under her shirt.

She was not shy with her hands and she whispered, "I can tell you have waited a long time. I, too, have been waiting."

She was like a wildfire and he wasn't sure if he could hold his end up for long. Connor was not sure how it happened, but he was naked first. She pushed him down onto the bed while murmuring into his mouth, tongues searching. She was correct, he had waited a long time. When it was over, he lay gasping as she lay on top, resting on her elbows and smiling as she studied him. He laughed, feeling relaxed but wanting more. Connor knew then he would have to share some part of her commitment to helping her people if he wanted to hold onto her. She knew it too. She counted on it, in fact.

Months later, in the following spring, he knew something was wrong when she didn't smile but motioned her head for him to follow her. Leading his horse, he followed her to a small adobe house not far from where he usually stayed. He unsaddled the horse and entered as a boy came to take the horse. He gave some instructions then followed her in.

She kissed him hard and he returned it though he was trail dusty and much in need of a bath. Searching his eyes, she gave him the news.

"Cajeme was captured and killed in Mexico. His Segundo, Anastasio Cuca, was captured here in Tucson and was returned to Mexico yesterday and no doubt will share the fate of Cajeme."

"Are you in danger?" he asked, glancing toward the door, which he hadn't locked.

"Quien sabe? But I must leave for a few months until I can figure out what next to do," she said. She searched his eyes, then looked down.

"Will we go together, Rosangela?" He felt an unexpected tightening in his chest.

"No, Mi Amor. Safer to go separately. I will leave tonight, and God willing we can meet again in Bisbee in four months. You will come?"

She told him where and when and then there was a knock on the door. Connor pulled his revolver as Rosangela moved away from the door.

It was just the boy, with two buckets of water. Connor tipped him and secured the door, setting his gun close by as he stripped, stepped into a shallow copper hip bath, and washed with a rag and a chunk of soap from the first bucket. Pouring part of the second bucket on his head, he cleaned his hair and rinsed. He patted dry with a small towel and moved to the bed. She was waiting and the urgency and anxiety didn't allow for as much finesse or time as he wanted, or truthfully needed.

"There will be more and better times soon," she said as they reluctantly prepared to part. They kissed again, dressed, and she was gone. He felt disconcerted and emotionally flat.

Later that evening, Connor went to the cantina, ate, then stood at the bar nursing a warm beer, thinking about what he needed to do. His back was to the door but the precipitous drop in the conversation volume caused him to look into the mirror and spot the two men moving toward the bar. It confirmed that he had made a mistake coming back here, but then, there was no reason why anyone should be looking for him. One of the men stood next to him at the bar, the other to the left of his partner. The closest was about Connor's height but heavier and his head seemed to sit on his shoulders without much of a neck. Mustache, clean shaven, his question in Spanish confirmed he was Mexican.

"Not many Yankees here, Senor," he commented as he looked at him directly.

Connor eased right, getting a better look at both. The other man was also from the other side of the border, leaner, unshaved, projecting confidence and a sense that, like his friend, he was no stranger to violent action.

Connor had his gun in a shoulder rig and with his left hand holding his drink chest high, he was confident he could have it out and smoking before his drinking companions.

That is, if they didn't move into him to interfere with his draw. His problem was that they were too close, but then, they had the same problem. He smiled faintly at them and replied in the same language that the prices were good and the cantina was quiet. They nodded and looked over the rest of the patrons, who obviously were not interested in meeting their eyes. They may have been involved in the arrest of Cuca, or not, but they had the aura of authority and that voice in Connor's head said he needed more distance from these two than just the length of the bar. He prided himself for being able to think clearly and act effectively when the situation demanded. Maybe they had been watching the bar, or Rosangela, her partner, or who knew? But their interest in him was not a good thing, and his best option now was to keep calm and hope they were not ready to make a play.

That seemed to be the case as they finished their beers and sauntered out without looking back. Connor had noted that Javier was not behind the bar and suspected that like Rosangela he had decided to maintain a low profile for a while. After a few minutes he looked at the bartender and nodded toward the back door. Receiving an imperceptible nod, Connor slipped behind the bar and out the back door.

He took a quick glance back as he passed through the doorframe and stepped out. He was immediately met by an air-stealing punch to the gut, dumping him on his ass and against the outside wall. An almost simultaneous kick to the ribs completed the rude greeting and he felt the barrel of a pistol against his head.

"I think we have more to talk about, Senor, and I think you will have more to tell us," the neckless cabron said.

Connor's breath wheezed out as his survival instincts accelerated.

The Mexican grabbed his shirt and started to lift Connor up like he was a rag doll. His partner, not wanting to miss the fun, slammed another fist into his side and plucked the gun out of his shoulder rig. The only bright spot was that he hadn't lost any teeth yet. That irrelevant but morose assessment was interrupted by the explosion of a shotgun in the alley, to his right. He was dropped back on his ass as his two drinking buddies ran around the corner and out of sight.

Gasping, he looked up to see Javier, shotgun in hand, staring down the alley and reaching down to help him to his feet. Putting his arm around his neck, Connor and Javier staggered off in the opposite direction. He felt like a complete fool for being suckered like that but also thankful to have been rescued. He knew that without Javier he would have been in for a lot worse at the hands of those two assholes.

"How did you know?" he asked.

"I have been watching them since one of our compadres spotted them a few days ago," replied Javier.

"I owe you," Connor gasped as his ability to breathe started to return. "I was a complete idiot."

No response was needed to that statement of fact. They arrived at the stable where the doors opened and the boy who had brought the water led a horse and a mule out.

"He packed your stuff and a little food—you will have to stop somewhere and get more but it is the best we could do. I suggest you ride and watch your backtrail.

Those men work for Governor Torres and are not friends to the Yaqui or anyone who helps them."

"How did they know about me?" asked Connor.

"A gringo, drinking in a Yaqui-run and frequented cantina, you are going to stand out. If you still want to help, we will see you in Bisbee. For now, leave and watch your back."

Connor shook Javier's and the boy's hands. He mounted, twinging with pain from the kick in the ribs, and guided the horse toward the west side of Tucson.

Leaving the city, he turned south; then, with the lights of Tucson behind him, he turned east. He maintained a steady but cautious pace, not wanting to injure the horse and mule while relying on just the moonlight for visibility. His ribs were hurting too. He was roughly following the railroad line and the sun found him stopping just south of the Rincon Mountains, about ten miles outside of Tucson. The Whetstone Mountains were in the distance on his right. He stopped and rested for a few hours and then turned southeast in the direction of Tombstone, about thirty or thirty-five miles away. He needed supplies and that was the best place to get them since Tucson was not feeling safe.

He had lost his pistol as well as some pride and was angry with himself for being such a dumb-ass. He was old enough not to waste a lot of energy nurturing a grudge, Irish antecedents notwithstanding. But this seemed somehow different, not so easy to shake off. Connor was burning with a desire to get even when the odds were better. He played a number of scenarios through his mind and that took his mind off the pain in his bruised ribs and sore stomach muscles. He kept his eyes moving over the terrain and his backtrail. Besides the two who had jumped him, there were still a few renegade Apaches ghosting through this territory, and bandits too. He had spent a lot of time in the triangle between Forts Lowell, Huachuca, and Bowie. By noon the following day he reached the San Pedro River and paused to rest, water, and let the animals graze in the lush grass along the banks. They seemed to be holding up all right. There was a profusion of birds, particularly quail, but they were safe from him at the moment. From there it was a relatively short ride into Tombstone where he would find a cheap place to stable the animals and a room to stay.

The next day, he wired some of his money to the bank in Springfield to pay down his loan for the land on the Blue River. With the rest, he needed to do some shopping. His first stop was a gun store to replace his lost single action. He had in mind a double action Merwin & Hulbert in a .44-40 caliber, matching the caliber of his Winchester 73 model. The Merwin & Hulbert had a new model out. The Model Four came in a variety of standard barrel lengths and Connor was interested in the 3.5-inch barrel with the Bird's Head handle.

The revolver had a folding hammer and, combined with the Bird's Head grip, the double action made it fast to bring into play. It also was unlikely to catch when pulling from a shoulder harness and firing. Nickel plated for corrosion resistance, it was one of the finest revolvers on the market. Connor dry-fired several times and practiced with some empty shells, expelling them and reloading. He bought ten boxes of ammo to allow him to practice when he got to his cabin site on the Blue.

He would have to modify his shoulder rig, but for now he would use the old one. Next, Connor stopped at the general store to pick up some other supplies to get him to Clifton and beyond. Loading the mule, he stopped at the blacksmith's and had him modify a seven-inch length of leaf spring, about two inches wide into a tight, deep U shape.

The next morning, Connor traveled northeast through the gap between the Chiricahua and the Dos Cabezas Mountains. Between them, near Apache Pass, was Ft. Bowie. He hadn't been to Bowie since the previous September, when he had been paid off for his packer services. The Apache Scouts under Lt. Gatewood had also been mustered out around that time and, unfortunately, shipped off to Ft. Marion along with the renegades they had chased. Connor had established a rapport with some of the scouts and over the years had learned a lot about surviving in this arid country.

Stopping by the post headquarters, he ran into Sergeant James Murphy, whom he had campaigned with on a number of expeditions and patrols. Broad shouldered and balding, Murphy sported a luxuriant handlebar moustache. They shook hands and then met after duty hours at Gibson's sutler tent and his makeshift bar. Standing at the wood plank stretched between two sets of stacked cracker barrels, they nursed the burn from their rye whiskey.

"Things have slowed down since we shipped the Apaches out, although there are still some out doing some mischief," Murphy allowed.

"Can't say that I miss those bastards."

After a while, talk turned to patrolling south of the Chiricahuas and the rampant rustling and general thievery in the Sulphur Springs Valley in the east and the San Simon Valley to the west.

"Galeyville and Portal seem to be where most of those crooks are holed up," the sergeant said. Those places also seemed to be centers for illicit traffic going both ways across the border, he continued.

"Who has the contracts for horses and beef?" Connor asked, then talked about his ambition to raise calves on his property on the Blue River as the evening wore down.

The sergeant found him a bunk for the night in one of the empty barracks and Connor slept well knowing he was safe for at least this night.

CHAPTER 5

He was still three miles short of the Southern Pacific Railroad tracks when he saw four horsemen coming out of a draw in the San Simon Valley, heading right for him. He stopped and pulled out his Winchester from its sheath and jacked a round into the chamber. Dismounting, Connor laid the barrel across the saddle of his horse and waited for the men to intercept him. They fanned out about twenty feet short of him and the lead rider asked for his name. All four had rifles out but didn't bring them up to their shoulders, feeling confident in their numbers.

"Connor," he replied to the leader. "Who are you?"

The leader looked to be in his forties, vigorous and fit.

"Where are you coming from, mister?" he asked, and another added, "You best put your gun up before you get hurt."

Connor gave him a hard look. "We can talk but I won't hesitate to sort you out if you bring that gun up. I am coming up from Ft. Bowie and going north to my place above Clifton. Now who the hell are you?"

The leader recognized he was out on a limb and at a disadvantage against a dismounted man with a rifle at such close range.

He eased up a bit in his tone. "We are working for a ranch not far from here and have been losing cattle to riffraff and rustlers. You seen any other strangers on your way from Bowie?"

"No," Connor replied, "and I suggest you back off and I will do the same. I am not looking for a fight but I am not going to get rousted for what someone else did either."

When the leader grunted at that and took off his hat to wipe his brow, Connor asked him if he had seen a couple of Mexicans in the last few days and described them.

Frowning, he replied he had seen the two, about ten miles outside of the Southern Pacific whistle-stop of Maley, not more than six miles from where they were now.

"They friends of yours?" he asked.

"Not likely. They tried to bushwhack me a few days earlier, outside of Tucson," Connor told him, noticing that they were losing interest in pressing matters further.

A few more terse words and they were apparently satisfied that he was not the problem. Connor watched as the four rode off. Apparently, they were satisfied he was just passing through or just not prepared to push their interrogation further. Connor was happy to move on, too, heading north for the Gila River, toward Safford. Northwest were the Pinaleno Mountains and one of the highest mountains in the territory, Mt. Graham, a sacred peak of the now subdued Apache.

As he rode, Connor thought about the two Mexicans who had given him the aborted beating in Tucson. If he had been in their shoes, he would have taken the train and got off either at Benson or Maley. They could even, if they chose, leave the train anywhere along its route toward El Paso, their horses unloaded from one of the stock cars. By asking around Ft. Lowell or Tucson, they could have learned enough to guess his general destination and get ahead of him. He doubted they wanted to follow him all the way to Clifton and beyond. That left an interception somewhere between the railroad and the Gila, the Pinaleno and Peloncillo Mountains to the west and east.

Halfway between the two mountain chains were the much lower Whitlock Mountains. A high point near the northern end would provide good observation to the east, west, and north. Connor couldn't be certain but, with a little luck, he might just turn the tables and repay the rough treatment he experienced in Tucson. He also suspected that they had carte blanche from their employer to shut down smuggling and suspected smugglers. He couldn't just keep looking over his shoulder; he needed them off his back if they were a threat. He had enough food to be patient and could find a waterhole in the dry San Simon Creek that slanted toward the Gila. With the sun dropping, he veered northeast then east toward the broken terrain at the base of the Whitlocks. Crossing the dry creek, he used his shovel to dig down enough to have water seep into the hole and water the horse and mule. He then followed another draw into the mountains in early evening.

He made a dry, cold camp, hobbled the animals, and then moved up and north on foot, hoping to spot a fire or a light. Nothing. Those two were probably too canny for that. In the early morning grayness, he repeated the process, without success. Moving slowly north, he was almost out of the foothills when he thought he spotted movement to the west and a little behind him. Connor settled into cover and waited. After a few hours, using his binoculars, he was able to confirm that there were a couple of men and several animals opposite his position. Taking his time, he slowly stalked their position. In ninety minutes, he closed to where he could smell their cigarettes. He was satisfied with his fieldcraft but wary of pushing his luck. He wasn't sure if he should damage them or their horses in a combination of payback and warning. Connor hoped running off their horses would be enough of a message. In any event, his luck didn't hold.

He disturbed a covey of quail, which caused them to burst low into the air with a *thruuurrrrr* of beating wings. One of the two men spotted him and snapped a shot at him with his rifle, then came close with another. These two were clearly prepared to kill, and that changed his response calculation. Now it was about more than sending a message and a little payback. Connor dropped into a low arroyo, and, angling left from their position and using the cover, sprinted toward them. Looking over the rim, he was less than a hundred feet out. He shouldered his Winchester and fired, ejected and fired again immediately. A shout told him he'd either hit someone or was close. Another ten feet and he popped up again, acquired one of his targets and fired, ejected, and fired again. At this distance, the trajectory was line of sight out to one hundred and fifty yards. If not rushed, the aim would be accurate and deadly.

Rounds were coming back from two weapons and Connor came out of the arroyo and low crawled to a group of boulders. A quick glance showed they were focused to his right and he ducked down and moved farther left. Looking around a boulder, through the branches of some greasewood, at ground level, Connor sighted, steadied, and fired. He heard an explosive grunt and got his head back as a half dozen rounds splashed around where he had fired from. Shards of rock ricocheted around him as he backed into a shallow fold in the ground and crawled at a diagonal toward where he expected to find the man he had hit.

Connor had six bullet loops attached to his rifle butt. He used the cartridges to refill his magazine while trying to relocate his enemies. One rifle was still firing, searching by fire, hoping to get lucky or provoke return fire and pinpoint his location. Connor estimated he was thirty feet out and eased up to a sitting position, head slightly exposed, elbows jammed into his knees to provide a supported aim. Another shot hit about ten feet to Connor's right. He fired through his opponent's smoke, and as the man came up, trying for a shot at the telltale smoke, Connor fired three times, steady and fast, knocking him back. Connor rolled from the sitting position to his knees, paused, and in the absence of fire, sprinted diagonally toward the Mexican's firing position. He stayed low, glanced quickly, and saw the burly Mexican agent with the short neck sprawled out and bleeding heavily.

Connor left him there and moved toward where he thought the other man had been when he received fire. He was extremely cautious and slow, his hearing limited from the noise of the gunfire, methodically moving his eyes and head then easing forward. He spotted blood and decided to just wait until his hearing recovered more. His hearing improved and he gradually became aware of labored breathing, maybe a dozen feet away but out of sight around a mesquite tree and some waist-high rocks. At the same time, he also located the horses, tied off but stomping and snorting, to the left and behind the tree. Connor circled around slowly until he reached the horses, rifle shouldered, head and rifle moving as if locked. They saw each other simultaneously. The man had one hand on the saddle horn and a boot in the left stirrup. His other hand held a pistol. Connor fired first, hitting the horse, which reared slightly, sidestepped, and collapsed. The man fired as the horse fell on him, the round pinging off the ground. Connor sidestepped and fired twice, moved more to be clear of the gunsmoke, dropping to a knee.

The horse was down, kicking, as Connor put a bullet into its head, effectively ending the misery. The downed man was forever beyond pain. Connor automatically reloaded his rifle from the bullet loops sewed on his vest chest pocket. The lean, unshaved Mexican from the Tucson cantina lay contorted, his leg under the dead horse. Kicking his single action colt away, Connor left him and went back to check on his partner. He was where he had left him, empty eyes staring up.

He went through their effects. The lean man had a letter hidden in his boot, attesting to his employment by the governor of Sonora. It directed the reader to render assistance for requests from his agents. His name was Sergio Menendez, his partner Jesus Torres, likely no relation to the governor. Connor went through their pockets, finding some money but little else of interest. Saddles, bridles, bags, and weapons he placed in the rocks and covered with more rocks. Pistols were .45 caliber, typical of those used by the Rurales, but not confirming the affiliation. They were on the wrong side of the border to have any legal authority. Still, they could have been on detached duty and he remembered their swagger when they had entered the cantina.

Their bodies he buried deep. The horse, he left for the vultures and scavengers. He kept the loose .44-40 center-fire cartridges from their rifles, and a bottle of mescal, less a couple of swigs. The pack horse and surviving riding horse he turned loose after retrieving his animals. He didn't want to have anything connecting him to the gunfight. Moving to a high point, he saw no one heading his way although he saw a few vultures gathering, circling. He would have to rely on the scavengers to further confuse the scene.

Crossing the Whitlock Valley, Connor skirted the Black Hills then descended to the Gila River. The two men had given him no choice in the gunfight, which eased his conscience. But if he were honest with himself, they were a threat if only by identifying him to the authorities in Mexico. The U.S. authorities were also not enamored with gunrunning. It was in his self-interest that they were in a better place. They may have sent a description south and maybe a name. Connor consoled himself with the thought that they had moved fast to get ahead of him, so communication and detail might have been limited. He suspected they saw an opportunity to gather intelligence about high-priority, Yaqui rebel support. Eliminating a supporter would have been a consideration too. Anyway, there was nothing he could do about it.

Connor thought about all this as he continued north. If he was smart, he would forget about another trip to Mexico. The woman, Rosangela, was committed to the Yaqui cause, and if he wanted her, he would have to provide some level of support. The money was important to his plans too. Was he being used? Was there really a future possible? Connor shrugged. It really didn't matter at this point. For now, he wanted the woman. And he needed the money. There was work to do to get his small ranch operational, so he pragmatically put the other thoughts aside for now. He crossed the Gila and then, on reaching the San Francisco River, he followed that toward the mining town of Clifton. Four days after the gunfight, he reached Clifton.

CHAPTER 6

Clifton, named after Henry Clifton who originally prospected for gold, was now focused on copper mining and production. Tight against the cliffs on either side of the San Francisco River, Clifton was a recently completed terminus for the narrow-gauge Arizona and New Mexico railroad. The railroad started in Lordsburg, New Mexico, where it was possible to change trains from the thirty-six-inch narrow gauge to the fifty-eight-inch Southern Pacific. A rough, rowdy mining town, the population already exceeded one thousand, including a number of smelter and mine workers who had come up from Chihuahua and Sonora, along with Chinese and Anglos. The main smelter and mining claims were owned by the Arizona Copper Company and were on the west side of the river, while commercial establishments were on the east side of the river, most notably along Conglomerate Avenue. West across the San Francisco River, and just south of Chase Creek, was Chase Street, where a number of stores, restaurants, and bars were located. A number of smaller claims were farther west along the creek but were fast fading as smaller miners were being forced out or selling out to the big guys. Two or three miles west, along Chase Creek, there was extensive copper mining at Morenci and Metcalf.

Connor stopped first at the Clifton Hotel on Conglomerate Avenue, paying for one night. Stopping at the livery, he paid for stabling both animals as well as keeping the packs secure. Saddlebags and bedroll over his shoulder, he made a beeline for the Clifton Hot Springs Bath on the west side of the river, walking across the bridge just north of the hotel. Frank Woodard had just opened the no-frills bath and Connor was ready, and truth be told, in need of a good soak. Walking up Chase Street, he was amazed at the number of new places and people along the narrow street.

He stopped at the gunsmith's and shook hands with his friend from the Fourth Cavalry, Ray Witherspoon. The reunion was warm between two men who had served together. Ray had retired six years earlier and had tried his hand at mining before deciding it was better to sell to miners than to be one.

"It's been almost a year since I saw you, Ray. I think you were made for this business," Connor said as they gripped hands. "The way this town is growing, you picked the right spot."

"Yeah, I am not missing those cold nights and hot dusty days riding for the Fourth Cav. But how about you? I heard from an acquaintance of yours from Ft. Lowell, Tommy Chadwick, that you have stopped your contract work for the Army," Ray said.

Connor watched as Ray rotated his shoulder a few times, then grimaced.

"Times are changing and I need to find something else to keep me fed," Connor commented. "Anyway, we are almost neighbors, my friend. I am heading up to build that cabin on the Blue. At least until I run out of money. But I got more than enough for dinner if you'll join me tonight."

"Love to," Ray replied. "Where are you staying?"

After being told, Ray said, "Hell, you can bunk with me when you are in town."

"Well, I don't want to interfere with your love life, Sarge," which caused both to laugh since Ray was a confirmed bachelor.

After catching up, Connor produced the U-shaped leaf spring that he had fashioned in Tombstone.

"Can you modify a shoulder holster for me so that the tension holds my Merwin and Hulbert in place but allows me pull it almost straight out to fire?" he asked. "It will need to be under leather so it doesn't catch or scrape," he added.

"Didn't know you had ambitions to be another Jesse James," Ray commented as he half smiled.

Connor was aware the M&H was a favorite of James, and for good reason.

"You never know when you need an edge, Ray."

With that, he left the gun with Ray, along with the shoulder rig, making plans to meet that night for a dinner and drinks.

The rest of the day went fast as Connor made stops at the botanica to pick up some medicinal dried herbs and teas, including willow bark and ginger. At the barber he asked about leasing a wagon along with where to go for lumber and tin roofing sheets. He also priced small cast iron stoves. Dinner was at a café near the hotel where he met Ray Witherspoon again. Ray had been a weapons armorer in the Fourth Cav., among other duties, and Connor had learned a lot about repairs and maintenance from him. After sharing stories about their former commander, "Bad Hand" Mackenzie, the conversation turned to the shoulder holster. Ray's curiosity got the better of him.

"I don't know why you are interested in being a fast gun, but you are a good shot and it is better to be accurate than fast," he said. "You're not planning on turning outlaw, are you?"

"With the Apache troubles over, my packing and scouting days are over," Connor told him. "I need some money to stand up my small operation on the Blue."

Ray gave him a long, steady look, waiting.

"I had a chance to pick up a year's pay in a few months, smuggling guns south of the border," Connor admitted, holding eye contact. "I want to be ready to survive any complications that might arise."

Ray gnawed on his mustache, then said, "Trust me when I tell you that the clamshell spring you gave me for a holster is not going to be the answer. What you are going to need is the right holster, technique, and a hell of a lot of practice. I can help you with the holster and technique. Even with a lot of practice, there are a lot of circumstances and just plain bad luck that make this crazy. Your best bet is avoiding those risky circumstances and start with a gun in your hand or on your shoulder, not relying on a fast draw. Counting on being first is a fool's game."

Connor nodded and told him, "I know that is good advice, but I made commitments to people and I have to do what I can to be ready if things go upside down. If you can help, I appreciate it. If not, then I understand and no hard feelings."

Ray shrugged. "Yeah, I figured. Shit, Connor, leave the gun and holster with me. When you come back in town with the wagon, in a couple of weeks, I will have the holster ready and we can work on how to use it. Not going to use the clamshell though. I have a medium-frame Merwin-Hulbert .38 caliber you can borrow 'til then. Leave me twelve dollars in case you fall in love with it and I will throw in two boxes of ammunition."

Connor forked over the money and they shook hands. A few drinks later, they stopped by Ray's store and he brought out the .38 caliber revolver, the ammunition, and a Mexican double loop holster.

The next day, Connor tied his horse and mule to the back of the wagon he rented and picked up supplies. Besides the wagon, he rented two block and tackles, bought more food supplies, loaded lumber for the roof, and tin roof sheets. He only had enough to complete half of the roof, planning to pick up the rest on a second trip and then boards for the floor. He was going to lay stone in the corner where he was planning to sit the cast iron stove. It would serve for both heating and cooking.

Last year, he had cut and trimmed the logs, using a draw knife to take the bark off, sitting them up on other logs to allow them to dry. He had also dug the foundation and used stones gathered to fill the two-foot-deep trench, using the largest stones for the corners and every four feet to elevate and carry the cabin's load. He had planned on a 24 x 16 ft. cabin and had set the first course of sleeper and sill logs on the foundation, allowing them to dry in place on the stone before notching. He had set in log stringers horizontally, both length and width, resting on stone piers. The cabin was raised on stone footings about one foot above ground level. On the interior, he had filled the gap between the ground and the piers with dirt, leaving a small air gap under the stringers and, eventually, the flooring.

It was slow going along the rough trail adjacent to the San Francisco River. The river was not that wide or deep but had a stiff current this time of the year. A day and a dozen miles up, he camped at a seasonal creek. Here, the trail petered out and he still had another six or so miles to go before he reached the mouth of the Blue River, where it emptied into the San Francisco. The mountains on either side of the river climbed to between six and seven thousand feet and it was cool at night. Heavily forested, there was plenty of game and also predators. Wolves and Grizzles were at home here. This had also been the haunt of the White Mountain Apache bands, now loosely settled in San Carlos to the west and Fort Apache to the north and west. He would need to sleep light and keep a close eye on his stock.

This area had been home to the Bedonkohe or the Gila band of Chiricahuas, of whom Geronimo was the most infamous and now deported to the east. East were the Black Mountains, lately dominated by the Chihenne or Warm Springs Apaches. Connor had spent years scouting and packing in the campaigns against Victorio. They were scattered, some held at Ft. Marion, Florida. Some mixed in with other bands at San Carlos as well as on the Mescalero Reservation in New Mexico. Victorio himself had been killed by the Mexicans at Tres Castillos. Others still ghosted through this area, going between the reservations to the north and east and their Nednhis cousins in the Sierra Madre.

Seven years earlier, in the summer of 1880, he had been employed as a packer with his old unit, the Fourth Calvary. Ray had still been on active duty then, as a sergeant with A company, under Major Noyes as acting battalion commander. The unit was working out of Ft. Cummings, in eastern New Mexico. It was while on a scouting trip, looking for signs of Victorio, that Ray and Connor had been caught in an ambush. There had been seventeen troopers, led by a lieutenant. Ray was the senior enlisted sergeant. Connor was one of three packers, each with three mules for the extended scout in the Florida Mountains and then farther south to the Tres Hermanas Mountains.

The mountains were oriented roughly north–south. They had passed through the Florida Gap and were a little more relaxed now that they reached the flatter ground east of the chain. Though flatter, there were plenty of folds and small arroyos and scattered rock formations as they moved south. Connor was near the middle of the file when there was a shocking, sudden explosion of gunfire. He instinctively moved east, farther into the flats and away from the gunfire toward slightly raised and rock-strewn ground. A glance to the front told him at least three horses were down and the rest were milling, while troopers tried to dismount and return effective fire. It took all his horse's strength to pull the mules in file, and Connor reached back to add his arm strength to the lead rope.

The Apaches had been concealed in a shallow arroyo and were using its cover to shift toward the rear of the column. He could hear the breech-loading single-shot Springfield rifles as well as Winchester repeaters barking as the soldiers fell back, trying to regroup. Reaching the limited cover of his destination, Connor dismounted and was joined by another packer, three troopers, and Sergeant Witherspoon. The rest of the survivors were falling back to the north and the Apaches were shifting focus to Connor and the soldiers taking cover and returning fire. No doubt, they wanted the mules, the provisions, and more importantly the ammunition on two of the mules. One of the mules packing ammo was in Connor's string and it was frantically trying to break free and flee. Connor unsheathed his Winchester and put a round in the beast's head, dropping him and holding the other two in the string, in place.

Facing forward, he started adding his fire to the soldiers holding the warriors at bay. They were moving from position to position, seeking any cover as they tried to close on their enemies. Some fired and moved, others stayed in the arroyo to provide covering fire. Some of the Apaches were trying to keep the remaining soldiers from reorganizing and counterattacking. They were intent on pressing their advantage. The other packer, Fredricks, was also firing now, and the combined fire was becoming more effective, the shock having worn off. To his right, Sergeant Witherspoon got one of the troopers to move farther to his right as it looked like the Indians were trying to get around on that side. The other two soldiers and Fredricks were in an arc to the left and it looked like the attackers had stalled. Their constant movement and volume of fire made it seem like there were a lot of warriors, but Connor guessed they were about the same number as the patrol. The sergeant was trying to direct the defense and fire when he was hit and knocked back on his ass, stunned.

Connor could see he was moving as he slid more rounds into the chamber. He guessed he had twelve loaded and focused on the closest Apache, about twenty-five yards from the sergeant. He had an angle where he was mostly covered from the front while he could engage the Apache. He started firing at him, taking time to be deliberate and ignoring the firing from the front, splashing into the rocks. He felt rock shards skin just above his ear as he levered and fired again and again. The Apache he was aiming at fired in his direction and then began squirming back, then rolling left and facing toward the arroyo. Connor fired again and saw him jerk then roll into the cover of the arroyo. He ejected the round and it was empty. Dropping the rifle, he took ten steps, grabbed Ray by the collar, and dragged him hard and fast to the closest cover. As he looked to see how badly he was wounded, he became aware of increased firing from the north, the distinct sound of the soldiers' Springfield rifles. The Apache fire lessened and then became desultory. They were breaking contact. The soldiers came up on line with the men around Connor. Sergeant Witherspoon had been hit in the upper shoulder. Three others were also wounded, one still able enough to function. The third mule skinner was dead. Smithson was his name. He had gone down in the initial barrage.

Seven horses were down or wandering and using the mules as spare mounts; the wounded were slung on makeshift stretchers between mules. The patrol set off toward Ft. Cummings, about twenty-five miles north. It was hard on the wounded, but there was no place for medical help closer. Except for rest stops for the animals, they kept moving until they reached the fort. Ray was in sad shape for a while but then recovered and in four months was back on light duty. The official report said the patrol was able to inflict significant casualties on the Apaches, routing them. No bodies were found although there were certainly some at least wounded, judging by the blood trails. Several mules and a couple of horses were lost, along with four or five hundred rounds of ammo. Connor was left with the task of informing Smithson's widow.

Smithson had a wife in Silver City, and a week after the ambush, Connor rode west from Ft. Cummings to inform Mrs. Smithson about her husband. It took two days of riding to get there. Part of the way he traveled with a calvary patrol that was headed west. The last ten miles, he was on his own. Arriving, he stopped at the sheriff's office and then two churches before he found someone who knew where the Smithson's lived. Silver City was primarily about mining, sitting at around six thousand feet elevation. The Pinos Altos Mountains towered to the east. Ft. Bayard was not too far away, and Buffalo Soldiers from the Ninth Cavalry provided protection as best they could for the civilians and miners in the area. Connor and Smithson had both worked out of Ft. Bayard so this was familiar territory.

His knock was answered by a middle-aged, midsized lady, brown hair tied in a bun with a few strands drifting over her ears. Mrs. Smithson was a little heavy but pleasant to look at with a round face, a well-developed bust, and a clear complexion. He remembered her name was Eileen from the occasional campfire conversations with her husband. She saw a clean-shaven, fit frontiersman with a clean blue shirt, shoulder rig, and canvas vest, hat in hand. He wasn't handsome exactly but the word *capable* came immediately to mind for some reason. He appeared calm but she noticed that he was rotating the brim of his hat as he introduced himself. She braced herself for bad news as her daughter and son hovered in the background.

"Ma'am, could we speak alone for a moment on the porch?" he said as he stepped back and Eileen closed the door behind her, heartbeat accelerating. "We were patrolling south of Ft. Cummings when we were ambushed by Apaches. Your husband didn't make it, ma'am. I am so sorry," he added lamely and she covered her eyes and stated to cry.

Connor was at a loss at this point but then softly put an arm around her and pulled her in. After a few minutes, she pulled back and scrubbed her eyes.

"I need to sit. Come inside, please; I will get you some water."

She stepped in and sent the children out; the boy was about nine, he estimated, the daughter maybe twelve or thirteen. She wasn't that interested in the details, and truth be told, there was not that much to tell.

"Mrs. Smithson, I respected your husband and want to help you if I can, based on what you want to do," he told her. "I don't know if you have family you would like to go to or what would make sense for you. I have your husband's pay and a collection the boys took up. It isn't much but it is a little over a hundred and twenty-five dollars," he said as he handed over the envelope.

He didn't tell her that, outside of the pay, most of the collection came from him.

"I need some time, Mr. Connor. You were kind to come here and tell me. Can we talk in a day or two?" At this point she was starting to tear up again.

"Yes, ma'am, I will return the day after tomorrow if that is okay with you," he replied. "I am afraid that I have to get back to work in not too long," he added a bit awkwardly.

Leaving, he returned to the room he had rented and cleaned up before discharging his self-assigned duty. He stripped off and lay on the bed, tired, but thoughts about his own prospects and future kept him awake.

Connor went over to Ft. Bayard the next day to see if there was anyone he knew at the post and giving the adjutant a contact point for any scouting or packing requirements. The adjutant, Captain John Williams, was an acquaintance and he got the latest information on the campaign against Victorio. Both agreed that the Mimbre

Apaches and their Mescalero cousins would likely have stayed quiet or at least restricted their depredations if the government hadn't tried to move them to San Carlos. Neither said, but both understood, that war was opportunity for some. Connor preferred working as an Army civilian rather than busting rock mining or working on someone else's ranch. The second transcontinental railroad was working from east and west just forty miles south of Silver City. The meeting of the Southern Pacific with the Rio Grande, Mexico, and Pacific would likely occur next year. No doubt there would also be a spur line connecting to this area. His experience working on the first transcontinental for almost a year with his brother's crew, prior to joining the Fourth Cavalry, might be enough for him to supervise a crew there.

Connor also ran into Sergeant Tom Jackson, a hardened Buffalo Soldier that he had worked with in the past. His wife did laundry and sewing at the post, adding to their income. Jackson was a tough NCO and part of the backbone of the Ninth. They shook and shared a few recollections before Connor asked him if his wife could sew some bullet loops on his canvas vest.

"Two rows, six each under a flap on the left side, right about here," he showed Jackson. "I also need a leather or buckskin wrap for the butt of my Winchester that I can lace on, with six bullet loops also. I need something more than a pocket full of cartridges," he said after telling him about his recent close brush with the Apaches.

They agreed on a price, he handed off his vest, shook hands again, and departed.

The next day he was back at the Smithson house, where Eileen welcomed him into the simple two-room home.

"Ma'am, I am so sorry about what has happened. Can I help you before I have to return to work?"

"Please. Call me Eileen, and thank you again for your kindness. You are a gentleman and I apologize for not being more hospitable when you came to the door."

She seemed a bit dismal but determined and in control of her emotions.

"Years have passed and I am not that close to my relatives back in Michigan. I have a job here and I will stay with the children and try to make a living, try to make it work, Mr. Connor."

"Just Connor. My first name is Paul but only my mother and brothers call me that," he told her. "I want to be helpful if I can, ma'am."

She looked at him directly. "I need a man, Connor, and so do my children. A husband," she added. "I hope we will have an opportunity to become better acquainted as time passes. I need time to grieve, though, and I know that you understand."

He met her eyes. "I am honored, Eileen. I know that was a statement of fact, not necessarily of interest in me personally, and I am sure that a handsome woman such as yourself will have many good options. I will visit again and I hope we can be friends. In the meantime, can I ask you to be my contact with Ft. Bayard for work contracts that come up? I will reach out to you or exchange telegraphs when I am able. I don't have a settled place at the moment, except for care of Ft. Cummings," he told her.

There was an awkward moment as he made to leave. In the end, she gave him a modest hug. She was sure that she had his interest, and liked the way he had left it. He was intelligent and a bit humble, a gentleman as she had told him. She watched him leave with a thoughtful look. On his part, he liked her direct and decisive way. He was physically attracted too. He may not have needed a wife but he did need a woman and a different type of insight. He put those irreverent thoughts out of his mind. It seemed inappropriate given the circumstances. He could come again later after time had passed.

CHAPTER 7

ARIZONA, 1887

Connor was back in Clifton to pick up another load of building supplies and food. He had been able to put up a course of logs each day. He had cupped the bottom of each log as he had gone up, adding moss and clay on which the linear cupped area would sit. He also mirrored the notches so that the fit was tight. It was slow, but when up, it would have few air gaps that would require more caulking. He periodically used his wood drill to auger holes between logs, driving rough-cut dowels through to additionally stabilize the walls along the end notches.

This was the first permanent place he had since living home more than twenty years ago. It felt good to have a place of his own, although he was starting to appreciate how isolated it was out here. Connor looked to the east, noting the gentle slope toward the Blue River, roughly half a mile away. The cabin site had been heavily treed and he took advantage of that in his construction. It thinned out, becoming more parklike as the property approached the water. Connor didn't mind the hard work to get the walls up, so different from the nomadic existence he had been living. Somehow, he felt more centered even if he wouldn't be able to spend a lot of time here until he built up more of a grubstake.

The cabin walls were up and part of the roof. He hadn't sawed out the window or door openings but had taken the top log length of the planned openings out so that he could insert a saw and cut down after he completed the roof. There were three lengths where a portion of one log was cut out. He would make the rest of the vertical cuts to the log walls for the openings, frame them to enhance the stability, and insert a door, crude vertical shutters, and a couple of windows behind them. The immediate task was to complete the roof and the tin covering.

Ex-sergeant Ray Witherspoon was glad to see him and went to the back to retrieve his holster and the Merwin & Hulbert. Connor was impressed with his work. The holster was sewn to a leather backing at a forty-five-degree angle. The leather backing was triangular, rounded at the corners, and slightly wider than the holster. It was a little thicker than the holster leather and would improve stability for a draw. The shoulder loop was about two inches wide with bullet loops above the area closest to the gun handle. A strap came off the shoulder loop in the rear, at shoulder-blade level, and buckled with a strap coming off the shoulder loop in the front. Two holes in the backing, just below where the end of the barrel would rest, allowed a tie-off to a pants belt. The gun would hang with the barrel almost at hip level, the handle above and to the right of the belly button, about five or six inches below the armpit.

Ray had formed the holster. Wetting the leather until it was pliable, inserting the greased gun until the leather dried, it had conformed to the shape of the pistol. The leather covering the trigger guard was cut maybe a third of the way back. With the leather in its desired shape, Ray had used a penetrating oil to saturate the holster leather, then let the excess dry.

"You can trim back some of the leather and backing after you wear it and work with it some. The backing will also conform to your body after you wear it awhile. The chest strap length can also be cut back. You will want to adjust it depending on whether it is inside or outside your coat and the thickness of your clothes," he told Connor. "I will go with you for a day or two when you head back to the ranch and we can work on your draw and fire on a few targets. Then it is up to you to practice if you want that edge you are worried about."

Putting it on, it felt different than his old rig, which sat higher in his armpit and required a more vertical draw.

"If your barrel had been longer than three and a half inches, I would have cut the area around the trigger guard back deeper, but you don't want to have the gun fall out of the holster. I like the folding trigger. I left the sight on. It helps retention in the holster without hardly inhibiting a draw and it will help with accuracy if you are aiming toward twenty feet and beyond. Tomorrow, when we camp, you can try it out."

Ray was as good as his word, and Connor enjoyed his company as they rode the wagon along the San Francisco toward the Blue. That day they stopped early and started in on his technique. If his target was on his right and close, say within eight feet, Ray had Connor bend left while pulling the gun. This accelerated bringing the gun out of the holster and the barrel in line with the target. If not to the right but still close, the right shoulder should be roughly toward the target. Simultaneously with the pull, his right arm moved up and back to get out of the way of his shot or keep his coat from interfering. As Ray explained, there were three parts—pull, acquire, and fire. In pulling, the index finger was extended parallel with the barrel at the level of the trigger. As the guard came free of the holster, the finger would drop naturally on top of the trigger and through the guard. The gun could be fired while the arm was still bent and just above waist level. This method worked well when seated.

The other technique was for targets at longer distances. The pull was the same but without the lean. As his left, gun hand cleared the holster, it was thrust straight toward the target. The right hand came out simultaneously grasping the left wrist to stabilize that hand and accelerate the extension to eye level. Using the right hand was not necessary, but Ray felt it helped, as did the smaller profile. Firing the double action revolver was simultaneous with reaching full extension and obtaining a rough sight alignment.

The first night, Connor practiced both techniques, first at half speed, then about three-quarters speed. After dry runs with the close target technique, Ray set up a target and loaded the gun. On the second live fire try, Connor hit the target. Moving the target back to eight feet, he hit it again. Using the extended range targets, Connor practiced the other technique. Once he had drawn and fired, if he missed, he continued to fire until he hit the target, which was out at about twenty feet. In every case, he was able to hit the target before he ran out of rounds in the cylinder. The second night was more of the same, but Ray was adamant that speed was secondary to hitting the target. Gradually, Connor picked up speed as he demonstrated he could strike the target. Firing with a bent arm, he estimated that he could pull, acquire, and fire in about a second. The other technique took about two seconds.

"Connor, keep practicing every day until you are done with your dangerous business. Work at different ranges, different target sizes, and add movement, both yours and the target. Also add additional targets—two, three, or four. Keep the .38 caliber M & H and practice using from behind the back pull. It isn't fitted for your holster so you will have to work out the right place to pull from. If you are in an active fight, just drop your .44 and grab the other gun. If you have cover, holster it until you can reload. After that, get a little practice using your weak hand.

Finally, he gave Connor the leaf spring, now sized for the .38. It was encased in leather, with an extra two inches of leather above the closed end of the U. The extended leather had two slots through which his belt could go. The clamshell configuration could be suspended from a belt, clamshell around the cylinder of the .38 barrel, parallel to the belt and the ground, butt down. He could face it either left or right depending on which arm he wanted to draw with.

"Ray, I can't thank you enough. I am reasonably good with a gun, but what you know is amazing. I hope I can avoid using what you taught me, but if I can't, you likely saved my life with all this."

Connor gave his old comrade a hug and a slap on the back. Witherspoon looked him in the eye. "If you get yourself killed, I am going to kick your ass. You still owe me for the gun and the ammunition and I expect to collect."

He squeezed his arm and mounted, heading back to Clifton. He looked back and had one word for Connor: "Practice!"

Connor nodded and raised his arm, already missing him. He swallowed and got the wagon team moving in the opposite direction.

Two day later, he was back at work on the cabin. He cut out the section of logs for the door, chopped out a groove on each side, about two inches deep and wide along the ends of the exposed log walls. He hammered in a piece of lumber to keep the log walls locked in place, then framed and hung the door. He drove two wrought iron, L-shaped spikes at an angle into the logs on either side of the door to hold the crossbar, keeping the door secure against uninvited guests.

During the next two weeks he finished the wood roof, nailing a second plank over each joint and using more clay and moss to make it more water- and draft-resistant. Finally, he used the tin sheets on top to repel rain and snow. Before laying in the floor, Connor brought in smooth rocks to pave the corner where he intended to put the stove. He used a couple sheets of roofing to panel and fireproof the corner, behind the stove location. He set the stove and extended the pipe up through the roof, using the last piece of tin sheet to surround the pipe. He celebrated finishing the major portion of the construction. Sitting in the doorway, he sipped a bit of rye whiskey and enjoyed a sense of accomplishment.

Each evening he practiced drawing and firing from his shoulder harness. Mostly he dry-fired, but he did go through a fifty-round box of .44-40 ammunition. He also practiced with the .38 Medium Frame M&H. He hunted a few times, taking a whitetail on one short expedition. He added a shotgun to his list of things he needed to buy when he had some money. Bird and small game were much more dependable as a way to stretch his supplies. He didn't have a lot of money left and knew he might need to work for a couple of weeks in the mines near Clifton, before heading out to rendezvous with the Yaquis and the trip back into Sonora.

He had been buying primarily used Winchesters at between five and ten dollars each, hoping to have twenty before he left. He was OK with any barrel length and type, round, octagonal, or half-octagonal. He also picked up a Colt-Burgess rifle and a Colt Medium Frame Lightning. All were chambered for .44-40 ammunition. Any malfunctioning rifles were left with Ray to repair. Connor found a seamstress to take a piece of canvas, line it with two blankets, and partition it into ten slots to scabbard the rifles. He had one for each side of the mule to balance the weight. They could be rolled and packed horizontally along each side of the mule or angled up like an A-frame, bottom ends secured in the aparejo. He hoped to net out enough money to have enough to get the ranch going.

Connor needed more time to finish out the cabin, but it was enclosed and roofed. Cutting the windows, fitting the framed glass, wooden shutters, flooring, a small pole barn for the animals, the list was long. Unfortunately, he needed to augment the small amount of money he had left and get to Bisbee. Reaching Clifton, he stopped by a smaller mine, west of town, along Chase Creek. The claim was owned by a big Swede, Harold Amundsen. The Swede was hoping to have his claim bought by one of the bigger companies. Until then, he was working a vein of turquoise. There was copper, too, but Amundsen lacked the finances to profitably extract it. Connor had worked for him from time to time, the longest period being about six weeks between contracts with the Army. He was fair and the daily rate included food and a place to sleep at the mine shack. Besides Amundsen, there were four other members in the crew. One was a Mexican who had worked mines in Chihuahua. There was a Chinaman who was experienced in dynamite from his time working on railroad grades and tunnels. The other two were prospectors and partners, trying to build a grubstake before a return to scouting claims for themselves.

The two prospectors, Bill Jacobi and Steve Newman, shared a shack near Clifton. Connor, along with Chang and Alcazar, used the toolshed near the tunnel as quarters. The mine had extended and branched since the last time

Connor had worked there. Two would work at the face, two would load the cart and haul it out with the help of a donkey. Amundsen would sort and do some rough crush and refinement, along with the fifth man in the crew. Connor knew from experience that the key was working at a sustainable pace that made progress but conserved energy. He normally was paired with Alcazar, less often with Chang. Conversation with the Chinaman was stilted somewhat by the language barrier. Connor gathered that the man had siblings and an aged mother back in southern China that he hadn't seen in over twenty years. Chang wasn't big but he was well able to handle his load. He and Connor, when teamed, had a largely silent but comfortable rapport.

Roberto Alcazar had been working in mines in Sonora, Chihuahua, and now the States. He was certainly not silent.

"Connor, we have to find a different kind of work or a better mine. I am starting to think even the Mexican Army would be better."

Connor had to laugh, well aware of the harsh discipline and endemic desertion found there. "Better to save your money and open a cantina or pulqueria, if you can avoid drinking up the profits," Connor told him.

More seriously, Alcazar told him, "I have a cousin with a transport business, hauling freight between the border and as far south as Moctezuma. He has been after me to join him but I need to save some money so I am more than just a driver."

"Don't wait too long," Connor advised him before coughing from the lamp fumes and poor ventilation near the tunnel face.

Disaster struck on the eighth day. The usual process was to follow the turquoise seam, wherever it led—up, down, or sidewise—and tunnel accordingly. Really no different from how silver and gold were often dug in small operations. Use a charge of dynamite, dig out the rubble, shore up, and repeat. After expenses, to include the crew's salary, Amundsen was probably making three hundred dollars a month or less. A small-timer, hoping for some luck and, eventually, a buyout from one of the bigger mines.

The Chinaman either used too much of a charge or the shoring was not spaced properly. Maybe his time and luck just ran out when the charge went off. Chang was buried in the rubble and parts of the shaft began to collapse. Connor and Roberto were around the bend in the shaft and started for the entrance when the rumble of the implosion began. About fifty feet of the shaft leading to the entrance collapsed in front of them. The Ferguson headlamps on their heads were extinguished as a wave of choking dust left them gasping and on their knees. Roberto got his lamp relit first. Connor was still hacking and struggling for breath.

Roberto was the first to speak. "I think we can dig out if the roof holds. I pray they are digging from the other end to reach us."

He shouted a few times, but heard nothing from the outside.

Fighting to stop the growing sense of panic, Connor asked him to see if the ceiling would hold if they dug along the top of the shaft. Clearing three thousand square feet of debris from the shaft to get out would take too long. Connor didn't know if the air would hold out, but he knew the headlamps had limited fuel. He got his lamp going and went deeper into the mine to see if there was lumber or supports that could be scavenged to support their tunneling back toward the entrance. Reaching to within twenty or so feet from the dynamited face, he probed the rubble slanting down from the new plug, in front of the working face. About halfway up, he was surprised to see a hand.

Clearing rock and dirt, he pulled Chang out and down to the floor of the tunnel. He was breathing but unconscious, his legs damaged, bone through the skin in his left lower leg. Hoisting him over his shoulder, he carried him back to the other blockage.

"Roberto, I found Chang. Give me a hand while we try to help him."

Roberto scrambled down and stared at the unconscious miner. "I think there are gaps along the top and we can dig through or get close enough that they can hear us," he optimistically reported.

"Hold his shoulders while I try to pull the leg out and slip the bone under the skin, then let's try to dig our way out," Connor told him.

The state of Chang's leg only added to their urgency to get out.

They set Chang off to the side, aware of his fast, shallow breathing. They took turns digging and scavenging for wood to shore up the narrow tunnel. There were places where larger rocks had fallen and they were forced to tunnel around. After about three hours, they were both exhausted, and the lamps were starting to flicker. Connor estimated they had advanced about eighteen feet. There was a small can of oil, about half filled, for the lamps.

"I think we need to pull more lumber near the tunnel before we lose all light; we can push the supports forward by touch if we lose the light," Roberto stated.

They pulled as much lumber as the could over the next hour, causing part of the tunnel behind them to further collapse. On returning, they could hear Chang groaning but still not conscious. It was hot and it was getting harder to breathe. Both men were tormented by thirst and, worse, the possibility that they had found their graves.

Six hours after the collapse, their lamps had nearly exhausted their fuel. Connor was in the tunnel behind Alcazar, fighting to keep from passing out in the darkness. His chest, back, and arm muscles were screaming. He vaguely registered Roberto calling for more shoring. Crawling up and pushing two planks, he had to stop frequently. Roberto was probably twenty-five feet in, maybe halfway out. It was slow going because they couldn't stand up and were working from back, knees, or stomach. He heard him swear as the lamp flickered out.

Outside, Amundsen had finished his twenty-minute stint digging. The next man was moving forward to replace him. After assessing the collapse, Harold had set his remaining two miners to digging while he went to the nearest mine to recruit more men to help with the rescue. He promised double pay and a bonus if the three men inside were pulled out alive. It was dark outside and lamps had been set up. News of the collapse had spread and miners were gathering from among the other diggings by Chase Creek. This was not an unusual event. But the miners accepted the risks and assumed this wouldn't happen to them, until it sometimes did. Amundsen had no idea how far they would have to go until they broke through. He prayed the entire length of the shaft had not collapsed, making this effort about just recovering bodies. They had advanced about thirty feet, and when the man digging at the face changed, they would listen for any sounds.

Back inside the tunnel, the Mexican had to be as close to the end of his strength as Connor was. Alcazar had impressed him with both his physical and mental stamina. They had wood for props to take them maybe another five or six feet. Connor guessed he had strength to maybe dig another three before he would only be able to lie in the dark and pray for rescue. He couldn't, didn't want to think, his mind deliberatively blank. This was not about coming to accept his fate. He was trying to quiet those dark whispers that would lead to surrender. Maybe later he would be able to think about his life. Or pray, or curse.

The crew outside heard faint scraping first. They tried to vector in on the sound. Shouting, digging. Shouting more, digging more. They broke through and pulled Alcazar out and poured water on him, leaving him sputtering, crying. Shouting down the tunnel, they roused Connor from his stupor. It took him a long time to crawl far enough along the tunnel to be pulled out too. He would have cried but was simply too desiccated. No one would go into the narrow, twisting tunnel to get the Chinaman. After a short rest and a slug of whiskey, Connor went back in. He came back through facing backward, dragging Chang. About ten feet from the place where the two tunnels had met, he felt someone grab his feet and pull him on out, while he tried to do the same with Chang. Once they were all out, they discovered Chang was dead. Connor and Alcazar were exhausted but deeply thankful to be out. Grateful to Amundsen for trying to get them out, Connor and Roberto sat together, quietly acknowledging a relationship forged in a near brush with a horrible death. They both looked like filthy physical wrecks, at least for the time being.

The next morning, Connor asked Amundsen for his money. He got forty-five dollars, way more than he had earned, and a small sack of rough-cut turquoise. He thanked Harold, gathered his gear, and rode up into the part of town inhabited mostly by Chinese. He delivered the wrapped body and Chang's meager possessions to a young man, also named Chang who seemed to be the closest thing to a next of kin. A small group of men gathered around him and patted him on the back, expressing thanks in their limited English. Connor was then led to a small shack where food was prepared and they ate, largely in silence. He shook hands all around, expressed his condolences to all, including the cook, who was a tall, thin, Chinese lady, and then made to leave. He didn't know if he had made himself understood, but it was the best he could do.

The lady stopped him with a slim but surprisingly strong hand and said in clear English, "Thank you; you will be remembered." Her eyes stayed locked on his.

He nodded and murmured, "Thank you, ma'am," not really knowing who she was, but impressed with her composure and noting the deference the other men seemed to extend to her.

He gave her the small bag of turquoise Amundsen had given to him and asked her to use it for a good purpose. He wasn't sure why he did it, but it seemed right. She nodded gravely and bowed slightly.

Connor was relieved to be away from the somber Chinese, and headed to the hot springs. He needed to simply sit and regain focus after the ordeal in the mine. Soaking for a couple of hours, he still felt without purpose. Roberto found him there and they went to dinner at a small Mexican cantina with a seven-foot ceiling and exposed vigas. Neither had much to say at first.

"What are you going to do?" Connor asked, reflecting on his own decisions.

"Going back to Mexico, maybe work in a smelter or work with my uncle, making mescal. But not underground," he said, holding up his glass of the burning drink.

Connor nodded. "I am also done with working below ground. Thank you, I was near the end."

Roberto smiled for the first time. "I understand, Amigo. I was there too."

They talked for a long time and Connor learned that Roberto had an uncle who was in the mescal production business and about the cousin who was working to establish a transport company in northern Sonora.

Roberto said, "I studied to be a priest until learning that I was totally unsuited, having been seduced by La Revolution against the French."

The allure of money available in the mining operations, and the fast women nearby, led to another type of seduction. Recently he had been determined to make a change and had been saving money to finance that. Connor was also ready to make a change and, although not spoken, both were coming to a conclusion that success might be more assured with just a trusted companero. They talked a while longer, discussing possibilities for a better way to make a living, shook hands, and hugged.

"Visit me in Mexico. We can find some new ways to make money," Roberto concluded.

In the morning, Connor headed for Bisbee. He needed the woman, maybe now, especially. The mines were another story.

CHAPTER 8

ARIZONA, FALL 1887

The trip to Bisbee was taken slow and easy. Much hotter in the lower elevations, the open expanses were a welcome antidote from the claustrophobic ordeal he had just survived. It was roughly one hundred and fifty miles to reach the town and Connor cut through the heavy pine forests of the Pinaleno Moutains via Marijilda Wash, south of Safford. The high peaks to the north were obscured by the dense vegetation, but to the south he could see Heliograph Peak.

Connor shook his head, thinking about the station at the peak where the Army was able to use mirrors to communicate with Ft. Grant to the west and Ft. Bowie, about forty miles southeast. There were a lot of deer about and he was able to shoot one, taking a half day to dress it out and cook some of the venison. Maybe because of the profusion of deer, there were a lot of black bears and he saw both sign and claw marks on some of the trees.

He also needed to make a side trip to the Whitlock Mountains, which were roughly the halfway point to Bisbee. Coming down from the Pinalenos, he turned due east. There, he retrieved the two forty-five caliber Remington revolvers he had cached and slipped them into his saddle-bag. Looking at them carefully, he replaced the handles with the used ones he had bought from Ray. He buried the original ones. He was tempted to take at least one of the rifles, but didn't want to risk them being identified. The pistols, with the changed handles, he thought would be anonymous enough to sell.

Reaching Bisbee on day eight, he found a small rooming house and a livery. Washed and bathed, he started his search for Rosangela and, less urgently, Javier. Bisbee had grown dramatically since Connor had come through here with the calvary in the late '70s and early '80s. Mule Gulch, as it was known then, was focused on gold and silver mining and a lot had been taken out of the ground. The mountain slopes were being steadily denuded of trees, both for fuel and trusses. Now, with the Phelps-Dodge Corporation owning the Copper Queen Mine, the mining was shifting to large-scale copper mining, like in Clifton. The town's growth was impressive and he guessed that there were several thousand people living in the area. The removal of the Apaches to reservations and to Florida had accelerated the mining, ranching, and growth of southern Arizona.

Bisbee was well over five thousand feet in elevation, but still, the temperature was pushing ninety degrees as Connor took a stroll up Brewery Gulch. He noted Sieber's Brewery and the adobe bar next to it as he stepped over garbage thrown into the street. Cowboys from the nearby ranches rode through the narrow street, mixing with miners that were off shift. There was no shortage of bars and many had faro tables and other games of chance for those willing to risk hard-earned money. Connor was not one of them, having learned his lesson early, losing a month's pay one night while still with the Fourth Cav. He stopped at a gunsmith shop and waited for the shop to clear. The owner took a look at the revolver he unwrapped and made him an offer. After some minor dickering, they reached an agreement. He would try another place to dispose of the second Remington.

He dropped his laundry off, took his ticket, and set off uphill to the two-story wood building that was one of the more famous establishments in Cochise County. Connor looked up when he reached the steps to the front door and read the sign: "Copper Queen Con. Mining Co. Library Reading Room." Entering, he detected that distinct smell that such places had. He was transported to his youth back East and the library in his hometown. He had always loved reading but had found little time to indulge in it. An older gentleman at a table near the door greeted him,

"Welcome, sir, books on this floor and above. We have periodicals and newspapers in the small room behind you and a few rooms for a quiet game of cards. I am Reverend J. G. Pritchard, the librarian. If I can be of assistance, please ask."

Connor smiled and introduced himself, then added, "This is a wonderful place, Reverend, and it is justly famous. I have heard much about it and you are truly doing God's work here."

The reverend was medium height, older with thinning hair, a bit long in back and clean shaven. "I can see that you are a man of culture, despite your rough-hewn appearance," the reverend stated with a noticeable accent, which Connor recognized as from the British Isles. Pritchard confirmed he was Welsh by birth and was delighted that Connor, being Irish, was from that same fine Celtic bloodline.

Entering the reading room to peruse the newspapers, Connor was surprised to find Javier reading one of the not-so-current Sonoran papers. He glanced up, then jumped up to embrace Connor in an abrazo and pumped his hand. They walked outside after Connor assured the reverend that he would return soon. Outside, they brought each other up to date. Connor told Javier about eluding the two Mexican agents, but didn't reveal that he had found a permanent solution. Javier and Rosangela had been here about four weeks. Before that, they had been to El Paso, gathering money and coordinating the next arms shipment to the beleaguered Yaqui. They planned on using Weaver and some of his crew again. They wanted to seed the contrabandistas with people they could more fully trust, like Connor. A meeting was scheduled with Weaver at the end of the week, to coordinate the next delivery. Javier wanted Connor to be there.

As to Rosangela, she was sharing a small adobe with Javier. They were raising money from a number of Yaqui working in the mines. Their contributions were being used to support operations for the rebellion. Connor had an ironic thought about the men breaking their backs, working deep in the mines while Javier read the papers. It was troubling, and probably wouldn't have crossed his mind if not for his recent close brush with death. His attention shifted as Javier told him that Rosangela would be happy to see him.

"Come by tonight after six. I will be out, but I will give her the good news about your arrival."

When she opened the door, Connor couldn't suppress a big smile, stepping through the door and wrapping his arms around her warm curves. Lips, neck, ears—was that her moaning or him? Into the one bedroom, lips and tongue chasing down her flesh as the clothes disappeared. They joined and merged, undulating like a couple of pythons trying to devour each other. He heard her cry out as they tensed, paused on the precipice, and then plunged over. Holding each other tight, they slowly recovered. Breathing slowed, soft chuckles, mutual relief.

She was surprised by his intensity and passion. It was reassuring and also exciting. Was this the one, or was he destined to disappear or be replaced? Was he smart, tough, and ruthless enough to propel her to another life? His body was firm and toughened by a life in the field. She liked it. He was resolute and intelligent. She liked that too. But love . . . she had been required to fend for herself as long as she could remember and that tended to make sentiment a luxury. She had been dedicated to the cause, but was it enough or was there something more for her than struggle? Could he offer something better, much better? For now, it was enough to just enjoy the moment and the mutual desire.

He was not a kid and he knew that there was a certain amount of infatuation that he was experiencing. He enjoyed it, knowing it would subside in time, perhaps not entirely. But there was an intangible something that combined with the physicality of their relationship that he wanted and needed. He didn't feel a need to analyze it further; it just was and he loved it. Maybe later he would understand it better or become more rational. He felt at ease, content for now, near her.

He reluctantly left before Javier came back and made plans for the next day. She was wearing a mid-weight gold cross around her neck, which he noticed and hadn't seen before, as they kissed goodbye. Javier was watching from the shadows as he left to return to the boardinghouse. He knocked on the door and slipped in as Rosangela opened it. She was smoking and Javier raised an eyebrow without comment.

"We need a backup for Weaver and I think he is tough and resourceful enough to be the one," she said.

"Well, Weaver is smart enough to see that he is competition, and ruthless enough to do something about it," Javier commented. "Do you like him?" he asked.

"Which one?" she asked, stubbing out the cigarette.

****

Issac Weaver was crossing the border back into the United States. He was bringing with him about seventy-five stolen horses that he figured he could sell for at least forty dollars each. Net of expenses and paying his crew, he figured he would walk away with eighteen hundred dollars. After this, he was going up to Bisbee to finalize the plans for running the guns to the Yaquis, in Sonora. He had met with their agents in El Paso and was looking forward to renewing his acquaintance with the Yaqui woman. Tall, voluptuous, and smart, she was the perfect partner for the smuggling opportunities that he was making his fortune on. She also set his blood on fire. And he was a man who appreciated women.

Weaver had served for the Confederacy during the Civil War, rising to the rank of captain in the calvary. Like many, he had been ruined financially by the war and had come west to rebuild and didn't worry about the legalities of how he made his money. After all this time, he had a good network to both sell and buy, on both sides of the border. He was agnostic about who he dealt with, Comancheros from his early days in Texas, Indians, bandits, and would-be revolutionists. He was sometimes the broker or go-between, taking little risk himself. Other times he was prepared to be directly engaged with the smuggling or stealing, taking the risk but maximizing his return.

The trade with the Yaqui had, of late, proved particularly lucrative. To protect it, he was not averse to tipping off the authorities on either side of the border about rival shipments. He had an expanding ranch, south of Winslow, and was smart enough to know that he needed another plan if things became too difficult along the border. The ranch was a good front for moving livestock and other stolen property, but also as an investment. Prior to this rustling trip, he had almost been caught by the Rurales.

Their new commander in Sonora was Major Kosterlitzky, a favorite of President Dias, and justly so. The major was incorruptible, his intelligence network was first rate, and he could ride as hard as his men. Issac smiled—he had a network, too, and it had served him well over the years. Weaver had just managed to cross into Arizona ahead of Kosterlitzky that time, retaining just a few of the stolen cattle.

Weaver had good instincts and was physically hardened, as was his crew. He planned carefully and hated to lose money once it was in hand, which made the close run from Kosterlitzky so galling. It had been a close race and, in the end, he had cut bait to reach safety. His time in this business was coming to an end. He estimated he had a few years left at most. Then he would let others take the risks and he would skim what he could. Money, and women, were his passions and he would semi-retire with both, soon. Making eight to ten thousand dollars a trip, he planned on a few more gunrunning expeditions.

He crossed the border west of Nogales. Reaching the old, abandoned presidio of Tubac, Weaver met his buyers just east in the Tumacacori Mountain foothills. Paying off his crew, he spent the night drinking and carousing, then resupplied and set off toward Bisbee. He took Haggerty and another reliable man, William Corwyn, with him for the meeting. Weaver had three men that he used as Segundos at different times, and these were two of them. They were dependable and loyal, smart, but not smarter than him. He made sure that they were well compensated for their loyalty and willingness to undertake any task or direction.

It took four days to reach the Mule Mountains and Weaver found a place to stay in a small adobe, owned by one of his associates outside of town.

He told the associate, Carlos Rivera, "Go over to make contact with the Yaqui woman and set the meeting. I want to maintain a low profile for the time being."

He stripped off and, using a couple of buckets of water, cleaned up and then went into town to get a shave. He also wanted to meet another contact.

Connor was back at Rosangela's place eating breakfast when Rivera arrived. He gave Connor the once-over and then ignored him, speaking rapidly in Spanish. Connor had no trouble keeping up, but saw no need to participate. The meeting would be the following day, at Rivera's place, with directions provided. After he left, Rosangela seemed moody, then, seeming to get over it, took him to bed after locking the door. Connor was reluctant to leave but agreed to meet the following day at the meeting place.

The meeting began with brief handshakes and the distribution of warm beer. Weaver looked at Connor curiously, but then turned his attention to Rosangela. Javier was present, as was Haggerty. Corwyn and Rivera sat outside the door. Javier explained Connor's presence. "We have two packers already lined up and Connor will be responsible for them." Weaver could recruit the rest or they could help if needed.

"Two other Yaquis will be traveling with the caravan and will make the final link-up with the lieutenant of the new Yaqui leader, Tetabiate. The two Yaqui are Anastasio Maldonado and his sister, Mariela."

Javier vouched that they were trail hardened and able to add to the fighting strength of the pack train, if required.

"They will also handle an additional mule with rifles that Connor will sell on his own account. This will compensate Connor for his additional duties with them and the Yaqui packers," Javier told him.

These last two items set off protests from Weaver, accompanied by glares at Connor and a harsh refusal. Connor was surprised at how these changes had been introduced. He had planned on working the additional rifles with Weaver directly and frankly, was planning on a lower number to avoid just this explosion. In the end, Weaver allowed himself to be manipulated by Rosangela's earnest entreaty and subtle flirting. As she leaned toward Weaver, her full breasts ballooned inside her shirt, the gold cross nestled irresistibly in her spectacular valley.

His resolve weakened, she delivered the coup de gras: "Maldonado and his sister are cousins of the new Yaqui leader, assuring his trust."

The final coordination and rendezvous points were made and Weaver and his man got up to leave. He gave Connor a brief fixed stare, then moved to the door.

There were no handshakes this time. Ignoring Connor, he looked at Rosangela and said, "We need to talk some more . . . alone."

Connor maintained his poker face and got up with Javier and Rosangela to leave. "We will talk later," she assured him and they left without further words. On the way back, she didn't respond when Connor asked if she was all right or needed help. On reaching the adobe where she and Javier were staying, she entered without a word and closed the door behind her. Javier looked at Connor and shrugged. Connor walked back toward his room, considering what he had seen and heard. He was unable to make any conclusions but felt certain that he needed to have a strategy to protect himself, physically and otherwise if things got nasty with Weaver and crew.

The plan was to meet mid-December at Potrero Creek, just north of Nogales, and cross the border to the east. He had asked Rosangela to set up a meet with Anastasio, his sister, and the two Yaqui packers two days before their scheduled arrival at Potrero. She had seemed reluctant but had agreed to do that. He wanted to assess them and have a conversation prior to meeting the rest of the group. He kept to himself the hope he could establish a rapport with them. He just might need their support if things got out of hand with Weaver and his guards. Counting on them was a weak strategy, but it was something. He also sent a letter to Roberto in Mexico, and hoped it would get through.

His parting with Rosangela was not as warm as his arrival, but still good. He hadn't wanted to stalk her like a jealous lover, but Connor reluctantly admitted he was a little of that. He couldn't help but wonder if there was some relationship beyond smuggling with Weaver. Perhaps Weaver wondered the same. She was a lot of woman and Connor was not new to losing a woman to a better-heeled suitor. Knowing, in truth, he was not in control didn't provide emotional relief. He felt like he was in that mine again, not having an answer for fate. He turned to what needed to be done at the cabin and decided to blank out the rest as he headed northeast.

CHAPTER 9

ARIZONA & SONORA, 1888

Arriving in Clifton, Connor picked up supplies and ammo and headed back upriver to his cabin. Nothing had changed and he went back to work, cutting out the window openings, slotting in the frames, and hinging the windows on top so that they could be pulled up and inside the cabin. The shutters he hinged so that he could push them up and out. Opposite the stove, on the short side of the cabin, he started digging a root cellar, five by five by six feet down. The soil he spread under the stringers for his flooring. About four feet down, Connor added a tunnel from the cellar and out under the cabin for about ten feet until he hit rock. He then changed direction and, angling upward, reached the surface near a bushy juniper. He installed a trapdoor about six inches from the surface and carefully covered it over.

Connor wrapped and set the rifles and ammunition in the tunnel and concealed the entrance from the root cellar with the small rock lining he used for the floor and the walls. He left a short ladder down there, some rough shelves, and put a hinged trapdoor over the top. Then he went to work nailing down the flooring to the stringers. He had a month yet before the trip to Potrero Creek. He returned to Clifton and purchased another mule and supplies. He was hopeful that this would be his last trip as a smuggler.

He did a little hunting and small improvements around the cabin. He heard the coyotes and wolves at night and knew he would have to thin them out once he brought in cattle. He also found sign of bear, thankfully black bear and not grizzly. He constructed a platform bed, bench, and a table from the leftover planks along with some shelves. Extra nails would have to do for his wardrobe.

And he practiced drawing, shooting, and reloading. The last step seemed slow, taking about thirty-five seconds for a complete reload. He hoped it wouldn't come down to that. He felt a sense of security and a foreboding that he was about to leave it behind.

The last morning, he loaded up, rifles rolled in their canvas sleeves and placed horizontally along the mule's flanks. Connor had four blanket-covered gallon canteens placed on each mule, one over his shoulder, and one more hanging from the saddle of his horse. The bullet loops were filled. Wool blankets inside oiled canvas and, in turn, inside a rubberized tarp were rolled and tied behind his saddle. Connor kept a bottle of Bacanora in his saddlebag.

Connor bypassed Clifton and Safford on the way south. He hid the mule with the rifles outside the town of Maley as he came in to pick up more supplies. He arrived outside of Tubac, met the four Yaquis, and proceeded to the foothills due west. The packers knew what they were about, but would clearly look to Anastasio for direction. They were armed with single-round breechloaders, and one had a single action revolver. Maldonado had a very serviceable Model 73 Winchester, chambered for the favored .44-40 ammo. He had a single action Colt with the same chambering. His sister only had a revolver.

Connor told Anastasio that he wanted to see the Yaquis fire, since their lives might depend on each other. Setting up some targets, he watched the packers fire several rounds. He looked at their rifles and on one made a sight adjustment, recommended some changes in hold technique, their trigger pull, and had them fire again. There was an improvement, although they would never be considered sharpshooters. They seemed pleased with his help. He told Anastasio he would loan his sister a rifle for the trip and, with his permission, work with her on basic marksmanship. Anastasio hesitated and looked at his sister. He must have seen some affirmative sign from her, because he nodded.

Connor retrieved a Winchester carbine, with a twenty-inch, round barrel and a twelve-round magazine. He took her through the basics and had her dry-fire from the standing, kneeling, sitting, and prone positions. When he was satisfied that she could demonstrate the basic firing techniques, he had her load a round, chamber it, and fire at a target. She was directionally correct but not much more. They worked through a box of ammo, loading one round at a time. By the time she finished the box, she was able to hit a two-by-two-foot target at ten yards, three out of five rounds. At twenty-five yards, she hit with two out of five shots.

The packers cheered when she hit the target. She frowned then smiled when she saw they were sincere. Connor showed her how to clean the carbine, supervising her as she did so. He asked her to practice dry-firing each day in all four positions. He gave her another box of ammunition and told her they would practice again tomorrow, if it was okay with her brother. After Anastasio nodded again, he thanked her for being a good student and quick study, and predicted that she would be hitting targets at one hundred yards. Mariela bobbed her head and couldn't suppress a grin, looking over at her brother.

They walked back to camp, ate, and talked around the campfire. Connor asked in a serious way about their lives and answered questions about himself. At some point, he poured the Bacanora in his cup and they passed it around. It helped with the rapport and the chill. They nodded when he said, "This trip is dangerous and we will have to depend on each other to be successful." Whether they understood or their nods just meant they had heard him, Connor couldn't determine. Anastasio looked at him more intently and perhaps more thoughtfully. The trail would sort out who could be relied on, he thought to himself.

The next morning, they returned to their makeshift range and he worked on their techniques as they fired at fifty-yard targets. Both packers were improved. Anastasio fired for the first time and he proved a competent shot.

His sister fired another fifty rounds, warming up at ten yards, then firing at twenty-five and fifty yards. The last five rounds were fired at the fifty-yard target in a rapid-fire mode. She hit two out of five times. The black powder residue smudged her face, but Connor found the word comely had entered unbidden into his mind. He would have to watch out, no complications, just get the job done and survive. He smiled and nodded to her and to the four Yaqui in general. He had done what he could; it was time to go.

The Yaqui packers had their own mules, three each, and Connor had two mules, one with food and water. Anastasio and his sister had two mules, packed with food and water. The rest of the mules would be provided by Weaver and would be sold after the rifles and ammunition were delivered. Connor expected to sell one of his mules and keep one for the return trip. They arrived at Potrero Creek the following evening. It was dry but there were some shallow water pools near, where they filled canteens. Weaver arrived early the next morning. He was business-like in his demeanor, which Connor appreciated.

They spent the day repacking, organizing, clarifying movement discipline and general preparation. Anastasio and one of Weaver's guards would ride point and lead. Weaver would be next with a guard/flanker out to either side. The last guard would trail the packtrain. One of the Yaqui packers was next with his three mules, followed by one of the packers that Weaver had supplied, again with three mules. Next, Connor and his three mules, Mariela with three, then the final three packers and their mules.

The guard riding with Weaver also had a mule trailing his horse, along with two spare horses.

When all were in file, they were thirty-eight animals in length. Terrain permitting, they would move the mules in a rough column of twos and the length would be twenty-two animals in length. The packtrain could be broken into two or three segments if needed to avoid trouble. He had seen the Apaches do this many times when pursued, breaking into smaller and smaller groups until they seemed to vanish. Connor would take Mariela, one of the other packers, and one of the flank guards with a total of nine mules in all. Weaver had the train practice breaking into smaller groups and then reassemble a few miles down the trail. They also practiced breaking into six groups with one guard and with Weaver or Anastasio accompanying a packer. Four days into the trip, the packtrain was becoming a functioning team, though still with room for improvement.

That turned out to be a good thing because, on day six, the rear guard raced by Connor and reported to Weaver that there was a dust cloud moving toward them, maybe seven miles back. He had to hand it to Weaver; he was cool under pressure.

Bringing in the flank guards, Anastasio with his gunman, and Connor, he issued his directions: "Split up into six elements and regroup in three days at the rendezvous point near the river. If delayed for some reason, go to the second rally point identified farther to the southeast in six days."

Weaver looked at each of them, then after receiving a nod of understanding, he immediately set out with his packer and Haggerty, not looking back.

Connor, with his three mules, and Mariela and her three, headed due east for several miles and then turned southeast. They started to climb into the foothills of the Sierra Buenos Aires, another subordinate range to the Sierra Madre. Cresting a hill, he could see that the dust cloud was also spitting and a smaller group was headed in their direction. Within another two miles they reached a tributary of the Rio Sonora. Connor sent Mariela upstream while he took his mules and tried to lay a false trail downstream along the northern bank. After about a quarter mile he entered the stream for a hundred yards and then moved in the water against the southern bank and started back upstream. He had barely passed the point where he had turned downstream when he heard the sound of horses.

Connor pushed around a bend and stopped to see what would happen. His pursuers were like hounds, hot on the scent, and seeing the hoofprints heading downstream, they turned in that direction. He counted eight, Guardia Nacional. At least it wasn't the Rurales, who were more accomplished at this cat-and-mouse game. Connor waited for about five minutes and then started upstream. There was abundant growth near the stream, but it thinned as you traveled out before changing to juniper and oak as the elevation increased. After about five miles the stream became almost dry. He stopped to fill all the canteens and let his animals drink, then stayed in the streambed as it became dry and then simply disappeared. At this point, he caught up with Anastasio's sister.

They continued up into the Sierra until dusk, then made a dry camp. This was the first time he had been alone with Mariela, and he found her calm and competent as they set up for the night. They talked about the men on their trail and what to do if really pressed by the Guardia.

The plan was simple. "Try and down the pursuit's horses to discourage them and then outpace them," he told her. "If we are really pressed, I will fire and force them to dismount, then catch up to you. It is better to wound than kill because that will slow them more. Neither of us can afford to be taken."

Connor hoped it wouldn't come to that. Later, he asked her what they would do after this trip. She didn't have any uncertainty about what she would do.

"I will fight for our land until we win or it becomes hopeless; then I will join those who have fled and work on a new life," she told him.

Mariela questioned him with more confidence about his ambitions. Somehow, his ranching plan seemed less exciting, maybe mundane was the word. They took turns sleeping during the night and then continued in the morning. Connor found himself speculating on what she looked like absent the baggy clothes.

Three days later, they came down out of the Sierra and, from the high ground, could see the Rio Moctezuma. They turned south and, a day later, reached the rally point near the village of Pera. Within hours, they were joined by Anastasio with Cruz, and then, later in the afternoon,

Weaver and Haggerty. Next in was Alfredo and finally the last guard, Emilio. In the morning they set off south, moving slowly and staying west of the river. The following days were uneventful, and some miles south of Nacozari, where the small stream with that name joined the Rio Moctezuma, they halted. Emilio and Alfredo were sent into town to buy supplies. They returned with another gunman who was part of Weaver's crew, an alert, hawk-nosed pistolero named Ramon. They continued south with greater caution.

Four days after Nacozari, they stopped again for a couple of days outside of Cumpas to resupply, and then again at Moctezuma. Weaver's intelligence seemed to be good. Although there were Army patrols from the Guardia and Rurales, he seemed to know when to wait patiently and when to proceed. Between Moctezuma and Batuc, they traveled in three elements, as they had practiced, a day or two apart, arriving without incident. Anastasio went into Batuc, meeting his contact, and returned with bad news. The Yaqui could not bring up a party to conclude the deal for at least two weeks. The Mexican Army was aggressively trying to isolate the insurgents in the Bacatete Mountains and more time was needed to exit the strong-holds and work north to conclude the exchange.

Weaver cursed and considered the options. He could go deeper into Mexico and deliver the weapons to one of the Yaqui strongholds all at one time. Option two was to deliver the weapons piecemeal, slipping in and out more discreetly. The third option was to wait it out and let the Yaquis come to him, as was originally planned. He thought

the first option was too risky. The second option opened
the possibility that he would only end up selling part of
the contraband. Weaver wanted the big payday. The third
option seemed most appealing to him, but ran the risk
that they would be discovered. Not surprising, Weaver
preferred option three and pondered how to mitigate the
risk. His solution was to cache the contraband in three
different locations. He also was determined that there be
no compromising leaks. Two members of his crew would
be with each group to enforce security.

Connor suddenly had a heightened sense of danger,
and not from the Guardia or the Rurales. He recognized
that he was particularly vulnerable at this point. With
the hardest part of the trip complete, his role with the
packers was less critical. His elimination would provide
a bonus for Weaver: twenty additional guns for sale and
no need to pay him the final two hundred dollars. The
added benefit of eliminating a potential competitor would
likely be the most appealing. Connor's assessment was not
misplaced. Weaver pulled Ramon aside, telling him to go
with Connor's group.

"If you find an opportunity to eliminate him, I will
give you his share," he told him. Weaver had watched
Connor closely and gave the pistolero some additional
instructions. "I don't want to upset our guide, so if you
can provoke him, that would be better than plain murder.
He knows how to use a gun but is not a professional like
you, so be smart."

Weaver was already considering a backup strategy if
his plan didn't work. He might achieve the same results

by taking action after the consummation of the deal with the Yaquis. There were five in Connor's group. Besides himself and Mariela, there was Emilio and Ramon, the recent addition. The other packer was also one who had worked with Weaver before and no doubt was considered loyal. His name was Lopez, no first name given, and he didn't appear overly smart based on Connor's interaction with him on the trail. Of the three, he thought Ramon was the biggest threat and most likely to initiate any action. His stare, when he thought Connor wasn't watching, projected a competitive hatred. He expected Emilio to back his play, when it came, and Lopez to stay out of the way. Connor decided that at the slightest provocation, he would do his best to put him down first. He would have to be alert for some kind of edge.

He didn't have long to wait. Having buried the weapons and ammo, they started back to their campsite, about a mile away. Ramon attempted to strike up a conversation with Mariela, who studiously ignored him. His quick glances at Connor showed he was looking for a reaction. Mariela dropped back to avoid talking. When she was parallel with Connor, he slowed further until the other riders were out of earshot. He explained to her his suspicion that Ramon was looking for an excuse for gunplay.

"Mariela, I need your help," he told her. "If he tries to put his arm around you, pull you to him, or is even a step away while I am there, I want you to put your shoulder into him hard and then immediately lean or go the opposite way. I am going to draw, and I don't want you in the way. Can you do that?"

Her eyes widened and were glued to his. She nodded. He asked her to repeat back to him his instructions, and she did. Mariela resolved that Connor's trust would not be a mistake.

"When you see me draw, you do, too, and if I miss, shoot him. Are you any good with that single action Colt?" She shook her head, no. "After Ramon, Emilio is the next dangerous so if Ramon is hit, be ready to shoot him if he gets his gun out," he continued. "They will be close so you won't miss; point and shoot."

She nodded again, lips compressed into a thin line.

Reaching the campsite, Connor noted two things— Ramon seemed unnaturally calm, eyes half hooded, and Emilio seemed very much on edge. It was cooling and Mariela began gathering firewood. Ramon started trying to talk to her as she brought each armload to the firepit. His right hand was out of sight behind his back and Connor, seeing this, put his hand on the butt of his revolver, covered by his open coat. He was on the opposite side of the firepit, about eight feet away, Emilio about five feet to his left. Ramon made a lewd remark, and when she turned to glare at him, he reached out with his left arm, putting it over her neck and pulling her toward him, keeping his eyes locked on Connor. Whether he was trying to provoke Connor or just use Mariela as a shield, the move started the chain reaction.

Ramon's right arm was already moving out from behind his back when Mariela's shoulder slammed into him, moving him right as she then rebounded to the left. The mechanics of Connor's draw were perfect. Shoulder toward Ramon, lean left to accelerate clearing the holster, right hand moving his coat up and right. Arm bent, barrel aligned, trigger snapping back, Connor's Merwin & Hulbert chambered and fired. He heard Ramon fire as Connor extended his arm toward him and fired again. Pivoting left, he aligned the extended gun barrel with Emilio, who had his gun half out.

"Don't," he commanded Emilio.

Only a few seconds had passed. Emilio raised his hands and started blubbering about trying to help. Connor shifted his eyes to Mariela. She had her Colt out and pointing toward Emilio, her eyes wide, breathing fast. He looked down at Ramon. The first round had hit him in the chest. The second had hit the right side of his neck. He was twitching but that eventually stopped. His pistol lay in the dirt to his right.

Connor turned back to Emilio and the stunned Lopez, in the background.

"Bury him, now," he told them, then looked at Mariela. "Are you all right?"

She lowered her gun and nodded.

"Thank you, that was perfect," he told her quietly. And it had been. Whether it had been Ramon's balance, timing, distraction, or overconfidence, it didn't matter. It was enough. They walked over to where Emilio and Lopez were digging.

"Empty his pockets and put what you find in his saddlebag, along with his guns," he told them. "When you finish, come over to the fire. We are going to eat, sleep, and tomorrow give his horse and possessions to Mr. Weaver for his next of kin. You can tell him what happened. He disrespected the Senora and then tried to cover it by killing me. I don't want to hear anything different."

Lopez looked at him wild-eyed, nodding. Emilio looked down. "Emilio?" he asked.

"Si, Senor Connor."

Connor nodded to him and, without a trace of irony, said, "Thanks for trying to back me up." Emilio didn't look up.

While they worked, Connor went over to Mariela and kissed her forehead, gave her a reassuring hug, and told her to sit down; he would cook some beans and beef. She walked out into the dark, returning after a few minutes, wiping her mouth, and started helping him. He put the gun at half cock, pushed the release, rotated the barrel, and opened the breech. Two empty shells fell out. He closed the breech, rotated and locked the barrel and cylinder in place, then thumbed two new rounds through the loading gate. Mariela watched him—he seemed calm, almost disconnected from what had just happened. Her heartbeat was still elevated but slowing. She had seen violence before; she was Yaqui, after all. But Dios!

"He was a snake, Senior Connor," she asserted.

"That was a little too close, Mi Querida," he replied and then said nothing else.

She blushed at the endearment, but thankfully it was dark, and she didn't want to correct him. Her brother's assessment of him had been right. He was worthy of her trust.

The next day they rode into Weaver's camp and Issac immediately fixed on the empty saddle. He knew the answer but wanted to hear it.

"Where's Ramon?"

The fact that he directed his question to Connor said a lot.

Connor shrugged and turned to Emilio and said, "Tell him what happened."

"He disrespected the Senora and Senor Connor had to intervene. Ramon drew his pistola but was slower," Emilio told Weaver, but his eyes were on Connor.

Anastasio was standing next to Weaver and looked stunned. Looking at Mariela, he asked if this was true.

"Si. Hermano, he grabbed me and pulled his gun on Senor Connor. Thank God, he saved me," she told him, trying to remain calm.

Weaver was sure there was more to the story and would find out later. He had clearly underestimated Connor, and was now more convinced that his elimination was essential.

"Where is his body?" he asked.

Connor continued to study him, face expressionless. Emilio provided the answer. Haggerty had come up alongside, bolstering his confidence.

"I will have Haggerty provide security for you, since you are a man short," he stated.

"We won't need him," Connor replied evenly.

Before Weaver could reply, Haggerty responded, "Listen, asshole, you don't call the shots—you do what the boss says."

Connor ignored him, staring at Weaver. This infuriated Haggerty, who seemed to puff up; he turned red and unbuttoned his coat. Connor's hand was resting inside his coat and his stance signaled his mind was made up.

Haggerty took a step toward Connor and was stopped mid-stride by the distinctive sound of a round being jacked into a rifle chamber.

"We are safe with Senior Connor," they heard Anastasio's sister say.

She was kneeling as Connor had trained her, carbine lined up on Haggerty.

He opened his mouth to give an angry reply but was left sputtering when Connor overrode his tirade, saying, "Don't be stupid, big man. Your help is not needed or wanted."

Needing to regain his authority, Weaver intervened. "I'm sure Emilio and Connor can protect the weapons. We will send a message when we are ready to meet the Yaqui."

Connor turned and walked by Mariela, who waited for him to mount before uncocking the hammer and walking to her horse. Anastasio met her there and they had a short, intense conversation in Yaqui before they went over to some provisions stacked on the ground. She selected cornmeal, beans, bacon, and a few other items. Putting them in a burlap bag, she mounted and the group, including Emilio, departed.

CHAPTER 10

SONORA, 1888,
RENDEZVOUS AND AFTERMATH

Connor spent the following days resting and tending to his animals. He intended to move quickly after the weapons were sold and he was paid off. He had no illusions about Weaver and his crew and the danger they represented. He wanted to be miles from Weaver and planned another route back that was much farther east than the one used on the last trip out and the two trips in. Connor sent Lopez with Emilio into Batuc, with two mules to buy supplies for the trip back. With those two gone, he took Mariela into a small, boxed canyon with a box of .44s.

He designated targets at twenty-five, fifty, and seventy-five yards. Taking his time, he had her first dry-fire, then fire ten rounds at each target. Her skill and confidence were growing and she hit the far target about half the time. After cleaning the carbine, he took a look at the Colt. Her holster was only good for carrying the pistol. He showed her how to cross draw, with the pistol in her belt. Connor shared the advice he had received from Ray: Better to start with the gun already in your hand and focus on accuracy over speed. He had her fire the last twenty rounds, emphasizing a two-handed stance. He identified targets at twelve and twenty feet. She hit the near target seven out of ten times; the far target, two out of ten.

They left the canyon, not wanting to be there on the off chance that someone had heard the firing and came to investigate. At camp, they waited for the other two to return, drinking coffee in silence. Connor, after the long trip and recent shared danger, felt comfortable in her presence, as did she with him. The clothes she wore were a deliberate effort to obscure her shape, and even her curves were masked. He guessed she was close to thirty, some fine wrinkles near her eyes, which appeared slightly Asian, like some Indians. Her nose was not as pronounced as Rosangela's and her face was pleasing, projecting a serious and intelligent demeanor. She had demonstrated stamina and grit, and without her actions, the showdown with Ramon might have been very different.

She appreciated that Connor had treated her as an equal and with respect, on the journey. The loan of the carbine and the marksmanship training had helped her confidence. Mariela knew that her brother liked him, and she thought Anastasio was a good judge of character. Connor was physically tough and trail wise, and she had found her confidence in his decisions growing. That was why she had determined to follow his direction in the run-up to the shoot-out. Ramon had seemed to radiate evil and arrogance. She had been shocked at the fast, deliberate way Connor had executed that demonio. It had been a close-run thing and she had felt like a spectator when the first round slammed into Ramon's chest. It was only after several seconds that she felt an almost overwhelming rush of relief. It did not help to think about the alternative result. That was why she had taken a stand when Haggerty threatened Connor.

She was brought back to the present when Connor asked her in a quiet, almost apologetic way, "How is it that you are not married?"

She had been a widow for years now and he apologized with condolences when she told him. He had died of a sickness, not the endemic warfare with the Mexican Army.

"I joined mi hermano after the disaster of the second battle of Anil. I needed to be near my only immediate family," she told him.

Connor told her he was unmarried because of how he earned a living and that, at present, he didn't have much to offer a woman.

Mariela surprised herself by saying, "You have yourself, Senor."

He seemed a little startled by her response, then smiled slightly and bowed his head, almost in gratitude. "You are both kind and lovely, Senora Mariela."

He added spontaneously while meeting her eyes, "I hope that I will see you again after this trip."

She replied demurely, "I would welcome that but it will be up to you."

They were interrupted by the return of Lopez, Emilio, and the mules. It was evident that they had made a stop at a cantina while on their mission. Unlike with Mariela, he would be happy to be shed of these two. Connor separated out the supplies he intended for his return and looked up to the sounds of another horse. It was Anastasio. He hugged his sister and greeted Connor as the others gathered.

"In three days we will meet with our people and make the exchange. It is farther south and we will move out tomorrow, early evening," he told them.

They dug the weapons from the shallow hole and brought the mules in so they would be ready to load up in the morning. The trip to the meeting site was uneventful, the distance short, and the precautions taken at this stage were high. After reaching the rendezvous point with the Yaquis, two days were spent working out payment. It was a combination of barter and cash. After saying goodbye to Anastasio and Mariela, Connor went to collect the final two hundred dollars owed for packing in Weaver's rifles and ammunition. Weaver's attempt to screw him out of his money hadn't ended well for either of them. He had recovered about half of the money he was owed, having tricked Weaver into a discounted sale of Weaver's remaining four rifles. As Connor nursed his chest wound five days after the ambush, he figured it had ended much worse for him. Still, with his fever down and, for the moment, infection at bay, he might yet survive. He needed to avoid any more contact with Weaver or his crew and he would need some help and time to recover before crossing the international border, into Arizona.

He had been about two days' north of the meeting point and west of the Rio Yaqui. His attackers had counted on him using the same general route back as they had used when southbound. Connor had planned on deviating from his previous route, but not until he was farther north. He should have covered ground faster, but it was too late for regrets. He needed to cross the river and go west to where he hoped he could get help. The Rio Yaqui was fast and deep and the crossing would not be easy. He thought he could get help to recover on the other side of the Yaqui. There was a crossing at La Estrella, but he would have to backtrack about half a day. If that didn't work, there was another at Soyopa. From either crossing, he could go farther east to the village of Bacanora where he had someone to help him. The trail from the crossing to the village was through rough mountainous terrain. He might be able to join a group that was traveling through to Sahuaripa. Renegade Apaches and bandits were a present danger on that journey. Connor thought he needed at least a few weeks to recover if he reached the town of Bacanora.

The wound, painful as it was, coupled with the pummeling he had taken rolling down the slope, were not his main concern. Infection and fever were the more critical danger, and at the moment, he felt weak as a kitten. The wound had compromised his ability to defend himself effectively with either pistol or rifle. He doubted Weaver would give up trying to kill him. Even moving slowly and resting frequently, he was exhausted by the time he reached the outskirts of La Estrella. He found a place where he could observe the crossing while staying out of sight and resting. Connor planned to cross early in the morning, while it was just starting to turn gray.

He slashed across the ford, water rising halfway up his thigh until he rode up the east side of the Rio Yaqui. He started almost immediately going up into the foothills and then into the Sierra. It was now light and he took advantage of the early morning cool to continue until about ten in the morning. At that point he paused to sleep and rest. He could see the trail winding through the mountains and he observed it for a while before he fell asleep. He traveled a few more hours in the early evening before finding a place to stop and rest again.

He could feel the fever returning as he repeated the process each of the next two days. Connor could barely stay in the saddle when he descended into a valley and arrived at the outskirts of a village. He could see many agaves throughout the valley floor as his focus faded in and out. He asked a farmer for the location of his friend Roberto Alcazar and soon arrived where his friend was staying with his uncle. Before leaving Clifton, he had sent a message telling him that he might come to Bacanora. Hailing the adobe house, he saw his friend and an older version come out. Trying to dismount, his legs collapsed as they touched ground and he fell, striking his head and shoulder.

He was delirious for three days, cared for by Roberto's Aunt Luz, and another older woman. Her name was Amelia and she seemed to be part midwife, Curandera, and Bruja. Which one of those skills were most useful to bringing him back was a good question. He first got a good look at her as she was spooning some broth into him. It seemed to be chicken, laced with herbs, giving it a bitter taste. Thin, with hair severely tied back, and of middle age, it was her eyes that commanded immediate attention. She stared at him intensely and then began speaking in a low volume, index finger tapping his forehead. Had he been stronger, he likely would have fractured it, because it was that annoying. He restrained himself, thinking he should be grateful, and besides, he could barely move his arms. Roberto entered at that point and smiled, seeing he was back among the living. He also translated the Opata dialect she was using.

"She is saying you are a lucky idiot and now understands how you survived the cave-in at the Clifton mine. She also says that she expects a generous gift for her skill and efforts on your behalf." Aunt and Uncle entered and introductions were made; he thanked them all and, exhausted, fell back asleep.

It was another three days before he could sit up and feed himself. There were no mirrors but Connor could see he was skeletal, having lost ten to fifteen pounds on an already lean frame. Roberto provided him with two canes and Connor started trying to walk with assistance. A few steps were all he could manage at first, adding to it each day. Roberto knew there was more to the story than bandits and felt confident Connor would level with him in good time. There was a steady stream of visitors, no doubt having heard Roberto's Clifton stories and wanting to see if the Curandera's skills were as she said. They also wanted to hear about the ambush and the bandits, and Connor became adept at weaving a satisfying tale. That proved to be fortunate because, at the end of two weeks, two Rurales showed up at the door.

One was a sergeant, the other enlisted, wearing their distinctive gray, whipcord trousers and jackets, with the black braid down the trousers. One had a black, the other a gray sombrero with the eagle and snake emblem on the front. Both had bandoliers with ammunition draped over their shoulders along with a pistol belt with a revolver. A crowd had gathered outside, but the Rurales seemed supremely unperturbed.

The sergeant began the questioning: "We heard there was a gringo here and we want to know how you came to be here and why."

What followed was a detailed interrogation, a search of Connor's possessions, an examination of his animals, and a subsequent talk with Roberto and his uncle. They took down his references in the States to contact and told him to report in three weeks to the Rurales' outpost in Sahuaripa for further questioning. Connor was glad that he had discreetly hidden most of his money and shoulder rig since both would cause more questions. There was no choice but to agree, and he was glad to see them ride back out.

Roberto's uncle, Alexandro, had a subsistence farm but his primary occupation was as a Vinatero, a distiller of mescal. Not any mescal but the justly famous Bacanora, made with only the agave pacifica. The plant had a large root ball with a lot of fibers and could be four to six feet in diameter, though more oblong than round. When harvested after eight to ten years, the pinas, as they were called, could weigh up to ninety pounds. It was hard work getting them out of the ground and cutting the two to four-foot leaves off. The tool used looked like a flat semicircular shovel called a Jimar. The work was as hard as mining, though less dangerous, and the men that did the work were called Jimadores.

The pinas were then split and baked in a large oven with a top opening, using mesquite firewood. After two days or so, they were taken out and crushed with a large grinding wheel, called a Tahoma. The pulp and juices were washed out with water and then put into barrels, topped off with more water. Wild yeast spores started the fermentation process, which was allowed to continue for about two weeks. Connor, besides increasing the distance he could walk and recovering weight and strength, was trying to be helpful. Alexandro allowed him to help with the distillation process. Using mesquite charcoal, a pot still was used to boil the fermented pulp and juices. The initial distillate had small bubbles and was barreled separately from the following distillate, which had fewer bubbles. Those two would be blended together to get the final product. The Bacanora was left in the oak barrels until decanted into jugs for sale.

Connor enjoyed helping, feeling his strength gradually returning. He still had ten days before he had to see the Rurales again. He had started gently stretching the scars, softening them with aloe and butter. He had begun practicing his draw, acquire and fire practice, knowing he had lost skill but determined to be ready when there was another test. After talking with Roberto, he determined that three goats would be the appropriate gift for Amelia, the Curandera, for her help with his recovery. When he came to her hut, he saw a small garden at the side and a drying rack with vegetables and desiccated animal parts. She answered the door and simply looked at him, then examined the goats and nodded to the small fenced area, which two goats already occupied. He released the goats to join the other two and returned to the door.

Connor thanked her again for her help with the wound and the infection. He pressed a ten-dollar gold eagle into her hand and turned to leave.

"Come in. I will try to help you," she said, taking hold of his arm.

Amelia had him sit on the floor and she sat opposite him, picking up a small basket. Inside were a collection of bones, shells, stones, and sticks. Connor knew from talking with Roberto that people went to her for advice about the future.

"What would you have me tell you about?" she asked.

He hesitated and then, not wanting to be insulting, said, "Please help me with the questions. You seem wiser than me."

To himself, Connor acknowledged that he neither believed nor doubted that some people might be able to peer into the future. He also was wary of the concept of self-fulfilling prophecies.

As to the questions, she stared intensely and said, "You place a heavy burden on me."

He pressed a five-dollar gold piece into her hand, hoping this would help with the burden, and waited. Amelia was acting now more as a Brujo, or witch, rather than a healer.

"I will ask about life, love, and threats for you," she told him serenely.

With that, she shook the basket and threw the assorted contents onto the floor between them. She looked intently, then looked at him. Repeating the process two more times, she appeared ready to share something.

"You are not meant to just hew wood and herd cattle. You are a leader and builder, searching for some prize even at great risk."

"What should I be searching for?" he asked. She offered no further clarification.

The process was repeated for the next question, and despite himself, he found his interest increasing.

"You are open and loyal—that attracts the good and the bad. Rely on what you see rather than on what you wish," she stated.

Threat was the last area of inquiry and he half expected to hear something relating to the upcoming meeting with the Rurales.

Instead, she told him, "Your enemies will get close; the solution will be intimate."

She gathered her tools for prophecy and then ushered him to the door, looked at him gravely. "Be careful, Senor."

She broke eye contact, gave his hand a squeeze, and eased him out into the light.

Roberto traveled with him to Sahuaripa. Connor was stronger but still not at full capability. The two-day trip through the Sierra was useful in assessing his true physical state. He felt another month was needed to fully recover, and Connor resolved to be patient. Roberto was contemplating what to do next—become a Vinatero like his uncle, or get into the freight hauling business with his cousin, currently operating out of Fronteras? The latter was somewhat less dangerous with the waning of the Apache threat. Roberto carried a Marlin, lever action, chambered for the government, .45-70 round. It was a good weapon, packing more punch and range than Connor's Winchester. The drawback was that it was longer, with the standard twenty-eight-inch barrel, and a heavier rifle. It had a nine-round magazine, unlike the fifteen rounds in the .44-40. Roberto was somewhat indifferent as a shooter, but if they had the time and ammunition, Connor thought he could help him improve.

While in the village, Roberto and Connor had talked a lot. With the Apache menace lessened, there were opportunities to make money hauling supplies and equipment to the isolated villages, ranches, and mines in the Sierras. It would be a long time before there were roads and rail connecting much of that. Connor was an expert packer and leader. Roberto had a cousin with a wagon transportation business between the border and along the western side of the Sierra Madre Mountains. There were possibilities for making money that both wanted to explore. Connor had also admitted to himself that he needed another one hundred and sixty acres and more cash for calves if he was going to have a reasonable shot at the ranching business. If pressed, he would confess that he wanted more human interaction than the ranch would allow. Providing transportation services might allow him to build a better financial base for the future. Given what he had been through, having a reliable partner at his back was appealing.

Arriving in Sahuaripa just before noon, they found a woman who would cook for them and she prepared tortillas with some shredded chicken, beans, and chile peppers. It was good but reluctantly they went over to the building that the Rurales were using. There were about a dozen horses tied outside and more than the two men Connor had met in Bacanora. Entering, his eyes immediately fixed on the tall, spare, middle-aged man sitting at the only desk. His posture erect, perhaps even characterized as uncompromising, he had the same gray whipcord uniform as the other Rurales. His uniform was immaculate, and the silver braid running down the legs of his trousers denoted an officer. Connor had seen him before, at a distance, during the more recent Apache campaigns when the Mexican and U.S. Armies had cooperated. He was looking at Major Emilio Kosterlitzky, the Russian-born veteran of the Mayo-Yaqui and Apache wars. He had enlisted in 1873 and was now a major in the Guardia Nacional. He had been seconded to La Gendarmeria Fiscal, or Rurales as they were known, in the Sonoran Squadron at the personal recommendation of President Diaz. Some called him the Mad Cossack, but never within hearing distance.

Kosterlitzky fixed his eyes on Connor, who focused on remaining calm, his face placid, although his pulse rate had accelerated. The major was deeply respected by his men, and that was saying something. Some of the enlisted had come from civil backgrounds, but many were conscripted out of the jails and labor camps and were given a chance at rehabilitation. They were tough, resilient men, not averse to cutting corners and exacting harsh methods in enforcing the law when tracking down criminals. Kosterlitzky exercised iron discipline with his men, and deserters faced summary execution. With President Diaz's authority, bandits captured were interrogated and, if reasonably sure they were guilty, executed. Anything of value captured with them whose owner could not be identified was sold. In the Rurales, the proceeds were split, with the largest portion going to the commander. Kosterlitzky was different in that he split all spoils equally, taking the same share as his men. He trained his men hard and shared the rigors and risks of the trail with them. When needed, he would lead from the front, and his personal courage was never in question.

He inspired respect and his men carried themselves with a certain swagger.

"Senor Connor, our messages have been returned and you seem to be a man with a commendable reputation. I have a few requests and questions, however. First, I want to see where you were shot by the bandits."

Connor responded, "Yes, sir," opened his shirt, and slipped out of the left sleeve. The entry and exit wounds were scarring and were an angry bright pink. The places where they had been sutured were clearly visible.

The major's eyes returned from their inspection and met Connor's eyes. "Do you think you could take some of my men to the site of the ambush?"

"I believe so if you think it would be useful," Connor replied.

"What do you think we would find?" Kosterlitzky asked.

"Shell casings and perhaps the remains of a dead horse; I would think the trail would be very cold at this point," Connor told him. "When would you want to leave?"

Kosterlitzky stroked his full mustache, contemplating the question. "It would be a waste of time, as you say. How long are you planning to remain in Mexico?"

"I am not sure. My friend and I are giving consideration to a transportation service, between Douglas/Agua Prieta and the mining towns in northern Sonora."

This was the first time he had voiced the thought that it might not yet be time for ranching on a remote spread. Connor felt relieved that the conversation was shifting to a safer topic.

The Rurale looked at Roberto, who was fidgeting with his sombrero. "You have experience with packing too?"

Roberto replied, "No, but I have a cousin in that business, in Fronteras."

That seemed to satisfy the major. "Please join me this evening for dinner. I would like to discuss other things with you," he said and then turned his attention to the reports on his desk, effectively dismissing the two.

Both were glad to get out, and bought some supplies for another week of travel to include a few boxes of .45-70 ammunition.

"What do you think he wants?" asked Roberto.

"I am not sure, but we should make every effort to comply. I would like to be in his good graces," Connor told him.

Dinner was modest, eating in the courtyard of a house where Kosterlitzky was staying. The weather was perfect and they had chicken and tomatoes. They sampled a small bottle of Bacanora that Roberto had brought one that had rested in the oak barrels for some indeterminate period. The major and Connor compared notes and stories of chasing Apache, agreeing that General Miles had come up with a good solution. He complimented the quality of the Vinatas, the distillery, and then got to the point.

"I have been appointed Chief of Military Intelligence by President Diaz for Sonora and Sinaloa, in addition to my other responsibilities. I have need of any information about illegalities, and smuggling in particular."

Connor tried not to react to the news and maintained an interested look on his face, waiting for another shoe, or in this case boot, to drop.

"We would be happy to help," he told the major. "Is there something in particular you want us to be alert to?"

"Arms and ammunition. We are trying to settle the Yaqui, but they seem to receive a flow that is not making easy their journey toward civilization. More broadly, anything you think that would be useful to upholding the law. I would like you to meet with my intelligence officer, Lieutenant Ortiz, tomorrow. He will explain how to send messages. You will have my personal thanks."

Meeting with Ortiz took about thirty minutes. Afterward, the major came out to say goodbye and Connor took the opportunity to tell him that he had a friend selling arms in Clifton, and would be happy to dispose of any weapons that the Rurales seized through that channel. Kosterlitzky understood that he was angling for more than just the major's personal thanks, which was to be expected. Further, he would use telegrammed messages referring to those transactions to convey any news on weapons smuggling going south, using the code that he and Lt. Ortiz had worked out. They shook hands and then they proceeded north toward the Rio Aros.

CHAPTER 11

SONORA, SPRING/SUMMER 1888

Each day found Connor a little stronger. It had been roughly five weeks and both strength and stamina were slowly returning. The infection and fever had been of more lasting damage than the wound, but his chest was still very sore and tight. The trail to the north would take them through some of the most Apache-haunted mountains in Mexico. The Nednhi, the southern cousins of the Chiricahua, were maintaining a lower profile but there were likely one to two hundred, maybe more, scattered through the northern Sierra Madre. Renegades from the reservations would still find their way to join them, and small-scale robberies, rustling, and the occasional murder persisted, on both sides of the international border. Their most famous leader, Juh, had been dead for about five years. New leaders would have to deal with the reduced circumstances in which they found themselves. The old networks that relied on the trade in plunder for ammunition and other useful things were disappearing with the raiding. Connor was sure that at least a couple of Apache

Scouts he knew were among them, having avoided the deportation and confinement to Ft. Marion, Florida.

He had been north and east of the Sahuaripa area before. In 1886 he had been down here as a packer supporting Captain Lawton and Captain Leonard Wood. The expedition was trying to run down Geronimo and either kill him or convince him to surrender. It consisted of one company of infantry, one troop of thirty-five calvary, twenty Apache Scouts, thirty packers, and one hundred mules. Tom Horn had been the Chief of Scouts, with Jose Maria, the interpreter. They left Ft. Bowie in the beginning of May and after four months had not been able to locate Geronimo. They had searched both north and south of the Aros River, up and down the mountains of the Sierra Madre. The heat and rugged terrain had worn out men and horses. The cavalry troop had abandoned their horses after five days. Captain Leonard Wood had been reduced to wearing cotton flannel drawers, his blue calvary blouse, moccasins, and a hat that no longer had a crown on it. The rest of the soldiers and packers were no better and, arguably, in worse shape.

The villages they passed through reflected the effects of sustained Apache raids and attacks. A number of villages were simply deserted, while others consisted of single-story adobe huts, concentrated behind thick eight- or nine-foot-high adobe walls. There were few men of fighting age visible, with a preponderance of the old, the young, and widows. Looking at the faces of these survivors, the fear was palpable. Weapons were of poor quality, dominated by single-shot breechloaders and old muskets. Livestock was scarce, with the exception of goats and chickens; most everything else having been driven off.

They had been joined by Lt. Gatewood and his Apache Scouts, escorted by Lt. James Parker and twenty-five troopers of the Fourth Calvary in early August. Gatewood had discovered that Geronimo was in fact many miles to the north, near Fronteras. He was sent in advance by Captain Lawton to locate him, the rest of the command following as quickly as possible. They had slogged through Nacori, about fifty miles north of where Lt. Crawford had been killed seven months earlier, then Morelos and finally to Fronteras. The pack mules had to rest frequently, and the men were mostly on foot. Lt. Gatewood, a couple of days ahead of Lawton, at great personal risk, met Geronimo and initiated negotiations. These proved successful in convincing the renegade to meet with General Miles and ultimately surrender in September at Skeleton Canyon.

The campaign had been the last one for Connor. When they returned to Ft. Bowie, the exhausted packers had been paid off. There might be other contracts but most knew that this was the end of an era. Like the rest, Connor was so worn down that it didn't matter. It had provided the money for the down payment for the one hundred sixty acres along the Blue River, along with tools and supplies to begin the cabin. Now here he was, struggling north again through the extremely rugged mountains and canyons, most still unexplored and isolated. They splashed north across the Rio Aros not long before it joined the Rio Bavispe to form the Yaqui River. From there they would cross the Rio Bavispe going west, then turn north, following the west side of the river. There was a rough, tortuous trail that led through Tepache, about one hundred eighty miles from the border. From there they would travel on to Moctezuma, on the river by the same name. The trip to Tepache would transit through another difficult part of the Sierra Madre, known as the Sierra Lampazos.

Tepache was located in a narrow valley, about six miles long, between mountain ridges. It was small, maybe one hundred and twenty-five families. Subsistence farming and cattle were the main industries here. Roberto told him the name roughly translated into "place of beautiful women." They were not in evidence as the tired travelers rode in. They found a hut to sleep in and purchased some atole, a kind of corn flour–based watery gruel with some chunks of meat floating in it. It took the edge off their appetite but was soupy and tasteless, even missing the ubiquitous green chiles.

In the morning they set off for Moctezuma. It had been renamed long ago, but most still referred to it by its old name, San Miguel Arcangel de Oposura. The river, having also changed names, was once the Rio Oposura. The large brick church there carried the same name. It was sixty or so miles from Tepache and it took three days. There were no roads, just primitive trails suitable for trains of pack animals, led by Conductas, who led the packtrains. The trail would follow a ridgeline then descend along narrow switchbacks. Reaching low ground, there could be streams or pools of water, especially since they were in the period of summer rains. They would grind back up over a series of gradually increasing ridgelines.

On the higher ridgelines were pine forests, giving way to scrub oak, then juniper. The lower slopes and flats seemed devoid of humans, although there was ample evidence of more ancient peoples. Connor spotted a number of javelina, some in herds of almost two dozen. They were edible, weighing around fifty to sixty pounds, but it took a lot of cooking to be really palatable. Now at midsummer, most of the blooms were gone although some ironwoods were still showing their pale pink blossoms. The wildlife was also diverse with numerous deer and small game. The lower elevations supported jaguar and ocelots, evident by their tracks near the streams and isolated pools of water. They heard wolves howling at night in the distance, but none came close. Roberto and Connor took turns sleeping at night.

On the east side of the Bavispe was a thirty-by-eighty-mile swath of the Sierra, isolated by the great loop of the Rio Bavispe. The river started on the Chihuahua side of the Sierra Madre then traveled north, turned west, and finally south. The Rio Bavispe was joined by the Aros, also shown on some maps as the Haros, becoming the Rio Yaqui. The Rio Moctezuma joined the Yaqui near the village of Batuc, where the Yaqui had been contacted on the recent smuggling run. The area inside this loop was known as the Sierra El Tigre. Connor was startled when, on the second day out from Tepache, Roberto brought the Marlin up to his shoulder, chambered a round, and fired. They were coming up a ridge with heavy growth of pine. Allowing his eyes to follow the direction of Roberto's rifle, he caught a glimpse of a deer staggering into the heavier growth.

"Got him," uttered Roberto, as both men urged their tired animals toward the spot where the animal had vanished.

There was blood, but no deer. From the amount of blood, the animal could not have gone far. Even if not a clean kill shot, the effect of the .45-70 would be fatal. Dismounting and tying off the horses and mules, they followed on foot. Breaking into a meadow, Roberto made to follow the blood trail out into it when Connor pulled him back. Moving with caution while skirting the opening, they moved counterclockwise around the meadow. Near the opposite side of the opening, they found evidence of a long-term camp. Just inside the tree line, there was a shallow gully, maybe twelve feet below the meadow's elevation. It was about one hundred feet wide and four hundred feet in length. It was forested but more parklike in nature with a six-foot, rocky natural uplift on the far side. On the near side, gaps between the trees, parallel with the gully, showed evidence of a crude fence, lumber wedged between trees to create a barrier. On the far side, above the rocky lift, Connor could see at least seven primitive buildings. A couple had sidewalls of stacked stone, held in place with mud or clay. The rest seemed to use split wood planks, some laid horizontally and notched to interlock; others secured vertically to a frame. Roofs were all supported by a six- to seven-foot-high forked stick on either end of the dwelling with a pole between the forks to support the ridge pole and thatched roof.

It was deserted, but showed signs of recent habitation, and Connor and Roberto went no farther to investigate. They returned to the meadow, found the deer, and dragged it back into the woods opposite the camp. They quickly skinned and quartered the animal, wrapping up the meat in the hide, and carried it out. The mules were skittish, not liking the scent of blood. They covered another two miles before stopping to slice the meat and cook over a small fire. It took about two hours to slice and cook what they could quickly prepare and take with them. They ate while they cooked, keeping watch around them.

Roberto speculated that the deserted camp had been inhabited by bandits. The more permanent nature of the buildings seemed to suggest that. Connor was not so sure. Even Apaches, maybe especially Apaches, could evolve. They had dominated this area for centuries. They had in their ranks a few who had been exposed to more sophisticated building practices, to include Mexicans, Navajo, and other renegades. Regardless, both agreed it was not a good idea to poke the bear, as they say, and moving on was essential. The camp's relative proximity to the trail, although it was well hidden, reflected the rugged nature of the region, where the next ridge over could be terra incognita.

Connor began scanning the trail ahead with his field glasses as longer vistas presented the opportunity. About three hours down the trail, his caution was rewarded. From the opposite direction, he spotted a group of five men and a single mule. As the trail widened at one point, he and Roberto moved off and tied their animals to a small stand of scrub oak. They moved to the left of the animals but close to cover if needed, and waited. Both chambered a round and replaced it with another through the loading gate.

The five men were not surprised to see them waiting, which told Connor they had been observed, at least for a while. As they nonchalantly spread out opposite them, both men examined them closely. They were not dressed as vaqueros and seemed well armed, to include unscabbarded rifles and bandoliers of ammunition draped across their bodies. They sat on their horses easily and seemed alert, eyes restless, evaluating Connor and Roberto while checking backtrail as well as the one ahead. Only one wasn't bearded, although he seemed to be cultivating some scraggly growth. The rider second from Connor's left was the first to speak, directing his statement to a point between Connor and Roberto.

"Good afternoon, amigo. This is a difficult trail, and one sees few travelers. Is the trail ahead clear?"

Roberto gave him a limited reply, not wanting to encourage conversation, nor wanting to precipitate any offense.

Three of the men dismounted, keeping the horses between themselves and Connor. He noticed that they didn't sheath their rifles, but this was dangerous country.

"Are you heading to Oputo or San Miguel de Arcangel?" the speaker asked.

When Roberto answered "Oputo," the speaker looked at the other mounted rider, who imperceptibly shook his head.

"We are going to make some coffee. Would you join us?" he said.

Roberto replied, "Forgive us, Senor, we greatly appreciate your hospitality but we must hurry north before the sun goes down."

With that, he and Connor moved toward the animals, cautiously mounted, and led their mules back onto the trail. The youth with the scraggly growth looked toward the silent rider, but receiving no sign, did nothing. Connor and Roberto wasted no time putting distance between them and the group. They were traveling upward over a series of ever ascending heights. At the third switchback, Connor had a good view back down the trail. He put the binoculars to his eyes and picked out the group of five slowly heading away from them. He focused on the second from the last man in the file, the probable leader. He was looking back at him. He couldn't see his eyes but couldn't escape a shiver of premonition.

That evening as they sat by the campfire, Connor told Roberto, "You did well. I think that if we had joined them for coffee, we might not be sitting here."

"Do you think they believed that we were going to Oputo?" Roberto asked.

"I don't think it matters. They took a good look at our animals and gear. They are valuable but not enough to follow us all the way to either Oputo or San Miguel. I think they will be back before the trail splits," Connor replied. "I think we should leave the fire going and move another half mile down the trail before we bed down," he added. "If they come for us, we need to deal with them without mercy."

Roberto, like Mariela in the showdown with Ramon, was finding Connor to be more ruthless than he had suspected. Roberto was about the same height as Connor and about fifteen pounds heavier, hard muscle from his time in the mines and then as a Jimadore. Still, Connor could project a sense of menace, without consciously trying. Roberto had observed him practicing with his pistol each evening, drawing and dry-firing. He had become progressively smoother and faster, the movement fluid and natural.

"Are you worried about bandits, or the ones who wounded you last month?" Roberto asked one night.

"I knew them, and they will come for me if they were sure I was still alive," Connor responded frankly. "I haven't decided if I should hunt them down. I am not sure that I could survive that. I have also been thinking about what Amelia, the Bruja, told me. She said, 'Your enemies will get close; the solution will be intimate.' I need to be ready," he added.

Roberto thought about that and after several minutes of silence, said, "I understand, my friend. I will help you if I can. You know your enemies may get closer than your gun can manage. I think that maybe you will need something more. There is nothing more intimate than a blade. I think that you should think about that. I am good with a knife, but my cousin is a wizard with a blade. I can help you with your skill and maybe he can too."

Connor nodded. "I think that I need to develop that skill. I would appreciate your help and instruction. I also appreciate your offer. I hope I can keep you out of any violence that may come out of this."

That had been four days earlier.

The five men were bandits and the pickings of late had been very limited. The men they had passed on the trail and the mules were valuable enough to rob and kill for. This was a lawless and difficult area for accumulating wealth. El Jefe had felt that the potential of losses was too high in overcoming the two men at the wide spot on the trail. They had continued down the trail and then backtracked to catch them at night. The deserted camp-site had been a disappointment, but they had persevered, locating the second camp just as the night was ending. They moved in file to within fifty yards of the camp and then spread out into a line. The leader had held back a few steps, moving as silently as he could. Surprise was critical as their victims did not appear to be sheep. This was the time when alertness tended to fade.

They took turns on watch, and just before dawn, Roberto woke Connor, whispering, "They are coming."

Connor took a kneeling position, just left of the camp, the low embers of the fire and the blanket rolls. Roberto was twenty-five feet to his right, the animals twenty feet to his rear. Whatever happened, they couldn't lose the horses and mules. There was gray on the horizon but still dark in the trees with deep shadows. The bandits were closing in, now fifteen feet from the embers and the bedrolls. One fired at the left bedroll. Connor fired directly at the muzzle flash, the sound drowned out by at least three other shots coming from the line of killers. He fired at another muzzle flash and a dimly seen silhouette behind it. Roberto must have selected the same one too. The bandits knew that they were in the hornet's nest. They were trying to break contact, evident as the muzzle flashes began increasing in distance. Bullets smacked into trees and the ground. Connor methodically aimed and fired at movement, flashes, and shouts or screams. Roberto started moving forward and then abruptly fell face forward onto the ground.

Connor moved to his sprawled friend and rolled him over, looking for blood as the scene slowly lightened. No blood, but next to him was one of the bandits and plenty of blood.

Roberto moaned. Connor shouted at him, "Where are you hit?"

"Not hit," he replied and Connor was up and moving toward the retreating men.

He walked fast, pushing more rounds through the loading gate and firing at sounds ahead of him, trying not to stumble. A muzzle flash, then another. Connor returned fire, pressed forward, then shifted right toward where he thought the trail was. Sounds of breaking brush, then the sound of horses. He broke out to the trail as a line of horses came out of the brush to his left. A man was clinging to a saddle, half on, half off the beast. Connor fired four times toward the man and the horse, bringing the animal down. The man avoided being trapped under the horse and staggered after the line of horses moving farther down the trail. He turned, bringing a pistol up, firing, missing, turning to flee. He heard the boom of the Marlin behind him and the man on the trail went down. Roberto came up alongside him, breathing hard. Connor reached out to hold him back. "Let's wait."

As the sun came up, they tried to see what had been done. The man who had fired first was shot through the chest and bleeding out. He was the one with the scraggly beard. The bandit that Roberto had tripped over was dead, shot in the side and gut. The growing light showed blood trails toward where the horses had been picketed. The dead bandit on the trail was the spokesman during the tense meeting, yesterday. That left two, including the leader. At least one was wounded, as evidenced by the fresh blood farther up the trail. Following them was out of the question. They would have the advantage of position and it was not worth the risk of getting shot. Besides, they were coming down from that kill-or-be-killed surge of adrenaline and feeling grateful that the worst was Roberto's bruised forehead.

They went through the belongings of the downed bandits, including the saddlebags of the downed horse. There was little money in their pockets, maybe the equivalent of forty dollars and change. Some food, which they added to their supply. Roberto tossed him a double-edged knife, about eight and a half inches long, inch and a half wide, along with a sheath. He also found a hide-out knife about three-quarters of an inch wide by six inches long. One of the rifles had a broken stock, but the mechanics were excellent and Connor decided to keep it. They only found one other rifle, a Winchester Model 1876. Connor tossed Roberto a Colt 45 double action in very good repair. He also kept a Smith and Wesson First Model, double action, chambered for .44-40. They also retained the ammunition that fit their weapons, along with bandoliers. They dragged the bodies deeper into the woods and left them for the wild creatures to dispose of. The dead horse they levered over the side of the trail, watching it fall about forty feet before coming to rest. They repacked and mounted, wanting to be away from this place.

A half day out from the campsite, they stopped and rested. Roberto brought out the jug of Bacanora and both took a swig. The burn felt good and both laughed as only men who have escaped a close encounter with death can.

"I thought you were dead, and the thought of trying to bury you was overwhelming," Connor told him. "Getting the horse off the trail was bad enough."

Roberto laughed and said, "I'm sorry we didn't get the leader of those bastards. We would have done a great service to Mexico."

"Now that we know how dangerous this transporting business can be, we will have to cut a good deal with your cousin," Connor told him.

In the back of his mind, he thought that the ranching business might have more charm than he thought. Whether he could make a go of it was another story, to be determined sometime in the future, he hoped. A day later, they rode into Moctezuma.

It was a decent-sized town, and Connor knew that Weaver had at least one agent here. Ramon had come out of here, so that was something. He was bearded now and his hair was longer. He would stay out of the cantinas as much as possible and try to keep his name out of any local circulation. The ride from here to Fronteras was going to be easier now—there was a road north, not just a trail. Roberto sent a message to his cousin that they would be there in a few days. Connor exchanged the S&W First Model for the Colt, wanting his friend to have the better weapon. He sold the pistol and the Winchester, then shopped around for a shotgun. He didn't find what he wanted, but there would be other towns.

Unlike Tepache, there were attractive women in evidence here. Connor, thinking about Rosangela and, surprising himself, Mariela, decided to delay immediate gratification. Roberto was not to be denied and they ended up staying an extra day. Resupplied, they set out in easy stages, with the next stop being Cumpas. It had been eight weeks since the ambush and subsequent infection. Connor felt he was between seventy to eighty percent of his old self. He had concluded that hunting his enemies openly was not the right approach, but neither was forgiveness. Weaver was clever and good at thinking ahead several steps. He had shown that on the two trips into Mexico. He also had a network that included tough and ruthless men with a degree of loyalty. Underestimating him would be stupid, possibly fatal. Weaver was greedy, and that was something. Like Connor, he didn't easily walk away from a grievance. Reflecting on that, Connor had to admit that part of his recent problems stemmed from similar impulses.

CHAPTER 12

They stopped at Cumpas, then traveled on upriver to Nacozari. It was a midsized town to the west of the Sierra Madre. There had been silver mining here since the mid 1600s, but the veins were mostly exhausted. More recently, there was interest in reopening the old mines but this time for copper mining. Potential new mineral deposits were being assessed to the east of the town and farther into the foothills. There was talk of extending a rail line from the Southern Pacific Railroad through Douglas, Arizona, to Nacozari. That would take a few years, though, in Connor's estimation. Currently, freight wagons brought supplies to Nacozari, and from here, packtrains would move supplies into the northern Sierra Madre. The advent of a spur line would not change that dynamic. Roberto would build that into a proposal to his cousin.

There were lots of small mines in the Sierra, and now that the Apache threat was much diminished, many were being reopened. The smaller claims were focused on gold and silver. Most deposits were small and tended to be exhausted after a few years. They were the result of the rock eroding, nuggets and flakes of the precious metal being washed from the quartz veins and collecting between the bedrock and the hard caliche and rock soil over the eons. In some cases, the quartz veins themselves were directly mined where found. The small placer deposits were often a point of departure for prospectors to look farther up in the Sierra Madre for the source and location of the veins.

Connor and Roberto thought they could build a business hauling supplies in on pack mules, trading for the precious metal as payment. The fact that they had no interest in the mines, mining, or the location specifically would inspire confidence in their service to the small-scale, secretive prospectors and miners. They would need to find some additional packers and invest in the mules, gear, and provisions. North of the border, there were men Connor knew who needed work now that the Indian campaigns were over. There was risk, too, but both figured that they were in turn cautious and tough enough to handle the challenge. Connor had come to the conclusion that he needed a lot more money to successfully launch his ranch. Roberto needed a good opportunity to build a life outside the mines. They had confidence and trust in each other and that was a good start. Connor had three problems: finding and lining up customers, dealing with any residual threat from Weaver, and seeing where he stood with Rosangela.

The trip to Fronteras was uneventful. The town was dusty and small, about forty-five miles north of Nacozari and about thirty-five miles from the U.S. border. There was an old presidio and a mission. The Apaches had frequently come here to trade plunder for a variety of supplies, although both sides did so with a high level of distrust.

Roberto's cousin had a place of business on the north end of town, close to the river. It consisted of a barn with adjacent corral, and two adobe buildings. One was two floors and used for storage. The other was used as both office and bunkhouse. Luis Alcazar, Roberto's cousin, would not be back for another day. There were a couple of wagons going out to Tucson and Connor took the opportunity to have one of the drivers carry a message for Rosangela. It had been over five months since last contact.

Taking a page from Issac Weaver on competitors, he also sent a message to Lieutenant Ortiz, Major Kosterlitzky's intelligence officer. He identified Issac as a possible arms smuggler, indicating that he might be operating out of Bisbee or Tucson. Connor indicated he would continue to investigate and update when possible. He asked Ortiz if he had any collaborating information. He also asked if, on a different subject, the Rurales had a list of any weapons that they were looking to dispose of. He gave his friend in Clifton, Witherspoon, as a point of contact for any response.

Connor was feeling mostly recovered from his chest wound. His muscle movement was still restricted but getting better by the day. That night he and Roberto finalized their proposal for Luis as they had dinner. The essence of the deal was simple. Connor would help line up additional customers north of the border for Luis and his wagons. Roberto, Connor, and Luis would look for customers needing supplies hauled by mule train into the Sierra, where wagons couldn't go. A ten percent finder's fee would go to any business identified and executed by the Roberto/

Connor team or Luis. After agreement, Connor would go north for two months and Roberto would work on lining up customers starting at Nacozari and farther east in the Pilares area. Roberto would also explore bringing mescal from Bacanora along with packers. Connor would line up packers from north of the border. Together, they would line up mules and gear when they were ready to start. Roberto also revealed that the Brujo, Amelia, was actually Luis's mother. Connor thanked him for the heads-up—he would keep his stories respectful. They both laughed at that and downed their drinks.

Connor liked Luis Alcazar. He was thin and had the same severe look as his mother. Roberto and Luiz had a warm reunion and shook hands on the deal. His transport company had ten wagons of various lengths and widths. The number of mules in harness would vary from four to ten, depending on the nature of the load. He liked to assign at least three wagons to a transport and two well-armed drivers per wagon to ensure security. His routes were mostly north, as far as Tucson, and south as far as Soyopa. Occasionally his shipments would go east to El Paso and west to Nogales or Ures, farther to the southwest. Basically, he was covering areas between the central rail line between Mexico City and El Paso and the line from Guaymas and Nogales. The packtrains would fit nicely with his current operation. Once operational, Connor and Roberto would base out of Nacozari initially.

Business concluded, the three, along with Luis's girlfriend, a plump, vivacious lady named Emelda, went out to eat and celebrate. She was from Fronteras and was happy, eager even, to introduce Roberto and Connor to eligible local ladies. Roberto seemed intrigued, but Connor demurred until he could return from the Estados Unidos. They ate and drank to excess, with Connor feeling more relaxed and optimistic than he had felt for a while. Persevering despite a throbbing headache, Connor rode out the next day after leaving Roberto with three hundred and fifty dollars to help with bankrolling the startup operation in the next two months.

****

In Tucson, Rosangela was surprised to hear from Connor. Weaver's comments about him had been terse and she doubted that it was just jealousy. Maybe a little. The other Yaqui packers had gone back into the Bacatete Mountains so there was no one to ask. From pieces of conversation, Rosangela gathered that there had been some kind of money dispute, but didn't most issues come down to money, power, or sex? In this case, maybe all three. She liked Connor and was flattered by his strong interest. The bedroom part was more than satisfying also. She wasn't foolish enough to believe that Issac would marry her. But he was generous and also gave her a kickback, which, along with the commission that she and Javier took, was adding up. She didn't question that he was the better choice. Still, Rosangela had to admit, it would be awkward and unfortunate if a betrayal had severe consequences for Connor. She would mitigate it if she could, but in the end, taking care of herself was the priority.

She debated whether to tell Weaver about the note she had received, but decided that it was for the best. He listened intently but didn't explode as she thought he might.

He gave her a warm hug and a warmer kiss, telling her, "Thank you for telling me. I appreciate your loyalty, Mi Amor. Don't tell that bastard anything about us. I think we may still have use for him, as may the Yaqui people."

"What are you thinking, Issac?" she asked.

"I need to think about it more, but for now, I want you to myself," he said, making her blush.

"What happened on the trail?" she asked, hoping for more insight.

"He tried to undermine me and upset our business, and that has to be addressed. He got away from me on the trail before we could balance the ledgers," he replied enigmatically.

He took her in his arms again, and after running his hands possessively over her derrière, slipped his arm around her waist and firmly guided her to the bedroom, effectively ending that part of the conversation.

Later that night, Weaver gave more thought to dealing with Connor. He had proved himself to be more resilient than he expected. This time he would take his time and make sure he went down with a satisfying thump. And not get up. Based on his experience, he would need a good plan A and B. Rosangela hadn't actually shown him the correspondence, implying something short of total trust. She might balk at murder, but wouldn't turn away from something less permanent. Javier might know more, and he would ask him to help. Javier liked his commissions too. Weaver decided he would play his cards close but make sure he had a winning hand. In the meantime, he had another rustling expedition that required his attention. He was already lining up the buyers.

After leaving Tucson the next day, he traveled to Bisbee to meet with Corwyn and Rivera. He kicked himself for not doing this sooner.

Over beer he told them, "I need you two to find out everything you can about this bastard, Connor. Corwyn, you talk to people north of the border—he was a scout and packer so check the military posts in southern Arizona and New Mexico territory. Tell them you are looking for a good pack boss. Rivera, you work the south side of the border. I want to know about him, what his plans are, and where he is going to be. Rosangela said he was in Fronteras. Once we know more, we will work out a plan to put him out of his misery. And mine."

"Do you want us to take care of him if we get a chance?" asked Corwyn.

"No, and don't tell Haggerty anything either. He has a hard-on for this shithead and I don't want him to do anything to alert him. Be careful. I don't want us to underestimate him again," replied Weaver.

He gave each two hundred fifty dollars for expenses and their time, planning on meeting them in forty-five days in the same place.

****

Connor followed the Rio Fronteras north to where it joins the Agua Prieta and followed that across the border. It was early September but still very hot. He went up Whitewater Draw and camped near a small pool of water. He took the opportunity to soak for a while and remove some of the dust. The next morning, he went north of the Mule Mountains, bypassing Bisbee and arrived in Tombstone at early evening. Stabling his horse and mule, he found a boardinghouse and then a bath. He also bought a set of gold earrings and had it wrapped as a gift. The next morning, he rode over to Fairbank, about nine miles from Tombstone. There he stabled his animals and, just taking his saddlebags with some clothes and miscellaneous gear, bought a ticket to Benson, then on to Tucson. Arriving there, he got a room, hoping he wouldn't need it, and headed out to find Rosangela. At the Pulcheria, he asked the bartender if he could get a message to her or Javier. After a coin and getting a nod, Connor tried to curb his impatience and sat down to wait.

Shortly, a boy showed up and asked him to follow him. The house he took him to was better than the last adobe, larger and with a front courtyard. A large mesquite provided shade and there were several large clay pots with flowers near the door. It opened before he knocked and she stared at him for seconds before putting her arms around him and pulling him close then stepping back into the house.

"I had given up on you," she said while unbuttoning his shirt. Connor slipped his shoulder rig off and she opened his shirt.

Rosangela ran her fingers over the fresh scars just below his left nipple.

"Who did this to you?" When he shrugged, she added, "Did you know them?"

Later, he would think the question curious, but in that moment, he replied, "Weaver's men."

She looked at him for a moment. "Why would he do that?"

"He hates competition. He needs to be treated always as the top dog," Connor told her.

Rosangela knew he was right about Issac. She also saw no reason to choose between them. He was here and she wanted to enjoy him—now. Connor loved her firm, substantial body against his. He returned her wet kisses with growing need and followed her into the bedroom and her bed. They were noisy in their lovemaking as they raced to the first conclusion.

Later, in the aftermath, she moved her hand over his stomach and asked, "What will you do about Weaver?"

"Avoid him if I can, kill him if he comes for me."

What Connor didn't say out loud was that he would hurt Weaver's operation if he could and wouldn't hesitate to take out any of his crew if he thought they posed the slightest threat.

Rosangela was actively raising more money from the expatriate Yaqui community and planned to send more arms and ammunition before year's end. She had several repeat sessions with Connor, and she admitted to herself that she was a woman with a good sexual appetite and liked to have a man around. Rosangela also acknowledged that an extended, permanent relationship with one man might not suit her nature. The gift of the earrings had delighted her but didn't change her belief that there was no reason to close the relationship with either man. Her bank account was growing, and at some point she would move closer to the border—Nogales or El Paso. She wasn't going to risk returning to Mexico.

Before leaving Tucson, Connor sent a telegram to Ray Witherspoon in Clifton, asking if there had been any messages. He got a quick reply that there were three—one was from Lieutenant Ortiz, another from Eileen Smithson in Silver City, and finally, a message from Sergeant Murphy at Ft. Bowie. The last two were about packing opportunities, which Connor felt were a surprising coincidence given his fledgling business with Roberto. The Ortiz message he would have to study before replying. Before leaving Tucson, he stopped at Ft. Lowell to ask about packers that might be looking for work now that Apache troubles were so reduced.

The post quartermaster was Captain Gil Wilson. They had both served in the Fourth Cavalry, but really knew each other from the times Connor was pack master on expeditions mounted from here. Ft. Lowell supplied posts throughout southern Arizona and used both organic unit transportation and soldiers as well as contractors to haul supplies. Besides uniforms, equipment, arms, and ammunition, the quartermaster also supplied draft animals, remounts, construction materials, forage, and rations. Wilson was busy but enjoyed talking with him in his office. It was located in the quartermaster and commissary office, which was a forty-by-sixty-foot adobe building. It was dwarfed by the adjacent quartermaster depot, which had almost ninety-five hundred square feet of floor and cellar space. The post was laid out with the officer quarters east–west along the southern side of the parade ground. The quartermaster depot and offices were along the west side, and the hospital on the east side. Three barracks were on the north side, going east to west with one additional barracks north of the hospital, facing west.

Captain Wilson knew Sergeant Witherspoon from his long service in the Fourth Cav. After the usual "whatever happened to and do you remember" small talk, Wilson told him he thought there would be opportunities for contract hauling, primarily wagon, but some mule packing also. Connor told him to use Ray as his contact point and then asked about packers, looking for work.

"It's funny you should ask. About two weeks ago, I had a fellow asking about packers and you in particular. He seemed interested in your background, but of course, at the time, I didn't know your whereabouts."

When asked to describe him, Wilson said, "About your height, heavier, maybe blocky is how I would describe him. Clean looking, but needed a shave. He wore a black holster on the right side, Remington single action 45. I noticed he had an open crown hat, black. He was well spoken but a little evasive about his business. He seemed capable, no tenderfoot."

Connor thanked him and asked if the laundresses still did some needle or awl work. He also asked if he had any surplus ammo belts for the standard .45-70 ammunition used in the Army-issue Springfield rifles.

"Yes, on both counts," the captain told him. "Go see the laundresses, and I will have the cartridge belt when you come back."

There were eight adobe buildings on the northeast side of the post where the laundresses lived and worked. He inquired politely about the service he needed and told them that the quartermaster had sent him over. An older woman, Mrs. Isobel, said she could do the work for fifty cents. He had her make an adjustable buckskin cover for the butt of his rifle with seven cartridge loops and a tie-down flap from a piece of buckskin he had brought. Secondly, Connor had her sew the sheath of the hide-out knife parallel and onto his belt so it would rest horizontally, below the small of his back. The blade was only six inches and, with handle, the total length was just over ten inches. She set it for a right-hand pull. Under the canvas waistcoat he usually wore, it would be invisible. Thanking her, he gave her a Morgan dollar, which she appreciated with a smile. He paid for and picked up the cartridge belt from Captain Wilson, said his goodbyes, and headed for the train station.

He planned to retrieve his animals then train to the stop at Bowie. He would ride the ten miles to the fort with the same name and talk to Sergeant Murphy about his telegram. Then take the train from Bowie to Silver City. It had been almost three years since he had seen Eileen. She had remarried, to a city council member and mine owner, John Potter. Connor had enjoyed her company for a while—she was an energetic and fun lover. He liked her children, too, and still corresponded with them sporadically. They had remained friends and he had continued to use her as a contact for work out of Ft. Bayard. He understood and respected her decision to remarry. He really didn't have much to offer at the time and she was ready for more stability and financial certainty. She had been honest from the beginning and Potter was personally and financially stable. Her new husband had been civil to him, too, which he should have, considering he got the better part of the deal. He looked forward to seeing her. From there, Connor would go back to Clifton, traveling on the narrow gauge.

He got his animals off the stock car in Bowie and set out on the well-used trail to the fort. It was strategically positioned near a spring and a pass through the Chiricahua Mountains. Connor expected that like a lot of the forts, it would be closing over the next few years, now that the Indian threat was largely, gone. As he rode, he thought about Luis's mother and her fortune-telling. His trouble with Weaver seemed to confirm her comments that he was not meant to follow other men's direction. Amelia's words on love and threats seemed oddly intertwined. Loyal and open, good and bad, intimate solution to threats, the words turned in his mind. Connor was not a big believer in prophecy but it was causing him to reflect, which he thought was okay. Maybe it was his recent time with Rosangela that had him thinking, along with seeing Eileen again soon, albeit platonically. Then there was Mariela and her brother. He liked her and hoped his schemes for Weaver didn't result in danger for those two. He would need to be very careful.

Rosangela was a puzzle. Their dynamics were great, but he had questions in his mind. She was going to ship more weapons and munitions to the Yaqui but hadn't

CHAPTER 12

raised the idea of him being part of that effort. If she wasn't going to use him, then that left Weaver. He knew from experience that business, her cause, and loving were closely mixed. He had made the two runs into Mexico for the money certainly, but also because he wanted her. He still did. Connor had to admit to himself that he was actually relieved she didn't push for another trip. He was convinced that gunrunning was increasing in risk, one that he didn't need to take. He had empathy for the Yaqui people and their struggle, but it wasn't his fight. He and Roberto were developing other options and the last thing he wanted was to have a run-in with the Rurales. He had found Major Kosterlitzky to be very smart, well informed, and not someone you wanted to cross. Regarding Rosangela, if it really came down to Connor or Weaver, wouldn't this play out like it had with Eileen when faced with a choice?

CHAPTER 13

ARIZONA & SONORA, FALL 1888

Like most Army forts in the Southwest, Ft. Bowie was organized around the parade ground. Connor rode across it to stop first at the headquarters to check in and see if there was anyone he still knew there. Coming out, he turned left to the adjutant's office, where he expected to find Sergeant Murphy. The sense of urgency and purpose evident during the Apache conflict had clearly changed and Connor wondered how long these posts would remain active. They had been a big piece of his life, but he felt a strong determination to turn the page and get Roberto's and his transport business profitably launched. With a healthy bank account, he could then think about ranching on the Blue River. He mentally winced at the knowledge that Rosangela would never be interested in that. With a mental shrug, he put it out of his mind.

Sergeant Murphy didn't have a lot of time to talk—he was preparing for a patrol around the northeast corner of the Chiricahuas and down the upper part of the San Bernardino Valley. There were a number of small mining claims now being worked and small hamlets and towns that supported them. Connor decided to ride with the patrol for the first day, dropping off around Galeyville and scouting for any business opportunities or information. It was only ninety to one hundred miles from Fronteras, fifty to the border. That made the area a hotbed for smuggling and rustling.

They camped that night at about five thousand feet in elevation, north of Galeyville. Murphy told him about the conversation he'd had with the potential customer that was similar to the dialogue with Captain Wilson. His description of the man seemed to tally with what he had heard before. Connor was starting to conclude that the mysterious person was not looking for just anyone, but specifically, him. He would confirm that at Ft. Bayard. He was reliable and good but there were a lot of mule skinners looking for work. What differentiated Connor was the proven experience on more dangerous trails or, recently, with moving contraband. That last category was only known to Rosangela, Javier, and Weaver, at least he hoped. He grunted at that disturbing thought. He needed to be especially alert if he was going to avoid being fatally surprised. Connor thanked Sergeant Murphy, wished him luck on the patrol, and secretly gave thanks that it was no longer his task. He decided to skip the mines and small towns on the east side of the mountains and return to Bowie, then catch the train to Deming, New Mexico, and on to Silver City. Connor felt a sense of danger building that needed resolution quickly.

Silver City was prospering and bigger than the last time he had been here. Finding a room and a bath was no problem and Connor sent a message over to Eileen's house asking when was a good time to stop by. That afternoon, he walked up to the house and knocked. The house was a two-story frame and a considerable step up from when they had first met. She greeted him warmly and invited him in. As with the first time, he asked for water and they sat in the parlor to exchange news.

Eileen looked at him critically and then smiled. "You look good, more rugged than ever!"

"I had to stay busy after you broke my heart," he told her with a smile of his own.

He skipped over the tales of scouting and packing and told her about his most recent plans for launching a transport business. She listened thoughtfully as he talked, and he valued her comments. Eileen had gained weight but it only added to her appeal. The laugh lines on her face were no distraction—she was still a handsome woman. She had picked up some gray but then so had he. He was interested in her children and she told him that her daughter was working in town and her son had just enlisted.

"Likely inspired by your stories," she pouted, then laughed.

She told him about the message from Ft. Bayard and told him the contact was Lt. Buckley. He thanked her, promised to return for dinner. He had some time so Connor went over to Ft. Bayard and talked with Lt. Will Buckley. The lieutenant was several years out of the academy and, like himself, had been active in the final

Geronimo campaign. As a verse of the old drinking song popular with West Point grads goes, "In the Army there's sobriety, promotion's very slow . . ." It was this latter part that was weighing on Buckley and, Connor suspected, a lot of officers. He was not surprised to hear the description of the man, calling himself Scott Thomas, matched with the other inquiries at Forts Lowell and Bowie. What was different this time was that Thomas had left a contact point, a Mr. Walter P. Nelson of Bisbee, 83 Shearer Ave. according to Lt. Buckley. Nelson was looking for an experienced hand to chaperone a high-value shipment into Mexico and had heard that Connor was highly reliable.

Connor would contact Mr. Nelson after he had looked through the other correspondence that Sergeant Witherspoon was holding for him. It could be legitimate, but it felt suspicious given the indirect approach and trouble taken to research him prior to the attempted contact. Well, forewarned, forearmed and all that ancient wisdom. The question was, could he turn this to his advantage in some way? Meeting with Nelson could be a trap, but Connor was willing to bet it was not that simple. He decided to test how badly they wanted him, sending a telegraph message to Mr. Nelson saying he was unavailable and identifying another mule skinner for the job. He asked for replies to be sent care of Ray.

Dinner with Eileen and John Potter was good—she had prepared roast beef with plenty of vegetables. John had also gained weight, looking a little paunchy, but then, he was not in the hands-on side of the mining business.

"Let me check with some of my business acquaintances and see what their transport needs are. I can act as a reference," John added generously.

"I am excited to get this business going, John, thank you," Connor told him.

Connor thought John was a bit stuffy but nevertheless appreciated any help at this stage. Eileen's daughter, Katy, stopped by after dinner, enjoying Connor's compliments and a few shared memories. She had a boyfriend and Connor told her he was jealous as they all laughed. They chatted and played a few hands of whist before calling it a night. John offered a firm handshake while Katy and Eileen provided softer hugs. Connor thought it was a short but needed change to his recent past months on the trail. He slept well at the boardinghouse and in the morning caught the train to Deming, over to Lordsburg, and then up to Clifton on the narrow-gauge, Arizona and New Mexico Railroad.

After retrieving his animals, Connor walked up to Ray's gunsmith store and looked at a couple of shotguns while Ray tried to close a sale with a couple of miners. He was interested in the newer hammerless models, but they were more expensive and harder to find. The hammers cocked when you opened or closed the breech, depending on the manufacturer. He was looking for a twelve-gauge, and Ray had a couple of models. Connor was reluctantly coming to the conclusion that, at least for the short term, he could best afford an "eared model," with exposed hammers. There was an old Greener side-by-side twelve-gauge that would do, and he set that aside along with two boxes of bird and a box of buckshot.

Ray concluded his business and shook his hand. "I'm glad you made it back in one piece—are you ready to do some honest work for a change?" Connor gave him a short, edited version of the last months, collected his messages, and made plans to meet for dinner that night. He stabled his animals and repaired to his room at the boardinghouse. In particular, he wanted to think through his responses to Lt. Ortiz's message and ponder his reply to those interested in his transportation business or services. He estimated he had a few weeks to rest and organize before heading south again. He still needed to make his mind up about Weaver and whether to pursue a vendetta with that bastard or simply congratulate himself on surviving a close shave.

Ray had collected about a dozen messages and Connor started with reading the one from Ortiz. He had collected twenty-five pistols in working order, which he proposed to sell for six dollars each. He also had a dozen rifles that he would part with for twice that, roughly three hundred dollars in all. Miscellaneous rifle scabbards and holsters he would throw in gratis. It was the other messages, buried in the content, that made Connor focus hard. Ortiz appreciated the intelligence on Weaver and definitely wanted more. Besides gunrunning, he was a prolific and known cattle and horse thief that the Rurales had come close to catching only once. Kosterlitzky himself had almost caught him and was still angry about Weaver's successful escape from the chase. The major wanted to know more about a rumored weapons run in the late fall / early winter time frame.

The fact that Connor was trying to put Weaver in a pickle with the Rurales made him wonder if Weaver, or someone else, was trying to do the same with him. The mystery man that had been inquiring about him at the Army posts came to mind. He resolved to learn more about Mr. Walter P. Nelson of Bisbee. To that end, he sent a message to the Reverend J. G. Pritchard, reminding him of their meeting and asking for his help. The reverend was well connected and Connor asked him if he could facilitate a few introductions with people at Phelps-Dodge or the mining community in general who might need his transport services, particularly in Sonora. He also inquired if he knew Mr. Walter Nelson, having had an inquiry from the gentleman. He also sent a telegram to Rosangela, letting her know that he might be back in Bisbee in the next two weeks. He wanted to visit his cabin on the Blue and enjoy the peace coupled with some hunting. Connor concluded that it would have to wait until after a visit to Bisbee.

Walking between the telegraph office and the boardinghouse, his attention was diverted by a tug on his sleeve. He saw it was a young Chinaman, who handed him a note. It was a message from Miss Li, who indicated that they had met when he had delivered Chang's remains and possessions after that cave-in, almost a year ago. His mind went back to the tall, middle-aged Chinese woman who had thanked him on that depressing day. The message asked if he would join her for lunch at a small restaurant, along Chase Creek. Being close to there and a little curious, Connor agreed. He followed the man to the small clapboard place and entered. There were a few men inside, predominately Chinese, and he was ushered through and into a back room, where Miss Li was already seated. She stood, smiled slightly, and with her hand gestured for him to be seated opposite her. She spoke to his guide in their language and within a minute they were joined by an older lady who poured tea for both and then left.

In surprisingly good English, she said, "Thank you for joining me. We will have food brought shortly. I wanted to thank you again for your kindness with Mr. Chang. We were able to send his ashes back to China along with money for his family. Please, try your tea. I hope it is to your liking."

While she talked, the older lady returned with an embroidered mat and a fork for Connor and chopsticks for Miss Li. She also topped off both teacups. Next, she brought in a succession of dishes and soups, starting with a cold chicken dish where the meat was chopped with the bone still in place. As they ate, Connor studied Miss Li and responded to her questions about what he was doing. She seemed quite interested in his transportation service endeavor and allowed that though she didn't have large requirements, she had correspondence with a number of people that he might be able to help with. She asked what he might charge to deliver that correspondence.

"As long as it isn't too bulky and you are not concerned with slow delivery, I will be happy to help; payment is not necessary," he told her.

Miss Li told him that she represented one of the Chinese societies who helped supply labor to the mines and railroads both north and south of the border. As such, they had insight into some opportunities for transport needs and would share that as it became available. Connor told her about his planned meeting with Nelson over in Bisbee.

She inquired more closely about that, telling him, "I have a contact that will look into this Mr. Nelson and share it with you. Are you interested in information about Ms. Rosangela Lazaro and her uncle, Javier?"

Connor was both surprised and taken aback that she knew that much about him, and it must have shown on his face.

Miss Li smiled faintly and told him, "Don't be alarmed. I inquired about you after we last met because I was grateful and interested in knowing more about you. I hope that I can repay your kindness at some point. Please accept my apologies for prying. I don't want to offend you. Believe me that I am and will be very discreet and only wish you well."

Connor knew about the Six Companies and the less savory Tongs that provided legal, employment, and money services to the Chinese community. They would loan money and transfer money, effectively acting like a bank. Borders didn't pose a restriction for them, nor did regulations. Connor thought that this might prove useful in the future. They also protected Chinese against the substantial prejudice against them that existed in America. The Exclusion Act of 1882 had largely codified those racist feelings into something worse. That prejudice also extended into Mexico and among some Mexicans who saw them as unwarranted competition. Connor, like many Irish, was no stranger to being on the receiving end of the irrational bias against his countrymen, and he felt an empathy for the Chinese. He had been exposed to them extensively while working on the railroad crew with his brother. He also knew that the Tongs had a seedy reputation for providing drugs, prostitution, and gambling services, backed by the use of occasional violence.

He didn't understand Miss Li's role in the Tong organization and suspected that knowing even less was for the best.

Still, he asked her, "Which Tong do you represent, Miss Li?"

Now it was her turn to be a little surprised by his question and underlying knowledge, but she controlled her expression and answered, "Kwong Duck," naming one of the societies.

She had entered the U.S. through Angel Island in San Francisco. Li was from Guangdong Province and her exposure to missionaries had enabled her to learn passable spoken and written English before being kidnapped and trafficked to California. If not for those skills and keen intelligence, she would have ended life as a prostitute. She had been sent to Los Angeles and the branch there, before traveling to Tombstone. There she worked for Sing Choy in what the Anglos referred to as Hoptown, along with about four hundred other Chinese. Sing Choy was also known as China Mary and controlled the labor brokerage business for the Chinese as well as less legal operations.

Impressed, Sing Choy had sent her to do the same in Clifton and the adjacent mining towns. Of this history, she shared only the labor brokerage leadership with him.

Connor was sure there was more, and equally sure he didn't want to know it.

"Does your offer still stand?" she asked quietly, locking eyes with him.

He nodded. "Yes, ma'am."

She handed him a letter with the recipient's name in English above the Chinese.

"You will find him at the address on the envelope. Could I impose on you to deliver a small gift to the same person?"

"May I know what it is, Miss Li?" he asked. She opened the small box as she handed it across the table to him."

"Two tea bricks," she told him, knowing he might be reticent to carry other, less beneficial items. Connor's face remained impassive, but Miss Li felt she had guessed right.

He confirmed the contents, seeing the almost black, pressed blocks.

"I am happy to help," he said as he met her eyes.

"My contact will have news for you when you see him in Bisbee," she said as she extended her hand to him.

Her hand felt cool as he lightly brushed his lips against it.

"I want our friendship to be mutually beneficial, Mr. Connor."

He paused at the door and turned back to her. "You are an impressive lady, Miss Li. Thank you for lunch and your help. We can look forward to helping each other."

Her eyes were a bit warmer as she nodded goodbye.

Connor stayed another few days in Clifton before leaving to reach Bisbee. During that time, he received and sent several more telegrams. One was from Walter P. Nelson urging him to reconsider his request to meet and talk about transporting "a high value" consignment, promising a good commission. He also heard from Reverend Prichard saying that he could help with meetings when he returned to Bisbee. He gave both of them dates that he would be in town and then caught the train to Lordsburg, then over to Fairbank. From there he followed the San Pedro River south, then over to the Mule Mountains and Bisbee, arriving three days before expected. Connor found a room and went out to drop off Miss Li's letter and gift. The recipient, Ah Lim, was expecting him and led him into the ramshackle adobe that he inhabited. Lim was about his size, though younger, and looked to be a man to whom hard physical labor was no stranger. He also sported a collection of scars on his arms and one, healed, thin cut line on his left cheek.

What he had to say about Nelson was not totally unexpected. There was no Walter Nelson. The resident at the address was William Palmer, more recently from Tombstone, whose profession was gentleman gambler. Lim provided a good description of Nelson, aka Palmer. Asked how he knew this, Lim told him that "Nelson" had a maid in twice a week, who had been induced to let another associate carefully go through his possessions and papers. Among those possessions were found branch insignia for the calvary along with the chevrons of a sergeant. Further, he had only been in the house for the past thirty days. Connor found himself wondering about Nelson's proposition and looking forward to the conversation.

The story on Rosangela set his mind racing. Lim told him that she seemed to be busy with meetings and raising money for the Yaqui cause. Javier, a little less engaged in raising funds, was more engaged in receiving and sending messages. Rosangela seemed to also spend time in the company of a man whose description seemed remarkably like that of Issac Weaver. Weaver had not been seen in town for several weeks. Connor had sensed that there was more than a business relationship with Weaver. He also was not expecting an exclusive relationship. The question was whether she was actively involved with actions that would put him at risk, or worse. He felt her affection for him was real at an emotional level but, intellectually, he needed to consider the possibilities and protect himself. He thanked Lim and returned to his room.

CHAPTER 14

The next day he went over to see Rosangela, but first he found a place where he could observe her house for a while, somehow feeling a need for caution. He was rewarded, seeing Javier come out around midmorning, and decided to follow him discreetly for a while. He broke off shadowing him when it became evident that he was heading to the library, up the hill. He returned to his position and, after half an hour, went up and knocked on the door. She answered and looked surprised to see him but, putting her arms around his neck, pulled him into the house, locking the door. The surprised look was replaced by one of pleasure and she kissed him repeatedly while making pleased growling sounds that intensified as she pulled his clothes off and piled them on the floor. Connor found himself caught up in the frenzy and pushed any doubts aside as he lifted her up and awkwardly carried her into the bedroom. She tried to climb on top but Connor was not ready to cede control. Breaking a kiss, he buried his face in that deep cleavage. God but she had an appetite and his was matching, both rapidly approaching the finish line and exploding across. She might be treacherous, but in that moment, it seemed irrelevant. Both panting, they looked at each other, content for the time being.

"You are crazy," she said and he grinned.

"Do we have a future?" he asked. "Because I need this and you, Mi Amor!"

She snuggled up against him without comment and began to explore with her hands. This time he was happy to let her have her way. Later, they got up and went to a restaurant for lunch. He told her that beside wanting to see her, he was going to meet some potential clients.

When he mentioned Nelson, she said, "I know him. I have been talking to him about another trip to supply the Yaquis."

"Did you ask him to contact me?" he asked.

"No, but perhaps Javier did," she responded. "I will ask him."

"What about Weaver?" Connor asked.

She told him that she didn't trust him and felt they needed to have another gunrunner available. Connor didn't pursue it, mentally vowing to think about that a lot more. When his judgment was less clouded. Walking her back to the house, she seemed disappointed that he couldn't stay but needed to see a potential client. He was disappointed himself but wanted to talk with Nelson and see what he had to say. They agreed to meet later that night for dinner.

Nelson was living at a well-constructed house, and as before, he found a place where he could observe for a while before approaching. After forty-five minutes, he approached, knocked, and waited. Nelson was clean-shaven but had a shadow of hair growth on his face. He was taller than Connor but not by much and his build was not as robust. Nelson had a slight southern drawl; he was sober and alert asking what Connor wanted. Connor introduced himself and noted that the man wasn't surprised to see him. He was wearing a shoulder holster and backed away from the door without turning when he invited Connor in.

Nelson seated him at a large dining table. "Do you want a drink? I have some rye or tequila."

"Water is fine," he told him, and after small talk, Nelson poured a shot of rye and got down to the proposal.

"Sorry that I am a day or so early, Walter—can I call you Walter?" Connor asked.

"I heard you were in town so I was half expecting you," Nelson replied, which Connor decided not to pursue.

Nelson then proceeded to lay out the proposition.

"I have a load of rifles and ammunition that I want to get to the Yaquis in the next few months. I know that you are reliable and can be trusted to get the job done right. I have a date and time for the delivery, plus or minus five days, and the location, of course. For delivery I will pay you five hundred dollars, half up front."

Connor thought about that for a moment before asking, "Why me?"

Nelson responded with a repeat of the generalities about high recommendations.

"Who did you talk to, specifically? I am curious since this is a dangerous proposition," Connor responded.

When pressed, Nelson added that he had talked to Javier and Roseangela.

"Anyone else?" Connor asked.

"No," was the answer.

"A thousand dollars," Connor told him.

"There is not that much profit in it," Nelson stated emphatically.

"How many rifles and how many rounds?" Connor asked.

"Two hundred rifles and forty thousand rounds," Nelson told him.

"One thousand dollars, half up front," Connor replied. "I will need fifteen mules, six packers, and three guards. Two hundred dollars per packer and three hundred per guard. Food and water for the trip, two hundred. Twenty-three hundred dollars plus my advance. I will need that up front because I will pay them in Mexico after delivery. You supply the mules."

Connor could see that Nelson was nervous by the way he tended to his drink, precisely rotating the glass after each sip. He was a gambler, though, and knew how to maintain his composure.

"I will have to think about it," Nelson replied after some hemming around.

"What's to think about? You are not putting up the money," Connor replied confidently.

Still, Nelson dug his heels in. "Tomorrow," he said.

"We can meet at five o'clock tomorrow at Sieber's. After that I will be moving on," Connor let him know.

They shook hands and Connor left. Connor waited at his observation point and, twenty minutes later, Nelson bustled out, through Brewery Gulch and on to the housing to the east. Connor followed at a distance and recognized his destination, Rivera's home, where they had coordinated the last run. After what seemed like a long time, the door opened and Nelson came through, followed by Rivera and Corwyn. They shook hands and Nelson left. Connor noted that Corwyn had a black holster and a black open crown hat.

Later that evening, Connor asked Rosangela if they were paying Nelson up front or whether he had some money at risk for the success of the run. She was evasive, saying he needed to ask Javier for the financials. Connor was certain that this was a setup. The only question was whether she or Javier were part of it. He expected that the Yaqui need was more for ammunition than it was for rifles. While he was willing to help them, he was not going to ride into a rendezvous with the Rurales with a load of contraband. He was even more concerned when he heard they had lined up Anastasio and Mariela to be part of the crew on the run. He expected that Weaver planned to use his crew as a disposable decoy while he made a run in a different location. Connor was going to change the game and outcome while avoiding disaster.

The next morning, he sent out a telegram to Belem and the contact point that Anastasio had given him. He told him not to set out for the north until he heard from him specifically, since the north was very lawless and dangerous. The trouble with sending telegrams was you were never sure who was going to read it and whether the content would remain confidential. Consequently, messages had to be circumspect. He asked for a confirmation that he had received his message and would comply along with some personal words from Mariela. That would serve as a bit of further security.

Connor spent the next few hours at the Clifton Library, chatting with Reverend Prichard. He had been as good as his word and lined up a meeting the following day with a Frederick Prior, who was responsible for transport coordination at Phelps-Dodge, and Mr. Tom Westman, who was funding and supporting prospectors and geologists on expeditions into Sonora. Connor was convincing about both his transport credentials and lack of interest in mining investment and thus confidentiality, sharing his story of having been trapped in the mine in Clifton. He left his contact points with the two, feeling confident that they would eventually provide some business.

He had dinner with Javier and Rosangela. Javier was vague on the financial arrangements with Nelson and how the man was selected to coordinate the smuggling. He was also vague about the man's contribution to the effort. He repeated his counter proposal to the two, and they seemed confident that they could help with mules, packers, and guards. As before, he told them he wanted to meet the crew before departure and make sure that all was in readiness and everyone understood their role and contingencies. Javier either didn't know or wouldn't share with Connor the point where the exchange would be made with the Yaquis. Javier had detected Connor's concerns but knew that, without working through Nelson, they would lose Weaver as a conduit. Weaver was competent without doubt and neither he nor Rosangela wanted to lose their lucrative commissions through him. Rosangela was confident she could convince Connor and looked forward to doing so that night.

Weaver had been informed about Connor's demands, debating whether it would be easier to simply track and kill him. Bill Palmer, aka Nelson, had served with him during the war and, years later, had participated with him in several rustling ventures. The amount of money the man was asking for was a lot, the greedy bastard. He liked letting the Rurales do the dirty work while he slipped through with the real shipment. He just wished he could be there for the ley de fuego. The lost lives would confirm for the Yaquis that a real attempt had been made, and they were philosophical enough to realize the dangerous business would have some losses. Javier understood what was going to happen. Rosangela didn't know about the planned failure and would not be happy when the event unfolded. She, too, would ultimately be philosophical when the dust settled. If, for some reason, this plan failed, Weaver had a plan B and C. One way or another, Connor was going to die.

The next day, Connor prepared to leave Bisbee and return to Fronteras for a meeting with Roberto and his cousin. He would depart after his meeting with Nelson. The advance payment would be a good sign from Connor's perspective. Without it, he worried that Weaver would try to come for him sooner, not waiting for some trickery planned on the trail. That argued for an abrupt departure. He planned to spend the remaining time in 1888 developing the business with Roberto and then return in early '89 to coordinate the smuggling run in a way that would allow survival for him and his crew. Connor also planned to upset Weaver's plan.

The meeting with Nelson went about as he expected. He agreed to pay two hundred and fifty dollars immediately as a retainer, another two fifty and the crew's pay on departure, the rest of Connor's money on return. There was some quibbling over any monies from the sale of the mules, and that was it. Connor pocketed the retainer, said a brief goodbye to Javier and Rosangela. He rode out with two mules toward the Slaughter Ranch in the east, then turned south at Agua Prieta along the stream with the same name. In two days, he was in Fronteras, Mexico.

Luis Alcazar was not yet back from a trip south and Roberto was even farther away, in Nacozari. Connor stopped by Emelda's house, Luis's girlfriend, to check in and get any messages. One message from Roberto asked him to join him as soon as was convenient. He was getting ready for his first trip into the Sierra Madre to visit a sequence of mines or workings. There was a contract offered from Tom Westfield to transport a load of supplies to Nacozari, then store and transport the load into the Sierra for the Phelps-Dodge geologists as requested. Luis would handle the shipment from Bisbee to Nacozari via wagon. Roberto and Connor would take it into the Sierra by mule train. It seemed they were off to a promising start.

He left a message for Luis on the contract requirements and sent a telegram to Bisbee, accepting the terms.

The following day he set off to join Roberto, moving at a steady pace, with his two mules and a third that Roberto had stabled with his brother. It took two days to get there, and at about four thousand feet elevation, at this time of year, it was cool and crisp out. There had been mining in this area since the 1600s and the town was well established and included some Colonial-style architecture. He found Roberto in one of those houses, facing north–south with stables across a wide courtyard and storage areas that likely were once workshops and accommodations. They shared a warm abrazo and Roberto said, "We have launched our ship, compadre!" Three packers were staying in two of the adobes along the wall. A fourth would join them tomorrow and they would set out. Roberto and Connor shared their news as well as Bacanora and then turned in.

The next day they started off, heading east into the Sierra. Roberto had lined up four stops, bringing food and sundries along with explosives, lamps, wedges, and other assorted mining miscellanea. Payment would be made in coin or precious metal. They would also haul out and bank or secure refined ore or samples. At this stage, they were expecting to net the equivalent of one hundred to one hundred and fifty dollars a trip. All four packers were armed with rifles, some with pistols. They had fourteen mules to manage. Roberto and Connor would lead the train and provide security. The mules alone would tempt bandits and renegades. Roberto would lead out, staying about fifty or a hundred yards in front of the mule train. Connor would rove left and right and, if needed, drop back to protect the rear. Both hoped to grow the size of the train, adding guards and packers as the business developed. At this point, this was what they could afford and were required to take more risk.

The first day was uneventful and on the second they reached the first of the mines. They exchanged supplies, took payment, and established the next delivery and any special requests. The second and third mines were repeats of the first. By now they were deep into the mountains and possibilities of ambush were high, given the broken, mountainous, and partly forested nature of the terrain. The last stop was near a rushing stream that Connor suspected fed into the Bavispe, farther to the east on its long loop to the south and the Yaqui River. The three prospectors paid with gold dust stored in quills and also had extra quills that they wanted to send back to Nacozari to safeguard. The gold was carefully weighed on a small scale that they had brought with them. The actual location of where the men were panning for gold was not revealed and might not even be on this rushing stream.

The trip back was expected to take three or four days if the weather held, cold and clear. Carlos Rivera also hoped the weather would hold. While Corwyn had worked north of the border to find out about Connor, Rivera had worked in Sonora. He had learned about the business that Connor and Roberto were starting and was confident there would be opportunities to kill both in the wild and unmapped areas of the Sierra Madre Occidental.

He had recruited five bandits through his contacts and brought two proven associates from Weaver's crew down from the Estados Unidos. All were well armed, experienced in breaking the law, and avaricious men. Weaver had decided to give him the chance to eliminate Connor here first, and if that failed, use the weapons smuggling as his plan B. Javier let him know when Connor left Bisbee and where he was headed as Rivera moved with his two men to Sonora to gather the others. He had two men follow the mule train while the rest held back. Weaver had cautioned him not to underestimate Connor, and he didn't intend to. He had seen that Connor was riding rear security and was looking for a place where he could be cut off, isolated, and killed.

The mule train was starting the second day of the journey back. The loads were light and they were making good time. Roberto had crested a ridgeline and they were moving downward toward a dry canyon, maybe four hundred feet below on the right side. The rumble of the boulders was the first indication of trouble. When Connor looked up, he saw a half dozen large boulders rolling down from at least a hundred feet above the trail. They were gaining momentum and precipitating a minor landslide as they wiped out the trail ahead, taking the rearmost mules over the side, braying frantically as they plunged into the canyon. As the noise from the landslide faded, the sound of firing could be heard. Connor wheeled his horse back up the trail, realizing that he was cut off from the rest of the men and the plunging fire from the ambush was finding the range.

He didn't know about this time but knew that the Apaches would frequently let the lead riders pass through the planned kill zone before firing and usually had a man stationed to pick off anyone trying to retreat out of the ambush. He wouldn't go back, and down was out of the question—so that left up. It was steep but not vertical. Not knowing if he would be back for his horse, he looped his canteen over one shoulder and slung his rifle over the other, dismounted, and started along, using his hands and feet to scramble upward. Zigzagging from cover to cover, he started working his way up. His efforts were rewarded with another set of boulders gaining speed as they slammed down the slope toward him. He hugged up against a small outcrop of rocks and hoped they would shield him. Several boulders coming down veered to the right but a couple hit the rocks he was sheltering behind, causing them to shift but not roll. One hit and bounded over, barely missing him as it plunged downward.

Roberto had his rifle out and was trying to return fire. He had turned to see the landslide take out the trail behind three of the packers. The shooters had knocked one of his packers off his horse when he tried to move past Roberto and up the trail. The other three had tried to move up the trail toward him, only to have another wounded. Roberto shouted to them to stay put, dismount, and look for something to fire at. He moved upslope and then moved to his right, above the trail, trying to find the ambushers who had shot his man. He heard, then saw, another bunch of rocks roll down the mountain to his far left.

Rivera had posted two men on either side of the ambush site and kept three with him. He wasn't sure if those last boulders had crushed or injured Connor, but he didn't see any movement as the dust cleared. The packers below him on the trail had started to fire, but their fire was totally ineffective. He decided to sit tight and let his victims come to him for the moment. He shifted to his left with one of his men, continuing to watch for movement in the area he had last seen Connor.

Roberto couldn't see either the attackers above him or up the trail. He decided to move higher and farther right. His foot slipped, sending some small rocks cascading down the slope. He dove toward a stunted mesquite just as several bullets spattered chips near him. Roberto couldn't see them but he saw the smoke from their guns, which gave him some orientation. Sitting with his back to the slope, he started to fire his .45-70 systematically in the area of the smoke. He emptied the magazine as he saw one man scrambling for new cover near his last shot. Connor had given him a sixty-round bandoleer that he had picked up at Ft. Bowie and he loaded a half dozen before acquiring and firing at his attacker. He missed but he had him on the move and his next shot hit him somewhere because he heard a cry before he had to scramble for different cover when the man's partner opened up again.

Connor could hear the sound of Roberto's rifle but tried to wait out his adversaries, above and maybe also to his left. He decided to move right so that at least he would not put himself between two groups of shooters. The packers were keeping up a desultory fire, but he doubted it was of any value. His movement drew fire but he was able to get to the next piece of cover. He paused a minute, kicked some rocks loose as rifle shots bounced off the slope behind him, then scrambled up about six yards and then moved right another ten.

Rivera sent the man with him to go bring the other two men behind the ambush up so that they could engage and bring this to a conclusion. So far, they had no losses and had the advantage of firepower and position. Connor was trying to work up the mountain but with five shooters, he would get up to move one too many times and they would have him.

Connor was sweating heavily even though it was cold. The range was too far, at almost one hundred and fifty yards, to rush the shooters. Better to shift down again and try to link with Roberto, who was about two hundred or so yards to his left. They were outnumbered and time was not on their side. It took him ten minutes to work the two hundred yards over to where he thought Roberto was. He heard Roberto firing again, now a lot closer, and he shouted to him.

"Can you move, or are you pinned down, compadre?"

"They got me pinned. I think there are two on this side and one is wounded," he heard Roberto shout.

"Cover me. I am going to rush toward them," Connor replied.

With that, he dropped his canteen and moved down and to his right as fast as he could. As he came around some man-sized outcroppings, he saw the smoke from the men firing on Roberto. He kept moving forward as fast as he could, trying to close the distance. He was about fifty yards from one of the shooters when he was spotted and the man tried to shift his fire to engage. Connor knelt and systematically fired round after round and Roberto zeroed in on the same man. It was too much for him and when he tried to find better cover, Roberto caught him in the side and Connor hit him in the shoulder, knocking him over and out of the fight. The second man, who had been wounded earlier, tried to retreat, too, but Connor caught him in the chest with the last round in the magazine. Reloading as he moved uphill, he saw more gun smoke to his left and higher, near the crest. Roberto had turned to his left now and was providing some steady, aimed fire with the longer-range rifle of his.

He was now only forty yards from the crest and it looked like two were providing covering fire while what looked like four others would fire and move. They were trying to close on him and their combined fire was effective in suppressing his ability to fire or move. He continued to crawl upward but the progress was slow. Reaching some good cover, he was now close to the crest and above at least one of the attackers. Focusing on him, Connor waited until he was within seventy yards and then he started to fire, adjusting his rounds systematically right up into him, catching his leg on the fifth shot.

Rivera could see that the dynamics were changed. The element of surprise was gone and the two on the slope were not panicked. Two of his men were out of the fight, maybe dead, and a third was wounded. He wanted to kill Connor, but it was settling into a stalemate as long as the ammo held out. It was time for a fighting withdrawal, and they started to pull back to the ridgeline and then over. Connor could see that they were trying to break it off, and as the last two pulled over the skyline, he sprinted as best he could to the top and sprawled down to see if he could inflict more pain on the bastards. He was too far away to do any damage and watched frustrated as they reached their horses in a partially concealed draw and started to work their way down the slope. He ran down, trying to avoid falling and then, standing, emptied his magazine at them. One round hit a horse, which staggered and threw the rider. The rider struggled to his feet and limped after the rest, one of whom came back for him. He mounted behind his benefactor, and riding double, continued out of sight.

Reloading, Connor walked down to the wounded horse and finished him, then started going through the saddlebags. There was nothing of value or any indication of where these men were from. The bottom of the saddlebag had the letters *JC* crudely burned into the leather but otherwise nothing distinguishable or personalized. On a whim, he decided to take the saddlebag with him. He returned to the other side of the ridge and retrieved his gear, taking a deep drink from his canteen. He stayed upslope of the ruined trail, retrieved his horse, and carefully walked the skittish animal up and around the rubble that had erased the track. Rejoining the trail, Connor walked to the remaining mules and the packers. They looked shaken but relieved to have survived and he shook hands with them and took a look at the wounded man. The bullet had passed through his leg, missing bone, but leaving him only able to travel over the saddle, his wound bandaged.

He sent the two unwounded men down into the canyon to retrieve anything of value from the two mules that had been swept off the trail and to retrieve Juan, the packer who had been shot out of the saddle. While they were gone, Roberto returned, empty-handed. They shook hands and each took a slug of Bacanora, as did the wounded man.

"I left the two we shot with their horses just up the trail. One was dead; the other is now," Roberto told him.

"I am glad you had my back; that was touch and go," Connor told him.

"My friend, we make a good team," Roberto said.

The two packers came back up from the canyon, with one of the mules that, amazingly, had survived. Apparently, instead of cartwheeling into space, the beast had mostly slid down the steep slope, stopping halfway down, braying piteously. Unfortunately, Juan Salazar, the fourth packer, had not survived his wounds. The mule had a noticeable limp and some nasty abrasions but likely would live and recover to haul again. They went up the trail, and where it widened, reached the two bodies and the horses that Roberto had left. They didn't have much of value—the pistols they gave to the two packers, along with the ammo. There was a bottle in one of the saddlebags that they shared on the spot and some food. The horses and gear they would sell and give to Juan's widow. They continued for another half mile and found a reasonable campsite and camped for the night, taking turns at guard.

CHAPTER 15

When they reached the outskirts of Nacozari, they were met by a Rurale. "We intercepted a group of banditos in the foothills as they left the mountains to the east," he said. And added that three were captured, but the others had escaped to the north. Two of the bandits had been riding double. The captives were being held in the Rurales' camp and they expected Lt. Ortiz to arrive from Arispe in a day to lead the interrogation. After a thorough beating, one of the bandits had confessed to the attack on the mule train. Inquiries in town had identified Roberto and Connor as the owners of the packtrain. Would they like to observe the further questioning?

The following day, the partners rode out to the Rurales' camp and found that Lt. Ortiz had already arrived. They shook hands and turned to the three men, manacled and sitting a little distance from the fire. They looked dirty, fearful, and cowed. A half dozen Rurales stood around them, along with Sergeant Lopez and Lieutenant Ortiz. One, maybe two, would die, based on the usefulness of the information supplied, they were told. The two riding double were cousins. Details of the other members of the gang were soon forthcoming. Names were of questionable value, changing frequently amongst men like these.

The fact that three had come down from the States got their attention. Unfortunately, one of those had been killed at the ambush, and the other two, along with one of their original band, had escaped north. The Jefe was one of those. He had known about the packtrain—how, they didn't know. He had been keen on killing Roberto and Connor more than looting the mules. They had been recruited four weeks earlier and given a small amount of money to be available when contacted. Their contact was local but seemed to know the Jefe.

After the three were taken away, the lieutenant had asked the question—why would they specifically want to kill Roberto and Connor?

Roberto answered first, "I hope they didn't know that we were helping the Rurales."

Connor added, "As you requested, I have been trying to get in with this man Weaver. I worry that Weaver may have changed his mind about using me in his gunrunning operation and decided to get rid of loose ends."

Both were plausible but disturbing possibilities. Connor hoped this would suffice as an explanation because he certainly wasn't going to tell him what he really thought. Which was that Weaver was intent on eliminating competition from his erstwhile associate.

Ortiz added thoughtfully, "We need to get eyes on this Weaver and bring him to justice soon. He is a very dangerous and clever criminal."

"If there is any way that I can be there when you close the net on him, I would like to be there. I am feeling a very personal desire to get this son of a bitch," Connor let him know.

Lt. Ortiz nodded but wondered about the relationship between Connor and Weaver. No honor among thieves? He also remembered the brief telegram he had received over a year ago from the two Rurales investigating gunrunning out of Tucson. Too bad they hadn't been able to supply a name before they disappeared.

Riding out of the camp, Connor was certain that Weaver could only have heard about his business venture from Javier or Rosangela. The timing of recruiting the bandits, and the arrival of the three from the north after his return, fit with his trips to Bisbee. Whether the information had been transferred intentionally or not, it came from those sources. He needed to use that conduit to learn more about Weaver's movements and plans, or plant misinformation that he could exploit. The man was a threat both directly and through what he could tell the Rurales. Maybe he was overthinking the problem. Maybe he should find a way to take direct action if the opportunity presented itself. Unfortunately, Weaver seemed to be surrounded and protected by a tough and loyal corrida of men.

The following weeks leading up to Christmas were busy. They took several more packtrains into the Sierra Madre without incident. The money allowed them to add more mules and two more packers to their operation. They also hired a guard, one of Kosterlitzky's former Rurales who had been mustered out after a leg injury. The man, Guillame Castro, was deceptive to look at. Forty-five years old, he looked ten years younger with a slight build although nearly five foot eleven. He had been an artillery-man during the revolution and had developed an affinity for explosives. He had been apprehended trying to blow a safe in an assayer's office in the early hours of the morning. Apparently, there was a woman, a soldadera whose affection needed funding. Like many of the Rurales, he had been given a choice between staying in prison or joining La Gendarmeria. He had proved to be loyal and thoughtful in anticipating the moves of the men they pursued. Guillame carried a Sharps breechloader and was good with it.

Connor celebrated Christmas Eve at the compound with Roberto and three of the packers, their wives and girl-friends, and Guillame. Roberto had a lady join him whom he had been seeing when not on the trail. She owned a nearby cantina and was likely the same age as he. Wine, whiskey, and mescal were all in plentiful supply and the conversations were lively and uninhibited. During the evening, Connor shared a conversation near the fireplace with Roberto's latest interest, whose name was Luz.

"I am glad to meet you," she told him. "I have heard a lot from Roberto. I expected a bigger but not more handsome man! I met a man in the cantina a few weeks before the shooting in the mountains who asked about you. He claimed to be a friend and asked what you were doing. Did the two of you ever get the opportunity to meet, Senor Connor?" she asked.

"Unfortunately, no," he told her.

Her description of the man made him think of Rivera and it occurred to him that the bandit's description of their Jefe, extracted during the interrogation, described him also. "Luz, I think you should keep a close eye on Roberto and avoid talking with strange men," he told her with a grin.

The next morning was Christmas Day and Connor reflected about the year almost complete and the one to come. There was some unfinished business yet for 1888 and he felt a need to complete it. Bisbee seemed the place that would allow him to begin tying off some of the loose ends and questions from this year. He was healed and his speed with the Merwin & Hulbert was fast and smooth. He had practiced with the short, thin knife taken off the bandit on the trip from Bacanora this past summer. Roberto had a skill with blades and worked with him, off and on. He thought he needed something longer, with a wider blade. Roberto was probably right, but Connor liked the concealed nature of the six-inch blade, sheath suspended parallel to his belt and behind the back. Set for a right-hand extraction, it would never be his weapon of choice. If it became his weapon of necessity, the practice had provided some level of confidence.

The next morning, he set off for Bisbee, taking one mule with supplies for the trail. It was two days to Fronteras where he stopped and stayed the night with Luis Alcazar, picking up the commissions from the Phelps-Dodge contract, per their agreement. He also gave Emelda a set of small gold earrings for Christmas, which delighted her and warmed Luis, who appreciated the gesture. In two days, he was back in Bisbee, and he appreciated the sheepskin-lined coat he was wearing. It was quite cold at that elevation this time of the year. Normally he would send a message before arriving to inform Rosangela. Given his doubts and suspicions, he decided to be more discreet. His first stop was at Lim's, where he had to wait about an hour before he showed up. Lim showed no surprise at his presence or his offer to carry a message for Miss Li if needed. He asked if Walter Nelson and Carlos Rivera were still in town and if not, where. Lim agreed to check on the two men and with Miss Li.

Leaving Lim's, he rode northwest in the direction of Tombstone. As Bisbee started to tail off, he found a boardinghouse and a nearby livery for the animals. He had decided to stay on the outskirts, not wanting to advertise his presence. Off-loading his gear, Connor returned to Bisbee and carefully worked his way to Rivera's adobe. Smoke from the chimney confirmed someone was in, although he saw no activity outside. Lim had news for him—Rivera was in town, with another man. They had returned recently, trail-worn, and their horses in even worse shape. Lim also knew the livery where the horses were being stabled. The description of the second man was a good match for what the bandits had disclosed to Lt. Ortiz about the others who had escaped from the Rurales. Nelson had been seen talking to a man who sounded like the guy who had inquired about him at Forts Lowell and Bayard. Nelson was currently in Tombstone, plying his trade at the gambling tables there. Connor felt he had a good understanding of the lay of the land now and was prepared to start squaring some debts.

The next day he sent a message to Clifton, asking Ray to forward any messages. The first was several days old, from Rosangela. It asked for him to meet with Nelson and finalize the details of a transport contract for a delivery in Mexico, by the end of January. Actual delivery to be made on February 28, in Moctezuma. He was told that they had lined up two reliable guards and twelve good mules. He would need to find four packers. The shipment was prepaid so the delivery was for a specific time and place. There was no personal message from her and, despite his suspicions, he was disappointed in that.

He sent a response to Rosangela via Ray, agreeing and asking to meet with Nelson on January 15 and to have Nelson bring the money due. He sent another to Anastasio and his sister, Mariela. He sent another message for Lt. Ortiz, asking him to meet in Mexican Nogales, and a final telegram to Roberto. With New Year's just three days away, he met with Lim again, picked up a package for Miss Li. He then rode north to catch the Southern Pacific to Lordsburg and then the narrow gauge to Clifton. Connor was distracted as he rode into Tombstone, on his way north to Benson to catch the train. He planned on spending the night there and riding the final twenty miles to Benson the next day. He didn't notice that Weaver's old Segundo, Haggerty, had happened to spot him coming in and decided that this was an opportunity he couldn't pass up. He had been sitting outside Brown's Saloon when he spotted Connor riding down Allen Street and hitch his animals outside the Cancan Chop-House and enter.

Haggerty had returned from a rustling trip into Mexico with Weaver and other crew members just three weeks earlier. He knew that Weaver still wanted to kill Connor and was frustrated that the effort in Mexico had fallen short. He knew that he was working on some scheme, but Weaver had told him not to worry about it—he would call on him if needed. Haggerty had his own issues with that smart-ass and would be more than happy to help. Recently, Weaver seemed to prefer Cornyn and Rivera for his projects. That might change, but even if not, he had his own score to settle with that Irish prick. He moved to where he could observe the Cancan Chop-House.

Connor had entered and sat at a table. A waitress came out and he ordered, remembering that old Army adage to eat when you can. He could see several Chinese working in the kitchen, and while he was waiting, he stepped over to the kitchen door and waved to one of the men. He handed the man the note that Lim had given him. He read the Chinese calligraphy and then nodded, leaving the kitchen after a quick word with his fellow cook. Connor returned to his table, enjoyed his meal of steak, mashed potatoes with a generous chunk of butter, and bread. Thirty minutes later, the waitress brought his check and a note. It had an address in nearby Hoptown, as the Chinese section in Tombstone was called. He paid, left a generous tip, and walked out the door. Turning right, he walked up two blocks to Second Street, turned left, and headed down a small alley on his right and entered through a side door into what looked like a brothel. An older Chinaman motioned for him to follow and he was brought to a small room with a table and chairs. He was reminded of his first meeting with Miss Li.

The lady sitting at the table assessed the fit, limber, and alert man before her. He was close to forty, although which side she couldn't tell.

His eyes were brown and clear, focusing on her. He offered a polite smile and a slight bow. "Mrs. Sing," he stated.

He was looking at China Mary, Mrs. Ah Lum or Sing Choy, take your choice. He wasn't sure what to call her, but she seemed OK with the address he had chosen.

"Please, sit. Would you like tea?" she asked with a pleasing accent.

She wore a brocade robe that effectively hid her figure, but she appeared a little plump. Her face was set off by jade earrings and a necklace. As she poured the tea, he noted that Mrs. Sing's face was mostly unlined but he knew she was older than he and in her late forties. She was good at sizing up people, especially men. Her business interests were both legal and not so legal. She was a force to reckoned with in the Chinese community and amongst the Anglos. She could be both kind and ruthless. Connor sat at her direction and waited for her to sip her tea before doing the same.

"My associates in Bisbee and Clifton speak highly of you and say that you are a trusted and honorable person," she said in clear but accented English. "Can I help you in some way, Mr. Connor?"

"I brought a message for you from Mr. Lim in Bisbee at the request of Miss Li. I know that you have helped her in the past and I know she appreciates that very much," he told her.

He handed over a letter and a package, which she set aside, continuing to study him. Connor felt that maybe he should be nervous but strangely felt at ease. Still, he moved to fill the silence as she calmly studied him.

"Miss Li has helped me in the past and I am grateful. You likely also have helped in some way and I appreciate your consideration too," he told her.

She smiled then at his manners and decided that he was, as Li had told her, a trustworthy person, worthy of cultivating for mutual benefit.

"Miss Li and I are in similar businesses and I value her opinion and friendship. I have a package and letter that I would like you to deliver to her. I hope that you will feel comfortable calling on me if I can help in some small way."

She reached under the table and handed him a package similar in size to what he had delivered. It was wrapped in plain brown paper with manilla string binding it.

"Please stop by again when you are in Tombstone. I hope to hear more about your business and maybe share some opportunities with you."

The door opened and a man, who Mrs. Sing introduced as Tan, entered to show him out. Connor stood, gathered the package and letter, and with a slight bow, moved to the door.

She liked his grace as he moved and noted with approval the wide back, shaped by his time laying rail so long ago now and his more recent packing and scouting. When the door closed, she opened the package, seeing the money inside, counting quickly, though certain it was the correct amount. The younger man re-entered. He was known as a Boo How Doy, a guard, foot soldier, an enforcer that helped ensure that rules and commitments were adhered to. This one was about twenty-five, recently arrived from San Francisco and good with hatchet, knife, and the more modern weapon of choice, the Colt 45.

"Please secure this, then follow Mr. Connor who just left. He will be going back to the Cancan to retrieve his animals. I want to be sure he leaves Tombstone safely," she directed him.

Leaving the building and heading into the alley, Connor noted the sun had set and it was growing dark and cold quickly. He adjusted his grip on the package and shifted the letter to the inside of his coat pocket. He heard a footstep behind him and as he turned to his right he instinctively reached for his gun with his left hand. He saw something racing for his head over his right shoulder and hunched forward, raising his shoulder and ducking. It wasn't enough as the fist glanced off his shoulder and slammed into his head, about where the right side of his neck joined his skull. Connor lost vision for an instant and staggered forward a step, not completing his draw from his gun holster. His vision cleared in a flick of his eye as he felt an explosion of pain when a massive fist connected to his right kidney. Red screeching pain enveloped his lower right back. He vaguely registered his grunt and the air was driven out of his body. A hand on his left shoulder spun him counterclockwise as a fist slammed into his gut and both knees gave out.

Haggerty had been waiting for him to come out of the brothel, waiting in the shadows just to the left of the door. At five foot eleven and weighing about two hundred and five pounds, he had thirty-five pounds on Connor. He carried a bit of a paunch but he was trail tough and most was muscle. Haggerty had been in his share of fights and a broken nose as well as a missing tooth attested to the fact he could take as well as give. His specialty was a kicking, punching, stomping melee where anything goes and the real damage occurs when a man goes down. He wasn't afraid of this little shit but wasn't going to give him any chance or quarter. The brass knuckles on his right hand were just the beginning of what he was planning.

Connor's brain was starting to process at a primal level as a hard, open hand slapped his head causing brief starbursts as it pivoted right from the blow. He felt a hand reach into his open coat and first grab, then pitch, his Merwin & Hulbert into the alley dirt.

"Now I am going to skin your sorry ass," he heard the large, shadowed bastard say with glee.

There was a slight pause and Connor saw a blade coming down in an overhand strike. He threw his forearm up at an angle and made contact with the other man just above the wrist, deflecting the blade to his right and away. He heard a curse and felt a boot slam into his left side, partially cushioned by his left arm, which took some portion of the momentum. His left side felt numb from the force of the kick and he vaguely saw his assailant bringing his arm down again with the glittering blade.

Connor used his left forearm to deflect the blade to his left again and got his right foot planted flat on the dirt, left knee still down. The deflection wasn't so clean and he felt the blade rip through his coat, shirt, and into the flesh, taking a shallow piece of skin off. The blade caught in his coat for just an instant as the killer ripped it free from the material. Connor rotated his left hand, made contact, then gripped this devil's forearm as the blade was disentangled, trying to slow the attack. The momentum of the other man's arm as it deflected left then jerked up caused Connor to twist left, pulling him up just a little, and the killer to bend over just a bit more.

Adrenaline surged through his body, making it impossible to think beyond the next second or two. Connor was consumed by the animal need to fight, tear, rend, survive. His right hand slipped around the handle of his hide-out knife behind his back. Palm out, he pulled right, feeling it come free from the sheath, six inches of razored, honed steel. Gripping his opponent's forearm as it pulled back up for another strike, he pushed off the ground with his right leg, corkscrewing up and left with all the strength and speed he could muster. His right hand and arm rammed up and the blade tip made contact with bone, sliding left and into flesh. The point went through the underside of Haggerty's jaw, through his tongue and into the roof of his mouth. It wasn't long enough to reach the brain and Connor ripped it back out, falling back and scrambling to get on his feet.

Haggerty was hors de combat, truly out of the fight. He staggered, stiff-legged, eyes glazed, with blood erupting from his mouth. He dropped to his knees then fell forward, hands at his throat trying to stem the flow of blood drowning him. Connor watched, still having trouble thinking, his kidney radiating fire and his body throbbing. Haggerty's feet were drumming on the ground as Connor wiped his blade off on the dying man's pants. He couldn't have helped him even if he wanted to, and he didn't. He recognized Haggerty in the dim light now. How he had happened to be in this spot was not comprehensible in the moment. Maybe never would be. Connor walked over to where his revolver lay in the dirt, started to holster it when the door to the alley opened.

Tan was shocked by the scene as he stepped into the alley.

He quickly held his hands shoulder high, signaling no threat. "Mr. Connor, Mrs. Sing sent me. I am Tan, no worries!"

Connor had a gun in one hand and a short knife in the other. He holstered the gun and sheathed the knife as his still fogged brain registered the words.

"He tried to kill me, Tan. I have to get out of here," Connor stated.

"Wait, I will help," Tan told him, abruptly stepping back into the building.

Connor leaned against the wall for support and his breathing slowed, his thinking accelerated. Tan returned with two other men who grabbed the now still Haggerty by the heels and dragged him diagonally to a livery across the alley.

"Come, Mr. Connor, we will walk to your horse and mule while you tell me what happened."

Tan didn't lead him directly to the hitching post outside the Cancan. Instead, they went a block north of Allen, then turned right until reaching Fourth Street, then back down to Allen. Connor gave him an abbreviated version of the events after leaving Mrs. Sing's, gradually settling into a cold anger as he thought about the repeated attempts to kill him. Before they turned the corner to the front of the Cancan, Connor brushed off the dirt and straightened his clothes, taking off his coat, feeling the cold air for the first time. It was bracing. The left sleeve was torn and there was blood seeping from the cut to his forearm. He took off his bandana and tied it off around the shallow wound.

As he put his coat back on, Tan told him, "It might be better to stay in Tombstone tonight. You don't look like you will ride too far."

He hurried on as he took in the "you must be crazy" look that Connor gave him.

"We have a safe place where you can rest and clean up. We will find out more. The body will not be found, I guarantee that. I will send someone with fresh water and we will mend your coat. I will take care of the animals."

Connor found Tan convincing and, more importantly, the thought of a cold night on the ground and the pounding pain in his kidney was compelling. He was feeling hors de combat, himself. He nodded. They went around the corner, unhitched the animals, and walked back up the street toward where they had just come from. One of the men that had dragged Haggerty off came up and exchanged words with Tan, then took the saddlebags and bedroll off the horse. Tan shouldered the load and guided Connor into another building and to a second-floor room dimly lit by a gaslight. Tan assured him he would be safe here, and within minutes a middle-aged woman, not unattractive, entered with two buckets of water.

"She will take care of you tonight and I will be back in the morning. Don't worry." And with that, he left.

The woman pulled out a small tub, more of a hip bath, poured in the two buckets of water, going to the door in answer to a knock.

Connor had the gun in his hand before she told him, "No problem, more water."

Two boys came in with hot buckets of water and completed filling the bath. She locked the door as they left. "I am Lee and will take care of you and watch while you sleep. We have a guard outside." Miss Lee helped him out of his clothes and into the bath. Connor was in too much pain to be self-conscious. She nodded approvingly at the muscled frame and tutted at the scars decorating his body. After Lee bathed him, he needed to use the brass pot to piss into, and she obligingly turned her back to him. It took a long time for the flow to start, and when it did, he noted that it seemed to be mostly blood. He slipped into the bed clothes provided, then there was another knock at the door and tea was delivered. She sat with him as he drank it down and then helped him into bed. She took a chair by the door, his coat, and some sewing essentials he hadn't noticed before. Despite the pain radiating from his body, he fell asleep or maybe just passed out.

When he woke, Miss Lee was still by the door, which she opened, said something to someone, and then locked it again. Connor had trouble getting up, slightly better but still an aching mess. After he was able to urinate, he grimly noted that there was a lot of blood. She helped him dress into clean clothes that someone had brought and helped him into his brogans. He sat on the bed, already tired when breakfast was brought in along with the ubiquitous tea. This tea tasted medicinal, which is to say, bad. There was a knock, and this time Tan was at the door. Miss Lee made to leave, but Connor stopped her, closing her hand around a ten-dollar gold piece and thanking her for her attentive and needed care.

She tried to return it but stopped when he told her, "Thanks, Miss Lee, for your thoughtfulness and kindness. I appreciate it very much and will be saddened if you won't accept this small gift." She looked at him directly and, without smiling, nodded and left.

CHAPTER 16

ARIZONA & SONORA WINTER 1889

Tan asked him if he was feeling any better. Connor grimaced and shrugged, saying all that was needed. He had brought with him all of Haggerty's effects, which included about three hundred and twenty dollars, about a third in coin.

Connor pushed the money across to Tan. "This belongs to you and Mrs. Sing."

Tan pushed half back, saying, "Our commissions are not that great."

The brass knuckles, a ring, the knife, and a single action Colt with a four-inch barrel were among the effects. Also included were some letters and a telegram, which Connor quickly scanned. It was unsigned but asked that Haggerty meet the sender at the usual place on February 24, ready for an extended ride. Tan and Mrs. Sing had been impressed with this unassuming Anglo and the way he had dispatched Haggerty. Given the size of his assailant and surprise attack, he should be dead, but the knife wound inflicted on his attacker was either genius or excellent luck. Regardless, a man with this kind of luck or skill was good as an ally.

Connor decided to ask for a small favor, knowing it was neither small nor a favor. He suspected that a man named Issac Weaver was going to smuggle arms into Mexico around February 24. It would take mules, packers, and guards. Other known associates were Rivera, in Bisbee, and Corwyn, of unknown origins. Weaver was known to operate in Tucson, Bisbee, and El Paso. He also currently had a girlfriend, it pained him to say, Rosangela Lazaro, of Bisbee. He provided descriptions and also threw Javier into the mix. He would appreciate confirmation of Weaver's intentions or what information that could be gathered. Miss Li could be the contact point or Ray Witherspoon, both in Clifton. Tan took it all in without resorting to notes. He also recommended that he rest at least one more day before continuing his journey. Connor knew he was right and agreed, falling back on his bed with a groan when he left.

If anything, the following day he was stiffer and the pain was now an incessant throbbing but maybe slightly muted. Miss Lee returned before he left in the morning with breakfast, the nasty medicinal tea, and a tincture of some sort. Connor suspected that it contained diluted opium or laudanum. She gave him six additional small bottles, telling him to restrict his intake to one per day and avoid seeking more. He understood the dangers of addiction and promised to be careful. After nodding and smiling this time, she departed and so did he.

He left Tombstone and alternated riding and walking, not sure which was more painful. The tincture helped but he was glad to see Benson that evening, finding a place to stay and sleeping like the dead. The next morning, he put his animals on the stock car and boarded for the ride to Lordsburg. The train was better than the horse but barely. He changed trains and arrived in Clifton the third day of 1889. He stopped by to see Ray, who offered to put him up for a few days, which Connor gratefully accepted. He had brought a couple of flasks of Bacanora, which were well received by the retired sergeant.

After stabling his animals, Connor went to see Miss Li. She was expecting him and his package. Like Mrs. Sing, she left it unopened and focused her attention on him.

"Before we talk, I have brought someone to look at you and assess your health. Please allow this as a favor to me," she told him.

Before he could reply, an elderly Chinese man entered and began his examination. He studied his eyes closely, then rotated his head with his hands behind his ears, cupping his skull. He checked his pulse much like a Western doctor might. He asked him to remove his shirt and the man listened to his heart and gently explored the area where he had taken the blow to the kidney. There was a huge bruise there and his left arm had a long, wide, but shallow cut that was not fully scabbed over. He asked if he was still urinating blood and, if so, was it diminishing? He indicated that he could put his shirt back on and left after speaking with Miss Li.

"He says that you were fortunate to not have received more strikes to the kidney. As it is, you will need to rest as much as possible for the next two weeks. He will bring some medicine that will reduce the internal trauma—you should take it four times a day. It is consumed like tea. Also consume lots of fresh water. And avoid alcohol," she told him.

"Now, Mrs. Sing was impressed by you and is working on your request. She appreciates your help from time to time. As do I," Miss Li added. "I hope that you can join me for lunch before you leave today."

As they ate together, Connor learned that, like Mrs. Sing, she was from Zhongshan, in the northern part of the Guangdong area. The doctor returned with paper packets of dried powders. Connor sincerely thanked him and Miss Li and took his leave. When she was alone, she opened the package he had brought and stored the opium in a safe.

As Connor walked from his meeting, he reflected on this improbable connection. Miss Li and Mrs. Sing had been invaluable in providing intelligence and help when needed. The expansion of rail and mining in Mexico and the Southwest was bringing a steady flow of Chinese into towns and camps on both sides of the border. At the same time, the racial prejudice in both Mexico and the U.S. ensured that the Tongs flourished along with prostitution, gambling, drugs, and labor contracting. Connor knew that he might continue to need their advice and insight, and it was not always possible to pick your friends or allies. They, in turn, appreciated his discreet transportation and communication services. Friends should be cherished.

During the next week, Connor continued to improve and the amount of blood he was passing was reduced considerably, along with the other aches and pains. Ray had received the shipment of seized weapons they had purchased from the Rurales. The price and quality were good and Ray expected to turn a decent profit on them. After eight days in Clifton, he was heading back to Bisbee for his meeting with Walter Nelson . . . real name, William Palmer. As usual, he tried to get there a few days early and observe before going in. He visited Lim and was rewarded with a couple of updates. First, Weaver had been located in El Paso and had met with men in the arms trade. He had also been with the Yaqui woman, and had been seen at dinner with her. They had stayed in separate rooms but at the same hotel. His source could not confirm anything beyond that. They had actually located Weaver through the woman. She had bought a round-trip ticket on the Southern Pacific, leaving before Christmas and returning on the eighth. One of Lim's people had followed her to the railroad station and another had been waiting in El Paso. She had met with a number of Yaqui in that area and perhaps collecting money. Javier had stayed in Bisbee.

Nelson had met with Rivera and apparently had been successful gambling, being generous with his tips around town after his return. Connor decided to call on Rosangela, because despite everything he was still attracted to her. Secondly, he wanted to stay in character, at least as far as she was concerned. He sent a message over first and then, after a couple of hours, knocked on the door. She answered and seemed aloof and cold, but invited him in.

"I thought you had forgot me, Senor. I expected you during the holidays," she told him abruptly after closing the door behind him.

"I am sorry, Rosangela. I stopped by twice but you were gone," he told her, wondering what she would say.

"Javier said nothing, Senor," she responded severely.

Connor responded in tone: "I didn't come to see Javier, and never have. I came the day before Christmas and then again before New Year's. I had a present for you and will leave it with you now."

With that, he presented a small gold broach in the shape of a rooster. That seemed to soften her attitude.

"Thank you, Connor. I was out of town a few days in Tucson on business. I am sorry I missed you. You should have told me you were coming," she added primly.

There was an awkward silence, which Connor filled with, "It is always good to see you and I apologize for the confusion."

He gave her a small bow and moved to the door, ready to leave, having caught her in a lie and feeling no joy in it.

"Perhaps we can meet again, tomorrow," she told him in a more conciliatory tone, as he smiled, kissed her hand, and stepped back outside.

He met her sooner than expected, when she and Javier showed up at the meeting with Nelson the following day. The number of rifles had been reduced to sixty, along with forty thousand rounds of ammunition, all .44-40 caliber, and ten mules. Two guards had been hired—the four packers were Connor's responsibility. Pickup was just outside of Bisbee at a stable not far from where, unknown to them, he had last stayed. He would pick them up on the first of February. The details of the delivery point in Moctezuma were provided. At the end, Connor received his next two hundred and fifty dollars, the remaining half after delivery, and the money for the packers. When he protested that he wanted his own guards, he was strongly overridden by all three of the others. He also questioned the fixed delivery point from a security point of view, but again was overridden, with Rosangela telling him that this was as the Yaquis had requested and there could be no changes. He understood a little how Weaver had felt after he had been forced to accept the arrangement with Connor. He looked at Nelson and told him to be ready with the rest of his money when he returned.

"You don't want to face the consequences if you try and cheat me after all this."

He gave them a hard smile, a handshake, collected the second payment, and left without looking back. Well, not exactly true. He looked at Rosangela at the end, but she was expressionless.

Connor spent the night in Bisbee, checking out the pickup point for the contraband, and then headed to Nogales. He had three meetings planned, one with Anastasio, the second with Roberto, and the third with Ortiz. The ride to Nogales was long, about sixty to seventy miles, and it took several days. He had plenty of time to think and test his plans as he made his way southwest, first to the San Pedro River, where he stopped to rest and water the animals. From there, Connor angled toward the saddle between Coronado and Montezuma Peaks at the southern end of the Huachuca Mountains. He dry camped on the western end of Montezuma Pass and then crossed the San Rafael Valley, reaching Lutrell in the early evening. There was a lot of cattle ranching in the valley, with higher elevations and good grasslands. Also, a lot of cattle rustling, sitting that close to the border. He was hailed several times by ranch hands, who were assured that he was benign.

Lutrell, now renamed Lochiel at the behest of the Scot Colin Cameron, who owned the huge San Rafael Ranch, was fair sized. It had a smelter that serviced the mines in the Patagonia Mountains to the west, a few saloons, and a brewery, boasting a population of around half a thousand. More importantly, from Connor's perspective, it had a boardinghouse owned by Dr. Lutrell and a livery. After getting a room, he picked up a case of the local beer and stopped by the temporary cavalry camp on the outskirts of town. There was a twelve-man patrol from the Tenth Cav. staying there as they patrolled the southern end of the valley and along the border for a few days. The Buffalo Soldiers were out of Ft. Huachuca, about fifteen or twenty miles away, at the northern end of the mountains. Connor had packed and scouted with the Tenth when chasing Apaches and they shared a few tall tales while finishing the beer, although he didn't know any of these soldiers. They were led by Sergeant Livermore who was closing in on retirement and they knew some of the same officers and fellow NCOs. There had been a stage robbery on the road leading through the Patagonia Mountains and

Camp Washington about six months earlier, but nothing alarming since.

Connor got an early start the next morning. Passing through Washington Camp, he was surprised by the number of mines, shacks, and tents in the area. The higher elevations had stands of pine and it was brisk outside as the trail took him to about six thousand feet and then the long descent toward Nogales. He splashed across the shallow Santa Cruz River a couple of times as the road meandered southwest to the border town. He decided to stay on the American side, then ride across to meet Lt. Ortiz in Mexican Nogales.

Ortiz was not in uniform when they met for dinner. They shook hands then ordered. Over dinner, Connor laid out what he knew, emphasizing his confidence that his contract with Nelson was a decoy to the real smuggling operation led by Weaver. He shared his conjectures around a departure by Weaver on the 24th, his route and general area where an exchange might take place. Ortiz confirmed that his agents were already picking up rumors of an arms shipment being delivered near Moctezuma. Both considered the possibility of a turncoat in the Rurale organization and how it might be neutralized. Ortiz was curious about his sources and Connor tried to share elements of his information without giving too much away about how it was gathered. Finally, Connor stated his desire to be at the finish of Weaver and his organization. He stated that, if need be, he would pursue him back across the border to see that threat eliminated. Ortiz thought the cold desire for vengeance stemmed from more than just the ambush and loss of one of his packers. He promised to talk favorably to Major Kosterlitzky about his request. He also thought to himself that he would discuss his suspicions with the major about this Connor. They finished with a shot of Bacanora and a handshake.

He met with Roberto the following day. He was happy to see him again and they reviewed the business growth and the opportunities that were opening up for them. The future looked bright if they could eliminate the cloud cast by Weaver, and they focused on their plan to eliminate the bastard. Connor needed four or five trusted and hard men to help with the decoy arms and munitions delivery and how to avoid being killed or captured by the Rurales.

Roberto told him, "I will be with the packers and, like you, want to see this to the end. If I get a shot at Weaver or that hijo de puta Rivera, I will not hesitate to pull the trigger."

Connor gave him the rendezvous point outside of Bisbee, the date, January 31, and asked him to bring three or four additional horses with stamina as remounts. He gave Roberto the money he had received for the packers and half of his last payment plus his share of the commission he had received from Luis.

In the morning he went to the train station and bought a round-trip ticket for Hermosillo, Sonora. The rail line had been completed in 1882 by the Atchison, Topeka & Sante Fe Railway and connected to the Southern Pacific at Benson. From there you could travel to Tucson and Los Angeles heading west or El Paso, going east. In Mexico it was called the FC, or Ferrocarril de Sonora—the Sonora Railroad. It took almost eight hours to reach Hermosillo with numerous stops in Imuris, Magdalena, and other mining towns. The line bypassed the main Sierra Madre Mountains farther east, but there were plenty of sky islands and limited mountain chains to negotiate. It roughly paralleled the Rio San Miguel, and where it merged with the Rio de Sonora was the location of Hermosillo. It had been the capital of Sonora for the last ten years, and with the rail connection both north and south, it was growing.

He was met at the station by Anastasio, who dressed and blended in with the numerous Mexican citizens and assorted Indios in and around there. Connor had left his animals in Nogales and they walked for about ten minutes until they reached the boardinghouse on a small side street. Anastasio had rented four rooms. There he met the other packers, one of whom, Alberto, had been on the last trip, and Mariela. Abrazos all around, especially for Mariela, and then Connor took Anastasio back over to Plaza Zaragoza near the Governor's Palace to talk.

"My friend, Weaver is using us as a decoy for his operation and, no doubt, will betray us to the Rurales. We will make the exchange long before that happens so there are some plans that we must make so that we are successful and survive."

Then, Connor took him through the plan for the exchange. "I believe that the weapons, now reduced to sixty, will be of little value. I will inspect them but I think we should get rid of them as quickly as possible if I am right. The real value is in the ammunition, and that will be easier to transport. When you receive that, I will have completed my agreement with the Yaqui, and I hope you feel the same. Two other things. This will be my last shipment. I will always wish you well, but I have to turn my attention in another direction."

He then talked about the business that he and Roberto were working to establish and grow. Anastasio listened with interest and wished him success.

"The second thing concerns you and your sister. I respect your fight, but at some point it may be lost, or it will be time to let others take up the burden. I will have a place for either or both of you if you choose to leave the active fight. I will tell your sister the same."

Anastasio nodded. "That time may be coming, and I thank you for your offer. The future looks dark, but there is still more to do. If I send my sister, you will protect her?"

Connor chuckled. "More likely she will protect me, and you know that she is a grown woman who makes her own decisions. But yes, I will."

They talked about more of the details and Connor gave him all the money for the packers in advance and more for expenses required. Shaking hands, they returned to the others and gave them an abbreviated version of what they planned.

That night, they had dinner in small groups, not wanting to draw attention, and afterward, he and Mariela went to the plaza to sit and talk. She initially talked about the state of affairs along the Rio Yaqui. The Mexican government was building canals and redistributing land to new settlers from the south and also those Yaqui that were ready to make peace. Their community land was part of that taken. The talk turned to his venture and he repeated the offer he had made to Anastasio.

"I don't know how things will work out between us, but regardless, this offer stands and I will help you get started if you choose a new direction."

"Do you like me, Connor? Do you find me attractive?" she directly asked.

"I do, Senora, both in the dress you are wearing now and when dressed for the trail," he responded with a smile.

She leaned into him and placed her arms around his neck and pulled him in for a warm and deep kiss. He felt weak then strong as he responded with his arms around her waist. It was all that they could do in a public place. It was enough for now.

The next day, he boarded the train to return to Nogales. Anastasio and Mariela saw him off at the station. This time he kissed her on both cheeks before receiving a fierce abrazo. Anastasio shook hands and he boarded. The trip back was no faster, and he was happy to be back on American soil by late afternoon. He had two weeks before the meet in Bisbee to pick up the contraband. His plan was in motion, but a lot could go wrong. He needed more insight to have an edge and that meant talking to Mrs. Sing, aka China Mary. He decided to take the train up to Fairbank and then ride from there to Tombstone. He sent a message to Tan, expressing his wish to talk, and soon received a place and time to meet.

He was taken to a room on the second story of a general store. Tan stayed, standing in the background as an older woman poured tea and then departed. Mrs. Sing inquired about his health and thanked him for his delivery to Miss Li. She turned to Tan and he began updating Connor. Weaver was leaving on the 24th as suspected, taking three hundred rifles and thirty thousand rounds of ammunition. Perhaps the most important information was that he was going to depart from somewhere near the San Pedro River. He had six guards, which included Rivera and Corwyn, and eight packers. He would be traveling with the mule train and would meet his Yaqui contact at Batuc. Weaver had an informer in the Rurales—Mrs. Sing's network had not been able to discover his name—but he was an NCO based in the old Sonoran capital of Arispe.

He confirmed that Rosangela had a warm affection for Weaver that extended beyond just business. Javier was a frequent go-between for Weaver and the Yaqui leadership. It was he who had made the arrangements for the mules and contraband weapons that Connor was expected to deliver. Connor was amazed at the intelligence that had been gathered. He was also sobered by the thought of what would be necessary to keep his future movements and trips into the Sierra confidential. He was glad that Mrs. Sing was an ally. He had to reflect on what the Rurales and Kosterlitzky might know or suspect about his own illegal activities. And what that meant in terms of risk, going forward. It would be foolish to count on any special treatment, given Kosterlitzky's reputation for strict enforcement.

CHAPTER 17

On January 31, Connor met with Roberto in Bisbee and talked about the risks when they reached Moctezuma. He brought four good men with him, including the ex-Rurale Guillame Castro, along with one of the packers that had been caught in the ambush, Juan Castro, who was no relation to the first. He told Roberto that he thought Guillame was a good man but shared his reflection about keeping plans and operations secret. Neither wanted to be among the two birds with one stone nailed by Kosterlitzky and Ortiz. Finally, they strategized about how to manage the two guards provided by Nelson.

The options ranged from using them as intended to outright elimination. They settled on the first, unless they proved unmanageable. On the first of February, they all arrived at noon at the livery. The owner took his leave, as he had been paid to do. Nelson had the two guards with him, both Mexicans, and by Connor's assessment, bright and dangerous. Their weapons were well cared for as were their horses. Alvarado was the senior of the two and he shook hands, flashing a disarming smile. His partner was called Cortez and he gave Connor a wave while sizing him up. Connor introduced Roberto as his Segundo and asked them to discuss the plans for organizing and protecting the mule train during the trip to the rendezvous. He and Nelson would go through the cargo together and agree on the inventory.

Alvarado looked over at Nelson, as if asking for approval. Connor took the opportunity to emphasize the pecking order.

"Senor Alvarado, we are leaving later today. I am in charge and Roberto is my Segundo. You will follow my orders or Roberto's if I am not present. If you have questions about that, then leave now; I don't need your help."

Alvarado and his partner bristled and squared up their shoulders like billy goats in a barnyard.

Connor simply said, "Decide, gentlemen. I have no time for further discussion now or later. This is a dangerous trip. Our lives depend on discipline. If you question my or Roberto's direction once we leave here, I will cut you down right there and then."

Out of the corner of his eye he saw Nelson slightly shake his head.

"Of course, Senor, you are the Jefe and it will be as you say," Alvarado said with a sober look on his face.

Roberto led them out, Nelson sat down, and Connor started to methodically go through the rifles. He pulled them, started from the barrel, worked down to the butt, and then worked back up on the other side. Just as he'd learned to do in the Fourth Cavalry. He worked the lever action several times, easing the trigger down each time with his thumb. As expected, almost none of the rifles were in good shape. Corrosion and dirt were evident, and the actions were less than smooth. If this trip wasn't actually a setup, he would be lucky to survive his customers' reaction to the weapons' quality.

He signed off on the inventory Nelson had provided, and repeated his earlier caution: "I'll be expecting payment in full when I return." Nelson agreed nervously.

Roberto returned with two of the packers, proceeding to repack and reorganize for the trip. The two Castros were with the two guards, checking the mules with provisions and the extra horses. Connor stepped out of the livery stable and smoked his pipe, quietly observing the guards. In an hour they were ready and they set out, traveling ten miles southwest of Bisbee, toward the San Pedro River. Because of the late start, they camped near the river for the night, planning on an early start in the morning. His plan was to replicate his first smuggling run in 1887. He planned to travel along the San Pedro River, south across the border and then to its headwaters above Cananea. Circling to the east of the town, they would transit to the southeast-flowing Rio Sonora. When it turned southwest, Connor planned to strike out cross country to reach the Moctezuma River.

Taking a page from the Weaver smuggling book, Connor had the band of smugglers practice breaking into two groups with the two guards, Guillame Castro, and three pack mules with the rifles, a spare horse, a supply mule, and himself. Roberto would take the other mules with the ammunition, two supply mules, two spare horses, and the other three packers. Rendezvous points would be selected with backup points if the first failed. The first time, they reunited at the eastern most stream of the three that made up the San Pedro, just northeast of the village of Cananea. The old Spanish colonial mines were back in operation, thanks to General Ignacio Pezqueira, the highest peak named for his wife, Elenita. The village, like Bisbee, was a mile high and there was snow falling when they regrouped near there.

Southwest of Cananea, they reached the first of the intermittent streams that formed the Rio Sonora. As they had operated in the past, they traversed in the less traveled areas to the east of the river to avoid contact and proceeded south and east. When the Rio Sonora veered south, they struck cross country, expecting to reach the Rio Moctezuma in a few days. Roberto was riding point, scouting the way and providing security. Connor was to the east, Alvarado was providing security on the west side of the train, Cortez at the rear. He had to admit that the guards were competent and had been compliant. After the snow, the weather had improved to around sixty degrees during the day but cold at night, going into the low thirties.

Three days after leaving the river, Connor saw dust from Roberto's horse as he rode up and told him he had detected a party of men to the southeast, which could be Rurales. A short conference and they broke into two groups, with Connor and his group moving directly east. Connor took the point, Cortez helped Guillame with the mules and spare horse, and Alvarado took up the rear-guard position. He guided them to more broken ground with heavier mesquite, greasewood, and scrub oak. They stopped after forty minutes to avoid creating a dust cloud and wait for whoever was coming to pass. After an hour they continued east, not having seen anyone, and made an early camp.

The next day Connor's party reached the Moctezuma River, cautiously let the animals drink, and refilled canteens. They then moved west of the river, traveling in the early mornings and early evenings to reduce chances of being spotted. Just outside of Nacozari, they reached the rendezvous point and waited for the others. Nacozari was not actually on the Rio Moctezuma, but both Roberto and he had good contacts and their business headquarters there. Resupplying there, given their transport business, would not draw any attention and they could rest there, being ahead of schedule. From here it would take about six days of cautious travel to reach the exchange point. As he had done with Weaver, they cached their contraband and then went into town. They turned the animals loose in their corral at the headquarters compound, quartered the guards there, and gave the packers a few days off.

Connor was happy to be back and ready for a rest. He felt he had been on the move since Christmas and was a bit trail worn. He had a surprise visitor waiting for him, Mariela. He couldn't repress a grin at seeing her again, and Roberto seemed to like her immediately when he introduced his partner. They had five one-room adobe houses inside the walls where they stored loads temporarily and bedded the packers occasionally. Connor and Roberto each had one that they used for themselves. He got some boys to clean up one for her, and bring hot water to each house so they could bathe.

Connor was soaking when the door opened and Mariela let herself in. She stood by the door, appraising and smiling at him, although he had some concealment from the tub.

He was a little disconcerted but happy, smiling back and saying the first thing that came to mind: "I missed you, Mariela!"

"I know. That is why I am here, Connor," she replied while holding her grin.

Seeming to make up her mind, she pulled a chair up alongside the tub, improving her view. From the scars visible, she could see he had been through a lot.

"I will help you clean up," she added, reaching for the sponge.

He made no move to cover himself, and she leaned forward, put her hand behind his head, and pulled him into a long, warm kiss.

He reached for her with an urgency but she leaned back, saying, Ummmmm, you need cleaning first, Mi Amor."

Mariela grabbed the rough sponge and a sliver of soap, scrubbing his shoulders, back, and chest. She was careful around the more recent wounds on his chest.

"Why didn't I get to do that for you, Senora?" he complained.

"You will have to be more thoughtful in the future, Senor. I will forgive you this time."

She stood up then and walked behind him toward the bed, directing, "Finish up completely and then join me."

Connor did just that, the sheets barely settling around her as he reached the bed, toweling off and sliding next to her. Her appetites were strong and she was fierce and uninhibited. He found himself wanting to merge with her and let himself be carried away by this force of nature. He was pleased that his speculation about what was underneath her frumpy trail clothes was at last proved correct. At the end, he was left holding her tightly and murmuring things that made no sense but were well understood.

Later, they talked about the near future and then she shared news of Anastasio. Mariela planned to rejoin him but first wanted to help Connor finish Weaver. Mariela was a woman with no reservations or limits when helping friends, family, and lovers. Not being able to talk her out of joining the smugglers, they agreed that she would join Roberto's packers with an additional two spare horses. Her presence would be explained as a translator, if required, at the rendezvous.

He started to say, "When this is over—" but she shushed him with a finger across his lips and then another kiss.

A few days later, the party of nine left Nacozari, picking up the cached contraband, and headed south. It was still cold, but spring was not far away at this latitude. At the end of the first day, they reached the Rio Moctezuma and paralleled the river. Reaching Moctezuma a day before the scheduled exchange, Connor sent the two guards into the town to check security, asking them to return and report the following morning. After they left, he conferred with Mariela and sent her into town with Alberto to take up watch near the site. If Ortiz didn't play his part, and they weren't executed outright, perhaps they could spring them. In the morning, Alvarado and Cortez returned, reporting that all was secure. He instructed them to take up a position and provide security from across the street to the livery where the exchange would take place.

They rode to the site in two groups, the spare horses and mules carrying provisions stabled by Mariela elsewhere. Connor and two packers reached the livery first and entered, followed by Roberto and another packer a few minutes later. Alvarado and Cortez watched with enjoyment as a dozen Rurales materialized from alleys and side streets to surround the building and entered, with guns drawn. Minutes later they watched as the Rurales marched out the now manacled Connor and the packers, kicking and cuffing them as they were led out of town, along with the loaded mules.

Roberto and Connor were initially glad to see Lt. Ortiz leading their captors, but the rough treatment as they were marched out to a grove of trees outside the town and near the river had their thoughts racing.

Lt. Ortiz separated Connor and Roberto from the others, telling them coldly, "You know that smuggling weapons and munitions into Mexico is a major offense."

"But, Lieutenant, you know that this was a decoy, set up to protect the real smugglers," Roberto stated with exasperation.

"So you say, and I wonder if this is your first trip," replied the steely eyed Ortiz. "Smuggling guns is a capital offense and you have violated the laws of the Republic of Mexico."

Connor, keeping his tone reasonable and calm, said, "But, Lt. Ortiz, there are no guns or other contraband here. We would never bring those into Mexico, even as a decoy to help you catch other smugglers."

"Then what are these?" the furious lieutenant shouted as he flipped back the tarps over the packs on the nearest mule.

Ortiz's eyes popped when he saw that he was looking at lumber and pipes. He stormed over to the next mule pack and the next one after that. More of the same, and in the ammo crates, olives and oranges.

"Where is it?" he demanded.

"We destroyed it north of the border and told the American Consul that we were trying to help catch the criminals to both Mexico and the U.S.," Connor told him.

Frustrated, Ortiz glanced over to Guillame Castro, the former Rurale. All he received was a careful shrug from Guillame, who couldn't meet Roberto's intense stare.

If Connor had a gun, he would have pistol whipped Ortiz for his treachery. He took a deep breath, knowing he was still on thin ice with this double dealer. Instead, he diplomatically reminded him, "There are still two observers that work for Weaver. It would be good if we continue as originally planned and you proceed with the fake execution. It is important that those two don't warn him. I still hope you will allow me to participate in his capture."

Lt. Ortiz was of half a mind to execute these two, even if there was no evidence of a crime. He was certain that they were no saints. The information about the American Consul being informed was a complication, though, possibly an embarrassment, which neither he nor Kosterlitzky wanted. President Diaz was eager for more American investment.

From a distance, Alvarado watched the furious officer shouting and throw back the tarps on the mules. He was too far away to make out the words, but based on the sounds of anger and stiff posturing, he placed a bet with himself that at least Connor and his bastard Segundo would not make it to prison. He watched with pleasure as the two were marched into the woods with six Rurales escorting and heard the subsequent explosions of pistol fire. He had played his part and now, along with Cortez, he mounted and started the ride to Senor Weaver and his bonus.

Roberto and Connor waited inside the tree line with the Rurales and their now seemingly indifferent and silent lieutenant. The manacles were removed, and when their weapons were returned, Connor inwardly sighed with relief. He had been honest about the rifles, but the ammunition had been swapped with Anastasio and his men when they had split into two groups following the false warning from about a Rurale patrol. Roberto had suspected that Castro had not really been invalided out of the unit and they had made sure he was not in the party that made the swap. He just seemed too fit and helpful. His employment was going to be ended as soon as they were back on their horses.

In the distance, they saw Mariela wave her carbine, indicating that the two guards had left. Connor had told her not to come close, in case Ortiz wanted to hold them. Besides, he didn't want Ortiz to get a good look at her or suspect that she might be Yaqui. Mounting, he asked the lieutenant where he would find the trap set for Weaver, and he was given a location description near Batuc. He hoped they would not be working together again soon. They rode toward Mariela after collecting the mules and then split into two groups. Connor, Roberto, Mariela, and Juan Castro split off with a couple of mules with provisions and extra canteens and the spare mounts. The others headed back to Nacozari. Guillame had decided not ask for his back pay and stayed with Ortiz.

Connor and company rode hard, initially wanting distance from the Rurales but also eager to put paid to Issac Weaver and his crew. He set a steady but not exhausting pace and stopped for the night still north of Batuc and the junction of the Rio Yaqui and the Rio Moctezuma. As they were preparing to leave the next morning, they were approached by three riders. One was Guillame, now in uniform as a sergeant. He also had another sergeant with him, Maldonado, from Arispe, and a private, Juan Reales. Lieutenant Ortiz had ordered them to accompany Connor, angry and frustrated by the poor intelligence from both sergeants and the embarrassment that ensued at Moctezuma. The least he could do was to make their life miserable.

Connor didn't want any more of their kind of help but at the same time considered what might happen if they ran into more Rurales and the utility of having them with him. After an unpleasant exchange, he agreed to their company.

"Keep up or be left behind. I am in charge, and if you have a problem with that, then leave. I want Weaver and we are not stopping until we run him down."

Without further ado, he mounted and moved south toward Batuc. His men all had a spare mount and supplies to last six or seven days.

****

Issac Weaver reflected, as he rode south from Batuc, that he was getting too old for this smuggling and rustling business. His earliest experiences had been under the command of Colonel John Hunt Morgan and the Second Kentucky Regiment during the Civil War. Morgan had been an accomplished raider for the Confederacy until captured and imprisoned by the Union forces arrayed against him. Weaver had avoided capture and later joined General Forrest in the final campaigns of the war. He had learned a lot, both good and bad, from both. From Morgan, the fine art of horse stealing and the concept of not pushing your luck too far. From Forrest, fast, aggressive action when confronted by the enemy, expected or otherwise. Weaver had not survived this long by being timid, and he could be ruthless when survival was at stake. He had brought with him six guards on this trip, and two of his packers had also been with him on rustling expeditions and had also been guards in the past. That was to say that they were well armed and, like the rest, were prepared to fight their way out if confronted by the law on either side of the border.

He had received some money in advance, which offset most costs, but the real payoff was at the exchange point with the Yaquis. Two Yaquis had met his man at the church in Batuc, San Francisco Javier de Batuc, and were leading them south to the rendezvous point just north of the pueblo of Soyopa. Weaver was extra alert since he had decided this would be his last trip personally, and mindful of the lessons from Colonel Morgan. The two Yaquis were also a source of concern. He had never seen them before, and they acted a little too nervous, which was not conducive to confidence. Given the nature of Rurale justice, they had reason to be nervous. They were camped about two days out from the rendezvous, resting men and animals. Weaver was reviewing his plans again. He couldn't help but keep coming back to contingencies, which he thought was another indicator that it was time to leave these risks to others.

One of the guards spotted the two riders coming in, waving with an upright rifle that these were friends.

Weaver waited impatiently for them to reach him, and started with, "Well?"

They smiled then, and Alvarado said, "They are dead, Senor!"

"You saw the bodies?" Weaver asked.

"No, Jefe, but we heard the shots and saw the Rurales treating them roughly as they dragged them into the trees. We couldn't get closer, but I am confident they won't trouble you further," Alvarado told him.

"I just wish I could have been there or you had seen the bodies. Still, good riddance!" Weaver responded.

He reached into a nearby saddlebag and pulled out a bottle of whiskey, took a good slug, and then passed it around.

"You two will ride with us and pick up your bonus when we are finished, along with a little more," Weaver told them.

Despite the good news that the bastard Connor was dead, Weaver still felt uneasy about closing out this trip. Riding south the next day, he called over his two lieutenants, Rivera and Corwyn, along with two other guards. One of the guards was Felipe and the other, Alfredo. Both had been relieved to hear about Connor.

"We need to be cautious. There are still Rurales out there, and you never know what will happen when you deal with these Yaquis. I want you two, Felipe and Alfredo, to ride as rear guards. As we get near the meeting site, I want you to swing wide of the column and scout farther out on the flanks. You remember the signal if you see something. If it is clear, take positions where you can cover us if there is any trouble with the Yaquis or anyone else."

To Rivera and Corwyn, he said, "You keep your eyes on me, and if I shoot or bolt, you and whoever is following you break left and right, respectively, and then circle back toward me. I may not go back up the trail, so stay alert so you can close behind in the direction I take."

They both nodded and then briefed their guards, which now included Cortez and Alvarado. The next morning, the two Yaqui guides led the way, followed at around seventy yards by the two, point guards. Behind them came the mule train, eight packers, and twenty-four mules. Two guards on each flank, and Alfredo and Felipe riding as rear guard. Weaver dropped farther back in the column, with three mules and a packer behind and seven packers and twenty-one mules in front of him.

The smugglers were riding into a low amphitheater, low hills to the front and sides, with heavy vegetation of greasewood, mesquite, and paloverde. Weaver looked back to see the rear guards extending left and right and reconnoitering as they moved out and forward. Because of the heavy vegetation, it was hard to maintain eye contact with Alfredo and Felipe. Turning back to the front, he saw the two Yaqui guides extend their lead on the column. They continued to move forward for maybe another one hundred and fifty yards when suddenly the peaceful morning exploded.

The Yaqui guides vanished from sight in the trees to be replaced by a dozen Rurales, on horseback, rifles leveled and arrayed in an arc that extended just a little less than halfway around the column. Weaver looked left and saw Alfredo racing down off a low hill in the near distance, rifle extended. His rifle was in the raised hand, barrel pointed in the direction of the enemy and parallel to the ground. He was pumping it three times, pausing, then repeating the three pumps. Three more enemy riders on the left. Weaver didn't hesitate, standing straight in the stirrups. He fired forward toward the arc of Rurales until he emptied his magazine. He noted the panic among the packers as they broke like quail to the left and right, trying to first turn their mule strings around then some throwing their hands up in surrender. Others began shouldering and firing rifles, still others cutting their string of mules loose and trying to ride back in the direction they had come. Weaver sheathed his rifle, turned his horse to the left, and, cursing continually, rode hard in the direction he had last seen Alfredo. The Rurales were returning fire and mules and riders were falling with confusion and dust prevailing.

He didn't know if there were more Rurales behind the packtrain, or even if the right side of the trap was weaker. What mattered was speed and aggression. They might be breaking like quail, but they were armed and dangerous. A Rurale appeared out of the dust on his right and Weaver simply slammed into him with his horse, knocking both man and animal over. Ahead, another Rurale appeared and Weaver drew his Colt and emptied all five rounds in that direction. The horse went down and he didn't care whether he hit the rider or not. Behind him, there were a number of riders and Weaver could hear the heavy firing as he leaned over the neck of his horse and savagely spurred the beast forward. Maybe two minutes had elapsed since the Rurales had sprung their trap. Weaver was heading east, to the Rio Yaqui, planning to cross near Soyopa.

The Rurales at the trap were led by Lieutenant Rodriques, who like Kosterlitzky had been seconded from the Mexican Army. He was an effective leader and had taken sixteen men with him to capture or kill these gun-runners. Having fought the Yaquis for a number of years, he considered these men the lowest of the low. His men were seasoned and disciplined and had chased bandits throughout Sonora. The reputation of the Rurales was such that criminal scum like these would seldom put up much of a fight, preferring to run or surrender. He had to admit that these smugglers were more desperate or just tougher than most he faced. The trap had been well prepared, ruined only by the speed and ferocity of the response. At the recommendation of Lt. Ortiz, he had recruited two "tame" Yaquis to intercept the mule train and lead them into the ambush. Three packers had been killed, three captured, one of whom was severely wounded. Two had escaped—one going west; the other, north. The weapons and ammunition were captured. That was the good news. It took Lt. Rodriques time to assess the gains and losses from the melee and reorganize.

The leader of the contrabandistas had been farther back in the column and had ridden through the east side of the trap. One Rurale was badly wounded and not ex-pected to live. Another had a broken leg from his horse going down. A third Rurale had been unhorsed when his horse had gone down under him. On the west side, two of the guards had been killed and a third, unhorsed and captured. One had been able to ride away. Two of the Rurales had minor wounds but three had their horses shot. The lieutenant sent three men after each of the two escaped packers. He sent one man to the nearest telegraph station to inform Kosterlitzky and organize forces farther north. He took five men and headed after the men that had broken out. Rodriques estimated that they had an hour head start. The remainder were directed to repair to the nearest town with the wounded.

CHAPTER 18

Weaver had not stopped cursing since he rode through the ambush. This did not keep him from calculating the odds of escape or assessing the men with him who had escaped. He expected the roads north to be infested with Rurales and the Army, telegraph lines alerting them to his likely direction of escape. His best bet was to travel through the rugged Sierra Madre, the primitive, still largely unmapped areas to the east, near the Sonoran-Chihuahua state lines. It was going to be a long, hard ride, with the worst danger near the border crossings. He had a few aces up his sleeve but he would be a fool to think this would be easy.

Of the five men with him, he had got lucky and the best had survived. Corwyn had made it, as had Rivera, Alfredo, Felipe, and, amazingly enough, Alvarado. Corwyn had received a shallow grazing wound on his right thigh. Felipe had a bullet pass through his left bicep and had lost some blood before Rivera had bandaged him up. To his credit, Corwyn had managed to lead one of the supply mules out of the fracas. Both could travel—hell, they had to if they wanted to live. They rode in single file, Rivera at point and Alfredo acting as rear guard. Weaver had wished he had Haggerty with him but he had mysteriously vanished without leaving any contact. They had been about twelve miles south of Soyopa when the Rurales had shown up and now, three hours later, were closing on the Rio Yaqui at the crossing just below the town. He sent Rivera into town on the west side of the river to buy supplies. He and the other four crossed over and came up the east side.

Connor and the six with him were not far north of Soyopa when they ran into Lt. Rodriques and his men. He was glad that he had agreed to riding with the three Rurales or there might have been a tragic misunderstanding. As it was, they compared notes, and since neither had seen the fugitives, the logical conclusion was that they had crossed the Rio Yaqui. They also now knew what they were up against in Weaver's group. Connor had his party change to their spare horses and lead the previous mounts. They took the lead, while Lt. Rodriques and his men looked to see if they could confiscate some remounts around Soyopa before rejoining the pursuit. Roberto conferred about the best way to catch Weaver and his remaining crew. They were close to Roberto's home ground and he wanted to try and get ahead of Weaver. Roberto took with him the other Rurale, Sergeant Maldonado. They crossed the river and headed northeast toward Bacanora.

Maldonado was glad to be away from Connor and with Roberto. He was a heavyset middle-aged man, with a preference for riding a desk versus pursuing bandits on these treacherous trails. He had been on Weaver's payroll for quite some time and had been instrumental in setting up Connor in Moctezuma. It hadn't worked out as planned and Lt. Ortiz had sent him on this fool's errand to catch his paymaster as punishment. He was shocked to learn that Weaver had been almost trapped. His own survival was now in jeopardy if they caught Weaver and he talked, or perhaps if he escaped and blamed him for the trap. Weaver dead was the best option at this point. His ass wasn't used to this hard riding, but he stayed with Roberto doggedly.

Roberto was planning to reach Bacanora ahead of Weaver and, with his uncle and other townsfolk, arrange an ambush of his own. He chuckled to himself about outwitting that bastard Ortiz, but even so, they had just skirted disaster. Connor's story about talking with the Consul had been the clincher. The ambush late last year and the dead packer were reason enough to kill that cabron, Weaver, but he knew that the bastard also represented a loose end for Connor. If a live Weaver confirmed the suspicions of Kosterlitzky and Ortiz, then Connor was done in Sonora. He wouldn't be able to escape their rough justice a second time.

Roberto reached Bacanora early the next morning, only to learn that the smugglers had already passed through. He learned from his uncle that a man had come in, looking for medical attention from a bullet through his arm. His aunt had treated him as best she could, but he was running a fever. She had extracted some silver pesos in the process and he had bought some food and rejoined a larger group, based on the tracks. They were traveling downstream toward the east–west passage of the

Rio Yaqui, in the direction of the small village of Santa Teresa, just short of the river. Roberto borrowed some fresh mounts and set out at a more careful pace behind them. He was impressed that the fat sergeant was able to keep up.

Splashing across the Rio Yaqui for the second time in two days, Weaver paused to rest on high ground north of the river. He uncased his binoculars and looked back to check for pursuers. If there were not too many, he might just give them a bloody nose to discourage them. He found a spot above the ford and positioned Alvarado to his left and Alfredo to his right. Rivera was with Corwyn, who seemed to be recovering. Felipe was flat on his back, panting from a fever. He likely would need to be tied to the saddle before too much longer. He had been a loyal member of his crew, and Weaver was not yet inclined to leave him behind. Two riders approached the ford and Weaver was surprised to see that one was his agent at the Rurales' Arispe station. Why would that son of a bitch give him up to the Rurales? It was a mystery that he felt confident he could resolve.

Roberto held up his horse when he caught sight of the river. He jigged a little to the left as Maldonado came up alongside and forward a few yards. The sergeant dismounted with his canteen in hand when he heard the boom of a rifle, then several more. The first shot caught him dead center in the chest and he was dying as a second shot hit him in the shoulder. Roberto was off his horse and leading her back from the river and into concealment in the brush, then into some cover. More rounds chipped wood around him as he tied off his animals and turned to see if there was a target for his .45-70. He returned fire at the smoke signatures, but was unable to get a clear shot. He fired two more shots before the firing stopped and eased close enough to see that Maldonado was done.

Weaver smiled with satisfaction for putting paid to that dog Maldonado. Unfortunately, one of the horses had been hit and they stripped the gear off of it, redistributed the supplies among the remaining six men, and set off. Whoever was behind that .45-70 was good but not enough to do them any lasting harm. Alvarado thought he had recognized Connor's Segundo, which worried him, but not enough to share that news with Weaver. No telling how he would react. Besides, he wasn't sure and didn't want to consider the implications of that. They paralleled the river for a while then turned north where the small Rio Sahuaripa reached the south bank of the Rio Yaqui. Heading for Tepache, about twenty-five miles to the north, the fugitives could then veer northeast to Oputo on the west bank of the Bavispe or northwest to Moctezuma.

About forty-five minutes later, Roberto was just splashing back to the south bank, after scouting forward to see which way the smugglers were headed. He had loaded the dead sergeant's personal effects onto his riderless mount when Connor pulled up. After hearing about Roberto's close call, they crossed north and took up the hot trail. Guillame told the private to bury Maldonado and then see how far back the other Rurales were and send them this way. Connor considered sending Mariela back, but her grim, expressionless brown eyes told him a Jefe's writ only extended so far. The sergeant's death was a message to not come too close, and Connor was going to be cautious until an opportunity arose.

Like Weaver, they turned north toward Tepache, and just before the halfway point, the trail turned very difficult with numerous switchbacks and constrictions through the mountains. Roberto and Guillame pushed to the front. The horses were winded but they pressed forward and were rewarded with the sight of the fugitives working their way around switchbacks, straight ahead. Guillame spurred his horse forward until the beast just came to a stop, trembling with exhaustion. He dismounted, pulled his rifle from the scabbard, and scrambled forward as fast as his burning lungs and legs would take him. By trail, they were about eight hundred difficult yards ahead, but the switchback had brought Weaver's crew to within about six hundred yards. The trail was narrow, with a precipitous drop on one side. They were coming around another switchback and would start to move farther out in range.

Guillame had pulled a single shot, .45 caliber Sharps-Borchardt Model 1878. It was hammerless and breech-loading. The falling block design made the rifle capable of withstanding the high pressures generated by the long cartridge, resulting in an effective range greater than one thousand yards. He chambered a round, taking a sitting position just off the trail, hand on a boulder, palm up to stabilize the weapon, and stared through the sight. He focused on slowing and controlling his ragged breathing. He adjusted the flip-up sight, released the safety, and triggered the weapon. The round missed, kicking up dirt low and about eight feet short. The rifle was chambered for the .45-100 round and Guillame chambered another, released the safety, took a deep breath, let it out, and fired again. This one missed but skinned the rump of one of the horses, causing it to rear. The panicked horse stepped off the edge of the trail and began to plummet.

The men on the trail could hear Felipe scream as he plunged with the horse to the killing rocks below. The smugglers were trying to get up the trail as fast as possible when the next round slammed into the rock just left of the trail. A fourth round also missed, but the fifth caught the last man in the crew between the shoulder blades, pitching him over the horse's head to lie still in the trail. Guillame fired twice more, but the remaining four were able to get out of range. Connor came up alongside Roberto as Guillame hit the last man.

"Incredible shooting, Guillame," he exclaimed. The Rurale grinned. "I hope I get a chance at the rest."

"We will," Connor concluded harshly.

Looking back, he could see the others straggling up. They looked as tired as he felt.

****

Weaver was too experienced to be shaken, but he pushed the horses as much as they could stand. His men were grim but, like their boss, determined to make it out. They stopped in Tepache long enough to buy more provisions, distribute them, and press onward. They took the left fork in the trail leading toward Moctezuma and the river of the same name. Four miles out, they found a good place for an ambush and took up positions, securing their spent horses behind them, and waited taking turns standing watch. After an hour, their patience was rewarded. Three vaqueros trailing two pack horses came down the trail. Rivera stepped out, rifle raised, and told them to put their hands up. There was a moment where time stopped, but the presence of three more men with rifles ready decided the issue. The men were stripped, tied, and abandoned as Weaver's men mounted the fresher horses and, trailing the others as spares, moved down the trail another mile before working over to the east and the trail to Oputo. Alfredo argued that they should kill the vaqueros, but Weaver decided that served no purpose. Outside of the animals, their victims had little of value.

Connor reached Tepache about two hours after Weaver had ridden through. He was elated that the odds were improving but frustrated that they were no closer to riding them down and finishing the pursuit. They decided to rest for a couple of hours, get food, and rub down the horses. Two were clearly blown and getting more in a small place like Tepache seemed impossible. While they were gathering their strength for the next push, the near naked vaqueros staggered into the town. One was from Tepache and, along with one of the others, was intent on joining them to exact revenge. The townsfolk produced two reasonably sturdy horses and a couple of well-worn pistols and a muzzle-loading musket.

Connor, with a lot of animated discussion with the others, decided that they would have to take some chances if they were going to catch the fugitives. He was convinced that the trail to Moctezuma was a diversion. The east bank of the Rio Moctezuma and Nacozari were likely to be well patrolled by armed men. He felt that Weaver would cross the Rio Bavispe, both north- and south-bound loops of the great river, and cross the border into New Mexico. As they prepared to continue northeast, a Rurale, with his horse near collapse, staggered onto the main street. He told them that eight more of the Rurales were half a day back. Connor told them the latest news and their course of action. He requested that one of the Rurales telegraph ahead from Moctezuma and have three of Luis's men bring supplies and half a dozen fresh horses out from Fronteras. They would meet where the Rio San Bernardino merged with the Bavispe at the northern end of the Bavispe's great loop in five days.

There was a trail from Huasabas, twenty-five miles northeast, on the south-flowing Rio Bavispe. The trail passed through the mountains and reached Bacerac on the north-flowing loop of the same river and they just might catch Weaver there. Three days of hard travel would be needed. Now seven strong, they plodded to the northeast. Many of the towns and villages of northeast Sonora had been destroyed by the great earthquake of May 1887, almost two years past. The devastation evident only added to the sense that they were in a different world as they pressed forward. At Bacerac, they found that the smugglers had passed through just hours before, en route to Bavispe, about ten miles downstream. Summoning what reserves they had left, they continued on as dusk approached.

Bavispe was not more than a large village, sitting on a spur of the Sierra Madre Mountains. It had a famous church, established in 1645 by the Jesuits, seeking to convert the Opata Indians. It had been turned into rubble by the great earthquake two years prior. The earthquake had extended into Arizona, doing a lot of damage. Connor had felt the tremors when returning from the first gunrunning trip in 1887. Most of the houses had suffered the same fate as the church, some being partially restored. The people were just barely holding on at a subsistence level. Reaching the outskirts in a state of exhaustion, Connor sent one of the vaqueros who knew the locals to see what he could find out. The rest wearily dismounted and checked their weapons. Too tired to even eat, Connor fell asleep after cleaning his weapons, Mariela with her carbine next to him.

CHAPTER 19

Weaver and his men were exhausted too. They were close to safety, less than sixty miles from the international border. They were sitting outside a small cantina, the light to their backs, eating beans and tortillas augmented with some mysterious shredded meat. The hot food helped and he refrained from drinking, knowing it would leave him befuddled. He felt safer being able to watch the streets rather than being inside. A couple of boys had brought fodder for the animals, but the animals would need a few days of rest before attempting the final run. Of the nine horses, only six were even remotely capable of going on. His plan was to follow the river at a very slow pace for a day or two, hoping man and beast could recover enough to improve their chances. When the river turned west, they would work their way northeast toward the San Luis Mountains in Chihuahua and then to the Animas Mountains, in New Mexico. The horses had been unsaddled and the tack was against the back of the cantina. Back against the wall, he caught himself dozing, coming awake with a start.

Connor was dozing, too, when the vaquero returned. He'd talked to people he knew and who had actually seen the smugglers from a distance, outside the cantina. Guillame was confident he could get at least one before they could react. The vaqueros were having second thoughts, now that these hardcases were at hand. Roberto agreed with Guillame. No one had much chase left in them. Mariela and Juan Castro just looked at Connor and waited for his plan. He stood up and started to talk.

Weaver awoke with a start. He had been dreaming of his time in El Paso, with Rosangela. With her wide hips and strong thighs, she was quite a woman. He missed her. The boy was touching him and trying to say something. He had paid the two boys who had brought fodder to keep an eye out for strangers with a silver peso as the reward.

"Senor, there are strangers on the outskirts of town. They are moving this way," he said.

It took a moment to register the boy's meaning.

"Go over to the man at the corner of the cantina and wake him. Ask him to come over here and you will be rewarded, Chico."

It had gotten cold, and by the position of the moon, he estimated it was still at least one hour before dawn. The wall of the cantina he had been sleeping against had long since given up its heat.

Rivera shuffled up, and Weaver noted that he had the presence of mind to have his rifle with him.

"Go through the cantina and out the back. Saddle the best horses and get ready to move. We may have company. I will wake the others," he told him.

He whispered to the boy, "Wake the gringo and have him come over to me."

Having seen the killing range of the sharpshooter on the trail, he felt very vulnerable. With one arm under his saddlebags, he started to slowly slide toward the cantina entrance, now eight feet away. From the corner of his eye, he saw Corwyn get up and walk toward him, obviously stiff and moving like an old man. Suddenly, he focused on a man walking across the small plaza, sombrero on, with a blanket over his shoulder.

Connor was walking across the plaza, maybe thirty feet from the reclining man he thought was Weaver. The light from the waning moon made it hard to distinguish features. He had borrowed a sombrero and blanket and was moving at a slow, deliberate pace. He had his drawn revolver in his left hand, under the blanket, all six cylinders loaded. He saw one of the smugglers get up and start to move past the cantina door toward one of the reclining men. A young boy leaned toward the reclining man, speaking into his left ear and, suddenly, all hell broke loose.

The reclining man fired his 45, the bullet zinging past his ear. Simultaneously, the .45-100 spoke and the gringo walking was thrown back against the wall. The man in the supine position struggled to get up and was hit by both Roberto and Mariela repeatedly, collapsing, smearing dark fluids against the wall. The reclining man rolled twice and was through the door. Connor pushed the boy to the right and stepped through after the man. A muzzle flash lit the room as Connor dove right and upended a table. The table splintered as two more rounds pounded into it. Connor took a deep breath and came out from behind the table, firing twice at where he had seen the muzzle flashes. When there was no return fire, Connor cautiously stepped out the back door. He heard horses thundering away and he emptied the cylinder at the fleeing men. His fire was joined with the boom of a musket then rifle and pistol fire from Castro and the men coming from behind the cantina.

Mariela ran up, leading two horses, and Connor mounted, not caring if anyone else was coming. He kicked his heels into the mare's flanks and bolted after the men trying to escape. He felt gripped with an almost reckless desire to bring this to an end. His left hand reached to touch the butt of his rifle in the scabbard. Reloading his pistol would have to wait. On his left he saw another rider coming up on him and he concentrated on the dim forms of the men ahead. Connor's horse was slowing as the sky was starting to lighten. He pulled up his heaving horse and admitted he had lost contact with the fugitives. He dismounted and reloaded all six chambers of his Merwin & Hulbert and re-holstered. He chambered a round and added another to his Winchester. Mariela came up beside him and dismounted. He hugged her, grateful she was unhurt, surprised at the intensity of the emotion. He heard nothing but the sigh of the wind. He put his ear to the ground but only got dirt in his ear.

Standing, he could see no movement as the sun started to illuminate the terrain. To the left he could see the denser vegetation along the Rio Bavispe. Leading their horses, they walked in that direction. He saw Juan Castro riding to his right and whistled to get his attention. Juan reported that Corwyn and another man were dead. No one hurt from their side. No Weaver or Rivera down. They reached the denser vegetation by the river and stopped to listen. Nothing, only birds. A flock of quail exploded about one hundred yards to his right front. As a kid, he had hunted quail and knew that sometimes you had to really press them to get them to take to the sky where they could be hit. He sheathed his rifle, took his revolver in his left hand, and, holding the reins of his horse, he started to jog forward, moving left and right around trees, catclaw, cholla, and greasewood.

Suddenly he heard horses moving to his front and he moved from a jog to a flat-out run. He saw a rider moving to his left and then disappearing as he went over the bank and into the river. Holstering his pistol, he grabbed his rifle and let the reins go as he suddenly went over the river's bank and slid on his ass toward the water's edge. The rider was holding onto the saddle horn as his horse tried to swim to the west bank. The man was almost across, the water becoming shallow. He put one foot in the stirrup and lifted up, swinging his leg across the saddle. Connor fired, the first round hitting water, the second connecting with the horse, and the third, fourth, and fifth hammering into the man, who cried out and fell into the river. Facedown, he was hit again, washing into brush and deadwood extending from the river's west bank. Connor thumbed rounds back into the magazine and retrieved his horse.

He was starting to swim his horse across to the west bank to look at the body when firing erupted from his right front. He had to dismount to get his horse back up the riverbank and then started to move toward the firing, not remounting. There were two repeaters firing, and the one closest suddenly stopped. He shouted, "It's Connor, Connor, Connor," not wanting to get shot by Juan or Mariela. He almost fell on Mariela, knocking her over as he ran to her position. She cursed as she reloaded and then they both started moving forward. He saw a riderless horse cantering to the right and then found Juan, shot through the shoulder and breathing erratically. "Help him," he shouted, which she ignored, as they spread farther apart and pressed forward. He caught his foot on some undergrowth, stumbled, and sprawled face-first before scrambling back on his feet.

Mariela had raced ahead and he watched with shock, unable to react fast enough, as Weaver stood up from behind a twisted mesquite and slapped his rifle butt up and into her ear and head. She dropped, stunned, carbine falling from her hands. Mariela was on her knees, struggling to shake off the fog and confusion from the blow. Confident that he had the upper hand, Weaver dropped his rifle and jammed his pistol against her head.

He shouted at Connor, "Drop that rifle or she is dead!"

He was enraged that Connor still lived, despite his best efforts to remedy that. They were about twelve feet apart and Connor simply stared at Weaver, seemingly incapable of thinking or responding to Weaver's command.

"Drop it," Weaver shouted again.

"Okay, don't hurt her. I am going to lower the rifle," Connor said and started to slowly lower the rifle to waist height.

Connor's voice seemed to accelerate Mariela's journey to the present and her movement caused Weaver to snarl, "Stay still, you bitch!"

Like most Yaqui women, she carried a cuchillo, a short knife that came out straight from the handle, maybe six inches in blade length. The top was straight for the first three inches then dipped a little before rising to a point. The three inches leading to the point were razor sharp, as was the belly of the knife that curved out and back. At its widest, the blade was two inches. She kept it strapped above her ankle, concealed by the soft leather uppers of her boots.

Connor made eye contact with her as Weaver shouted for him to drop the rifle. Maybe he was expecting her to bang into his legs as she had done with Ramon, she thought, still fuzzy from being hit.

For his part, Weaver was not moving the barrel from Mariela's head until Connor was standing in front of him without a gun in his hand. When that happened, the Irish bastard was a dead man. Weaver was used to being obeyed and Connor's hesitation made his temper flare higher. He suspected the man was fast but not as fast as a man with a gun in his hand. He was about to kill the woman and then turn the gun on Connor, when the standoff was broken.

"OK, you win. I am going to set the butt down and then release the barrel."

Connor could see Mariela was reaching into her bootleg and he suddenly was sure about what she was intending. As he released the butt of the rifle to rest on the ground, he hesitated to release the barrel.

"Let it go, you son of a bitch," Weaver shouted, frustrated and ready to end this game.

Connor could see Mariela's hand slowly coming out of the bootleg, and then time accelerated. Pushing the barrel right as he released it, his hand continued in the same direction to wrap around his pistol grip. Mariela felt the barrel of Weaver's gun shift away from her head, his left hand still holding her hair. She brought her cuchillo out and down savagely through the top of Weaver's boot. He felt an explosion of fire and pain as he jerked left and looked down in pure shock and surprise. The Remington fired and he thumbed the trigger back to chamber another round despite the screeching torment in his foot, feeling like he had been stung by a dozen scorpions. Connor was already clearing his gun from the holster as he had done thousands of times, his movement liquid and fast, his finger dropping over the trigger as he extracted the barrel, left shoulder in the direction of his target, arm already extending. He felt a ripping pain across his chest and heard the bang of Weaver's 45. Connor was working with embedded muscle memory, too, and his left arm extended, joined by his right, and pushed out, firing. He heard Weaver's gun go off again, then Connor fired three rounds in an almost continuous roar.

The pain in Connor's chest made him gasp as he sat down abruptly, smoke clearing, the sudden silence leaving him stunned. Weaver curled on the ground, on his side, then rolling facedown. Mariela threw herself on Connor, ripping his shirt, trying to assess the damage, jabbering incoherently, tears streaming. "Damn," was all he could say. "Damn." There was blood from the groove across his chest, half an inch deep and six inches long, but no froth or arterial damage. She tore a strip of linen from under her shirt and wrapped it across the bleeding furrow, tying it off in the back. He closed on her hand, causing her to stop and look at his face, eyes wide.

"Bring my horse, Mi Amor. I need a drink and a clean wound," he told her, voice hoarse. "We also need to find Juan and see how he is. Are you able to think more clearly than me?"

"Of course," she said, then kissed him hard and went to find his horse.

While she was gone, he took a look at Weaver. Connor's first round had caught him high on the right shoulder, causing Weaver's second shot to go wide. Connor's second shot had caught his hip, and the third or fourth had hit his chest. One round had missed completely. That narrow, perpendicular stance had likely saved him—that and Mariela's cuchillo. He suddenly recalled the Bruja's words: "Believe what you see, ..." He got it—he had seen enough to know that this woman was very special.

He stayed in Bavispe for three days, resting and allowing his wound to stop seeping and scab over. It gave Connor time to think about the future after that exhausting chase. He sent Mariela and Roberto to meet the packers with the horses and supplies at the designated spot and return. He didn't want her around when the Rurales came up, which they did the following day. Juan was not in great shape, but he would survive. Both Rivera, when they recovered his body, and Weaver were carrying a good sum of money. He split it privately and evenly among himself, Mariela, Juan, Roberto, and even Guillame. He gave the two vaqueros a fair amount along with their pick of weapons from the dead. Most of the horses were in bad shape and Roberto gave those to the townsfolk. He expected to be back and you could always use goodwill.

Connor was done with the gunrunning business, confident he would sleep better transporting legal shipments even if the compensation was significantly less. There were less dangerous opportunities to make money and to avoid Mexican and American customs if need be. He reflected on what Luis's mother had told him: "You are not meant to just hew wood and herd cattle." The cattle ranching business would have to stay on the back burner for a while. Maybe a long while. He and Roberto were going to work this other opportunity and see if they could prosper in this transport partnership.

They rode back out, around the northern loop of the Rio Bavispe, across the Rio Fronteras and down to Nacozari. Mariela met them outside of town and stayed close to Connor. Mariela knew she wanted the Americano and had no doubt he needed her. Maybe there was love too, and she would find out for sure. It seemed that she would help him with the business for a while and maybe buy a dress. He grinned when she told him, and she found she couldn't suppress her smile either.